Queen of the Night

By: Vatalini Sahar

First edition, 2026
Published by AX Creative

Cover art: Vatalini Sahar
Editing: Jennifer Fink

ISBN# 979-8-234-00536-6

For Dr. Tufo -- Thank you for making me feel seen and for giving me music. I didn't make it to the stage, so I wrote my own score instead. With love and endless respect.

Content Note: This is a dark romance. It explores obsession, control, and morally gray desire. Content may include explicit sexual content, power imbalance, coercive dynamics, manipulation, and emotional abuse. Please prioritize your well-being and read with care.

— Vatalini Sahar

In the Maestro’s darkness, her voice was not worshiped it was claimed; and when the Queen of the Night rose inside her, it sounded like desire sharpening into a vow.

Prologue
The Lesson

The Final Test, Tuscany, ten years ago

He had told her to wear nothing at all only the silk black robe he sent for her.

The villa received her like a cathedral that had learned the usefulness of silence. No music. No footsteps. Only the breeze carrying the scent of Cypress trees through an open window. She could smell beeswax and oil rubbed into old wood, the devotion of hands that kept the place immaculate and untouched.

Lucia waited at the closed piano, her pulse a delicate staccato. She was twenty-one old enough to be chosen, young enough to still believe discipline was a kind of love if you wanted greatness badly enough. She stood very still, unsure whether to sit or kneel, knowing stillness was the only way to wait.

Her beauty had always been the kind that startled people into softness: dark hair that caught in the low light like satin, lips too full for innocence, eyes that could pass for calm even when she was shaking inside. Tonight, the robe made her feel like a secret wrapped in prayer.

He arrived on the hour as if time had opened the door just for him. A soft shut of the door fell behind him.

She did not hear footsteps, but she felt his presence heat without touch, authority without noise. The mask came into view first. Venetian. Full-face. Enameled midnight black so deep it held a sheen, as if water were cascading down it. Gold leaf was set across the cheekbone in a pattern that only a trained eye could read as staff and notes. She heard the tune in her mind.

His mouth was expressionless, but his eyes were not. There was something new on the mask tonight: a ruby she hadn't seen before. It caught the light and made the darkness look expensive. Power. Wealth. Music and blood.

He rested his gloved hand on the piano's edge, claiming it as an altar. "You are a singer," he said, circling her. Her robe suddenly felt like a confession. She resisted the urge to pull it tighter. He would notice. The secret would be revealed, and the robe would fall. "Your body is your instrument," he continued, "but you have not yet learned to suffer for your sound."

"I want to," she said bright-eyed, foolishly brave, determined to be the best.

He touched the tie of her robe, gently, at her waist. In the beat of a rest, it was undone. He gazed at her the way a man who had waited too long does not with hunger, but with possession. The silk slid down her body and pooled elegantly on the floor. She shivered, listening to the wind move through the Cypress outside.

Lucia held his stare. He was not lusting for her. He was studying her like a sculptor studies raw stone calculating what she might become.

A click of his tongue. Her hand was lifted closer

to his body. Her nails were bare. "No," he said. "From now on, you will wear only red. Red is the color of the passion you will sing. Red is the color of the blood that will be spilled. Only red."

The baton. *His* baton.

No longer white almost pink now, as if it had been rinsed and stained in private. It tapped across her knuckles like a metronome with teeth.

"Remember," he said. "You will forget the applause. You must forget the praise, the audiences, the curtain calls. This is a lesson. These lessons will take you anywhere I let you go. You will perform on stage for many." He circled her again. "You must remember you only perform for me." He stopped behind her and brushed her hair over one shoulder, exposing her neck like an offering. "Lie across the piano for me."

He slid the bench away and patted the closed lid once, an invitation that was really an order. She obeyed, climbing onto the piano and laying herself back across the lacquered surface, spine aligned with the length of it. The cold shocked her skin. For a moment she arched, ribs flaring as instinct fought the chill, then she forced herself to settle, shoulder blades pinned, throat lengthened, her head turned to the side so her airway stayed open. Exposed, altar-still. Like an offering laid out for a god who preferred obedience to prayer.

She inhaled low and wide anyway, the way he demanded. Diaphragm expanding against the constraint of her own posture, breath made difficult on purpose. Heat gathered lower. Terror lived higher. She held both and waited for his signal to turn it into sound.

"Trattieni," he told her. *Hold*. "Rilascia solo

quando senti dolore. Questo sarà il tuo ritmo." *Release only when you feel pain. That will be your rhythm.*

"Sì, Maestro," she whispered.

This was not the conductor's baton he used in public. This one belonged to his private lessons. The bruises were rumors. The color told the truth: discipline, not time, had stained it.

A rest. Then... crack.

The first strike startled her breath to the top of her throat. She kept it there the way he had taught her: hold the note until stars pressed at the edges of her vision. He waited. He tapped her gently again. She exhaled.

"Again," he said, and the baton found a different angle. She inhaled sharply, held her breath until a faint tap on the piano granted her freedom from the stars. "Bene," he murmured. *Good*. "Ora canta." *Now sing*.

She inhaled, her abdomen rising as her diaphragm filled with every ounce of air she could hold. She sang, cheek flushed, jaw angled for precision, her tone a bright blade that sliced through the hush.

"Higher," he said.

She listened.

He began to circle again not to admire but to measure. His hand hovered above her mouth, feeling the pressure of her sound run through his fingers. His body pressed lightly into hers, challenging her breath while his other hand found the side of her ribs, reminding her where sound begins and ends.

He was young enough to be devastating, old enough to be certain. Even beneath the mask, his beauty felt like a weapon: a hard jaw, a mouth that looked sculpted for cruelty and restraint, the kind of presence that made rooms obey him before he spoke. Italian, unmistakably dangerous in that elegant way, as if sin could wear a tailored suit and still look holy.

"You are a vessel," he said, only kindly. "An instrument that must be tuned. Our justice will be precise. The world has forgotten morality. They have built cathedrals from lies and call them ministries, cabinets, and courts. False gods walk amongst us in stolen robes." His voice lowered. "You will humble them. We will take their breath away with beauty and truth. We will correct the world."

Lucia believed him. Her soul burned with his words. Their music, her voice, would right the wrong. Stop the greed. The injustice. Bring the powerful to their knees.

"Hold," he said.

She held her breath wide as a bell under her ribs. The baton touched down another clean, consonant beat across her flesh and the release was almost a relief. Her breath turned into tone, a note that traveled outward, spilling into the Cypress trees like prayer.

"Again." The Maestro did not soothe. He did not apologize. He directed. As her breath went ragged, he stepped back and waited the way a conductor waits for a section of his orchestra to end. Through the mask, he watched her, focused on the rhythm of her breathing, the tremor in her discipline. "You will not sing to be loved," he said. "You will obey me to sing." The sentence felt like a rule the room had etched into its walls. He closed the distance by one step. The metal of his mask touched the side of her cheek, cool and precise. "Guardami," he said. *Look at me.*

She opened her eyes. Across the room, a gilt mirror caught them both. In it, she saw two women at once: herself laid out on the piano lid, his pupil, practicing breath as punishment. And the other, upright and commanding, wearing his mask. The Maestro lifted the baton again, and her breath lifted with it. She did not count. She sang, understanding at last the difference between her body and her instrument. This lesson taught her hands how to stop shaking, her throat how to open into darkness, how to let her sound bloom.

"Dimmi cosa sei," he said. *Tell me what you are.*

"La tua cantante," she answered. *Your singer.*

"Dimmi chi sono io." *Tell me what I am.*

"Il mio Maestro." *My Maestro*. The words did not feel like surrender. They felt like alignment the way notes align into a chord.

He rewarded exactness with the smallest gift he permitted: he ungloved his hand and rested it on her lower back in approval. The touch was brief. Devotional. Almost tender. "The world worships applause because applause is cheap," he said. He lifted his hand away, capturing one last controlled caress before putting the glove back on. "We will deal in fear and wonder. We will correct the immoral." He turned away with a slight wave, allowing her to lift herself from the piano.

Delicately, she found strength in her legs, ignoring the sting of blood returning, the aftermath humming beneath her skin. She reached for her robe and placed it over her body carefully mindful not to stretch fresh marks.

"You will take the stage soon," he said, his back to her now. "And you will sing until the powerful forget the names they gave themselves."

“Sì, Maestro.” Her gaze lowered as she watched him at the desk.

He opened a dark wooden box for the baton. Her breath caught when she saw the ribbon at the back of his mask loosen just for a moment, just enough to remind her that the face beneath existed.

Lucia turned her eyes to the window instead, to the valley of Cypress. His footsteps came closer. She kept her gaze down. The black sheen of his leather loafers stopped beside her bare feet. He inhaled above her. Her body reacted. Excitement braided with fear, want braided with devotion. Then his footsteps shifted away, leaving her standing alone. At the door, she heard the latch click and the deep creak of mahogany yielding.

“Il mio cuore è tuo, Lucia. Ma non devo dirlo.” *My heart is yours, Lucia. But I must never say it.* “Devi essere la migliore che darò al mondo, per bruciare ciò che deve bruciare.” *You must be the finest I give the world, to burn away what must burn.*

It would take ten years for the Maestro to hear what she said back.

Chapter One
The Queen Returns

Ten years later, Lucia barely remembered his face, his real face. In private lessons, he wore the elaborate Venetian enamel mask. In public rehearsals, he sometimes appeared unadorned, and the nakedness of his humanity startled her more than any cruelty ever had. To Lucia, his bare face had become almost ordinary, stripped of myth by repetition. To everyone else, he was still the Maestro. Still devastatingly handsome. Still unmistakably Italian. People softened in his presence without knowing why. A man. Not a myth. He wasn't a villain, she told herself. He was a Maestro. The best in the world. And she had been chosen.

When she was younger, she used to imagine loving the man behind the mask. But he only let her close in measured doses, just enough to keep her hungry, never enough to mistake longing for permission. He trained her to want him the way singers want air: desperately, silently, on command. That was what she wanted once. She knew better now. Between them, there was respect, and there was duty. Allies, not lovers. Love was a myth, like a fictitious note no soprano could ever reach.

Fog dragged across San Francisco Bay like smoke pulled from a smoker's mouth. Lucia stood on the service terrace behind the opera house, a trench coat belted tight around her waist. Her hair was braided over one shoulder. She took one final breath of cold air, then opened the stage door and headed inside.

Lucia had sung on the world's most punishing stages. She'd been reviewed, worshipped, and dissected. Tonight, she was back in San Francisco to open the season as headliner, crown and all, stepping into the role that had first made her famous. Queen of the Night in *Mozart's The Magic Flute*. The part that, in her youth, had turned her dangerous and untouchable, a woman the audience feared to desire and dared to worship. This was the aria that taught her how to sound like a blade wrapped in velvet. This was where the Maestro's plans stopped being theory and became choreography. She should have felt the clean thrill of it, the uncomplicated pride. Instead, she felt the old lesson threaded through muscle and memory.

The Maestro had taught her to remember through pain, to perform through surrender, to control by letting go. She could still feel him in the phantom ache of her throat, the ache that lived behind certain notes. In the swell of her breasts beneath a corset. In the heat that sometimes rose between her thighs when she was alone and furious and bored with being good.

And yet he was not here. She was without him. Tonight, she would return to the stage as if she had never left it.

Lucia reached her dressing room and shut the door behind her. The opera house hummed on the other side of the walls, laughter, murmurs, the orchestra tuning like a city gathering its thoughts.

Inside, the room was too quiet, all velvet and

bulbs and lacquered wood. Lucia stood at the garment rack as a young dresser crossed the room with a bundle of pins between her lips. The girl's hair was a deep, wine-dark red, the shade Marina used to wear when she let it down. Freckles dusted her nose, faint as a constellation. For a moment, the sight hit Lucia like a note held too long. Not pain exactly. Something sharper. Memory.

The dresser looked up and met Lucia's gaze, startled by the stillness of her attention. Lucia gave her a small nod, an almost-smile that meant nothing and everything. When the girl turned away, Lucia undressed, leaving only her undergarments and pulled silk with her as she walked to the vanity and sat.

She wore a red silk robe, the fabric pooling around her thighs like water. Her fingers found the corset laces coiled beside the powder tray and worried them once, twice, a habit from years of tightening herself into something unbreakable. In the mirror: olive skin still warmed by Tuscan sun, smoothed by time into something richer; long jet-black hair pinned into dark coils; lips bitten and ready for rouge; cheekbones more carved than soft now, refined rather than hardened. Her eyes, clear green, held a steadier kind of danger than they used to. Not the brightness of youth, but the polish of a woman who had survived every room she entered and learned how to own it.

Her palm rose to her chest, just above her heart, as if she could hold it in place. Red nails, slick and precise, caught the vanity light.

Only red. Even now, even here, she wore his command like a signature.

It had been a year since Lucia had performed

onstage. A break to heal her voice, the papers would say. A polite lie, the Maestro would allow. The truth was simpler and uglier. She had spent the year hidden in Berlin, tasked with bringing Marina's voice back before the world noticed it was gone.

The Maestro gave her twelve months. Not as a kindness, but as a limit. Twelve months to return Marina to herself, to steady the tremor that had begun to betray her, to place her back under the lights as if nothing had ever cracked.

Lucia went because he ordered it. Lucia stayed because Marina was the only person whose breath had ever softened her, the only heart she had ever learned to hold without flinching.

In Berlin, she found Marina under stage makeup and borrowed gowns, bruises hidden where the lights would not catch. Sleep came to her in fragments. Breath came wrong, as if the air itself had become suspicious. Not the kind of illness doctors named. The kind that arrived when faith broke quietly and the body had to carry the sound of it.

They shared a home to heal. They shared the bed the way women do when the world has made sleep feel unsafe. Lucia warmed tea. Marina forced laughter. Lucia pressed her hands over Marina's ribs during breathing drills, feeling for the moment the rhythm returned. Marina braided Lucia's hair when Lucia's fingers shook from exhaustion. Some nights they lay shoulder to shoulder while the city murmured outside, and Lucia listened to Marina's breathing until it found something like safety.

"Do you remember what we said we were doing?" Marina whispered one night, her voice raw at the edges.

Lucia stared at the ceiling. "We correct the immoral."

Marina made a small sound that might have been a laugh if it didn't hurt.

"He calls it correction," Marina said. "But he is starting to choose like a man who wants to be worshipped, not like a man who wants justice."

Lucia turned her head. In the strip of light under the window curtain, Marina's face looked older than it should have. Beautiful still, but sharpened by something Lucia did not want to name.

"You're tired," Lucia said.

"I'm awake." Marina's eyes were open. "That's the difference."

Lucia wanted to argue. She wanted to defend the Maestro the way she defended her own technique, fiercely and reflexively, devotion dressed up as certainty. Instead she said, softly, "Rest."

Marina swallowed. "I'm afraid of what he is becoming, Lucia."

"What he hates," Lucia replied without thinking. Then she regretted it immediately.

Marina's mouth tightened. "Exactly."

Lucia reached beneath the duvet and found Marina's hand. She held it there, palm to palm, as if warmth could be instruction. Then, because Marina had asked her to rest and because Lucia did not know how to deny her anything gentle, she lifted Marina's knuckles and kissed them once, soft enough to be mistaken for gratitude. Lucia had been there because Marina needed her. She returned to the stage because the Maestro commanded.

A knock sounded at the dressing-room door.

Before Lucia could answer, it opened. Another

stagehand stepped in, holding a garment bag like it contained something holy. The girl hesitated, eyes wide, then crossed the room to hang the gown.

Another knock followed, heavier, more deliberate, at the inner door that led toward the administrative corridor. Sergio entered without waiting to be invited.

He wasn't the Maestro's handler. Not exactly. Sergio called himself "protettore della musica." *Protector of the music.* And the title fit him better than any job description could. Late fifties, compact, a gentleman's severity softened by careful hands. He carried a slim leather folio and a thermos of tea brewed by his own hand. San Francisco water, he'd decided, could not be trusted.

"Program order," he said, tapping the folio once. "Light vocals in ten. Your call is in twenty. The house opens on the quarter." He paused. "The guild wants photographs after the curtain, not before." Then, quieter, he added, "A note from abroad."

Lucia's attention sharpened. "Australia?" She lifted her chin. "Has Greta delivered?" Her mouth curved, pride clean and bright. "Brava, mia sorella." Well done, my sister.

Sergio inclined his head as if she'd sung the correct pitch. "The Health Minister," he said. "The one who sold private care for public bonuses." His frown was delicate, almost polite. "His caduta is complete." *His fall is complete.* He slid a paper from the folio, clipped articles, a photograph blurred at the edges. "Anonymous," he continued. "An 'unknown woman' who may or may not resemble anyone we know."

Lucia kept her gaze on the mirror. "His wife?"

"Standing by him," Sergio said. "Per loro, fama è

una religione." *For them, fame is a religion.*

Something like pity touched Lucia's lower lip. "She will defend a man who would sell the breath of his people for a new house."

"Sì." *Yes.* Sergio poured tea into a cup, added a wedge of lemon the way she liked, and set it down without looking at the skin beneath her robe. He was old enough and careful enough to make her body feel like an instrument he'd been paid to insure.

"The papers call the woman a temptress," he said. "They always do." A beat. "The Maestro calls it correction."

Lucia heard Marina's voice in her head, sharp as a snapped string. He is starting to choose like a man who wants to be worshipped. "And what do you call it, dear Sergio?" Lucia asked softly.

He lifted one shoulder. "Accountability with a better soundtrack." His eyes found hers in the mirror. "And a cost."

Lucia drew in one slow breath, the old way, low and wide until pride and pity settled into the same place in her chest. "And the rest?"

Sergio opened the folio. "Two short press hits after the curtain. No director in the room, only the head of the Opera and a photograph. Tomorrow is recovery day." He hesitated. "From Germany," he said carefully, "no letter from Marina."

Lucia's posture did not move at all. "No?"

"Not yet," Sergio said. "I will keep asking."

Lucia nodded, small and contained. A stage movement meant to read as stillness from the back row. "Grazie, Sergio." *Thank you.*

"Prego." *You're welcome.*

He stepped toward the door. "I'll return for

warm-ups."

The stagehand exhaled a breath she'd been holding and crossed to hang the gown. Lucia stood. Her robe slid from her shoulders to the floor. She didn't bother to cover herself. Her body was not a secret. It was a weapon. That was the mission, if you stripped it down to its spine. They called it many things, depending on who spoke. Correction. Justice. Art as consequence.

The Maestro had started with men who were easy to hate. The kind who spoke about morality in public and bought silence in private. The kind who built reputations on philanthropy and paid for them with other people's bodies. He did not kill them. Not directly. He made them unravel. He made them confess with their own hands tied behind their vanity.

Lucia had been taught to be the lure and the blade, the aria and the trap. Beauty used as bait. Truth used as the final note. It was supposed to be precise. It was supposed to be deserved.

Germany had shown Lucia the cracks in the idea. Not in the mission itself, but in the hands guiding it. Sometimes the chosen were not the worst, Marina had said. Sometimes they were simply the closest. Lucia had told herself Marina was wrong because it hurt too much to imagine she was right.

The rest of her dressing team arrived in pieces: hair, makeup, wardrobe, hands deft and a little tremulous. They touched her like she was porcelain; powdered her like she was a ghost; wrapped her in midnight and glass-like fabric. The corset tightened until breath became currency. Then the final piece: her crown, placed carefully on her head, wired with thorns.

Lucia said nothing until they finished. Then, softly, "You may leave."

When the door closed, she turned back to the mirror and saw him again. Not in flesh. In posture. In stillness. In the shape of her mouth when she didn't allow it to soften.

"Non per essere amata," *Not to be loved,* he had whispered once, the night before she left his villa in Tuscany. "Per essere obbedita." *To be obeyed.*

She had walked away. But not free. Never free.

"Tonight, you will sing," she told the woman in the mirror, voice low. "Tonight, you will be worshipped." A beat. "And tonight, someone will be chosen."

She didn't know who yet, but she felt it in her blood. Maybe a woman. Maybe a man who wouldn't understand why he wanted her. Someone out there in the audience was already marked. Pleasure had never been the Maestro's gift to her. It was the weapon she stole when he wasn't looking.

Sergio returned on the minute, standing behind her just out of the mirror's frame. "Pronta?" *Ready?*

Lucia rose. "Sì." *Yes.* She glanced at the folio in his hand. She couldn't control the next line. "Marina should have sent something by now."

He considered, then answered as if reciting from a score. "Germany is quiet. Marina is... working." His mouth tightened on the word. "The Maestro has you here to continue the mission."

Lucia felt the old contradiction, devotion braided with doubt. Germany had taught her how to hear the tremor in Marina's breath that didn't belong there. Lucia had wanted to stay, to fix it, to put her own hands over Marina's ribs until the rhythm returned.

But the Maestro had pointed at a map and written: San Francisco.

"You think she's angry," Lucia said.

Sergio's gaze softened, just a fraction. "I think she is frightened," he replied. "And I think she has reason."

Lucia swallowed. The crown's weight felt suddenly heavier. "Curious which of the elites he'll choose," Lucia said, forcing her voice into steadiness.

Sergio's mouth tightened. "Curious which of them deserves it," he corrected gently. "And careful that deserve is the word we mean."

Lucia met his eyes in the glass. "Capisco." *I understand.*

They moved into the corridor, past framed posters and gilded donors' names. The opera house hummed on the other side of the walls, laughter, murmurs, the orchestra tuning like a city gathering its thoughts.

Onstage, Lucia stepped into the wing and measured breath against darkness. Two counts. Then four. Then eight held, then released. The house lights dimmed to a rumor. A note sounded from the pit, thin and bright, like the first star deciding it had the right to exist.

Backstage, the same young dresser whispered, "In bocca al lupo." *Good luck.*

Lucia smiled, automatic and true. "Crepi il lupo." *May the wolf die.*

Sergio took his place just off her shoulder, a shadow that refused to be menacing. "One more thing," he said, opening his folio. He slid out a square of manuscript paper. Not words. Notes. The melody traced a shape her body knew before her mind did.

A private motif the Maestro had given her once, and never given anyone else. A mark of ownership disguised as music. "He sends his blessing," Sergio said, and the word tasted wrong in his mouth.

Lucia's thumb found the first bar and stayed there. "Of course he does."

She heard Marina again, but this time it was an older memory, months ago in Germany, when Marina's voice had turned suddenly fierce.

"If he asks you to take someone who is not guilty," Marina had said, "what will you do?" Lucia stared at her friend, stunned by the question. "Tell me you'll refuse," Marina demanded. "Tell me you're not just an instrument he can lift and point."

Lucia answered too quickly. "He wouldn't."

"Warm-ups," Sergio said gently, bringing her back.

Lucia closed her eyes and began. Lip trills. Sirens. Vowel ladders that built a cathedral inside her ribs. Breath gathered beneath the corset's tyranny and made a friend of it. The body remembered even when the mind tried to forget. On the last slide through her register, she held until the edges of the world brightened, then released into a silence that felt like obedience and something more dangerous than obedience. When she opened her eyes, Sergio was watching her with the careful expression of a man timing a fuse.

"Andiamo," she said. *Let's go.*

"Andiamo." *Let's go.* He offered his arm. She didn't take it. But she let him walk close enough to count as care.

The curtain would rise. The aria would come. And somewhere in the house, the first pair of eyes would find her and not yet know they had been chosen.

Chapter Two
The Selection

From his villa above Tuscany, the Maestro watched her sing. No orchestra feed. No podium. No audience on the primary screen. Only Lucia, isolated in a rectangle of cold light of his monitor, her voice made visible by the way it cut through silence.

She moved like smoke made elegant. Black tulle over something that flashed like glass, catching and losing the spotlight with every breath. Her arms didn't lift to "act." They floated; hands curved like calligraphy. Her eyes never fixed on one section of the house. She gathered the whole room. She pulled everyone in.

She was the Queen of the Night. "Der Hölle Rache..." *The vengeance of hell burns in my heart...*

She didn't perform the aria from Mozart's The Magic Flute. She became it. Every high F sliced clean through the hush. Every run held its nerve. When she reached the final note, she didn't blink or tremble. She stood in the light and made the world meet her there.

The Maestro did not clap. Applause was cheap. "Bravissima," he whispered, nearly voiceless.

He slid to the second monitor, the house feed. A human sea. Rows of parted mouths and widened eyes. He wasn't looking for awe. He was hunting for exposure, the soft places a body forgets to hide. Who leaned forward. Who clutched at their chest. Who held their breath. He slowed the capture, frame by frame, until the smallest betrayals revealed themselves.

Row C, aisle: a widow in sable, pearls knotted tight at the throat, Mrs. Eleanor March. Next to her: Alex Chambers. Sharp suit. Sharper eyes. A man who came to be seen was now distracted by her. His Lucia.

Perfect.

The Maestro leaned forward, still as Alex watched the aria unfold. Captivated. Seduced without consent. The Maestro smiled with one side of his mouth. This was the method. Not knives. Not bullets. He didn't kill men. He unmade them.

Alex didn't care about Lucia's technique, not really. Lust sat behind his fixed stare like a second face. He was handsome in the clean, dangerous way: a jaw you could balance a lie on, a suit that didn't ask forgiveness. He had the manner of a man who never waited his turn. Even now, boredom flickered at the edges of him, the impatience of someone who believed the world existed to respond.

Alex had built an app that fed on attention. Legal enough to sell. Immoral enough to thrive. It blurred the edges of consent in the name of entertainment, then called the blur "innovation." Money came next. Then donors. Then the photos. Then a podium. Now Alex wanted more. He wanted the mayor's office. He'd been quoted as saying it was his duty. His service.

The Maestro called it theater. San Francisco deserves better, he thought, and felt how close that sentence came to prayer. He cut the house feed and returned to Lucia's close-up. The camera found her on the last syllable, mouth parted, note not yet relinquished. For a moment, he forgot the room he sat in. Forgot the wall of clocks that stitched together feeds from other cities, other sopranos singing like banners across the globe. He stood inside her sound and let himself love her. A moment too long.

His expression tightened. He reached for his private baton and brought it down once, quick and clean across his own forearm. Mercy was not for him. "Basta," he said to the empty room. *Enough.*

A memory rose, one he didn't want. The vineyard. The Cypress line. The one time his mouth forgot its task and remembered hunger. He had kissed her once, only once, then punished her for his weakness. He set the baton down with the care one gives a blade.

He opened a drawer of black folders with neat labels, a catalog of ruin: politicians, heirs, clerics, men who believed their titles made them untouchable. Each file was a fall. Each fall had a price.

The powerful were learning to fear being seen clearly. They were growing insular, more careful, more paranoid, aware that someone out there wanted to strip them down to their worst truths. Rumors of a Maestro were usually met with laughter. Humiliation. A myth people repeated at dinners because it felt safer than admitting the world had teeth again.

At St. Barths' last holiday, he'd been invited to one of the dinners people pretended didn't exist, the kind where too many powerful bodies in one room should've been dangerous. But it wasn't. Not to them.

His compadres suffered under propaganda and economies engineered to keep people tired apart, not together, surviving, not rising. The Maestro would remain their leader. He would take them down one by one until something like a revolution had a chance to breathe. Maybe. Just maybe. He hesitated, then pulled Lucia's folder from the drawer. He could finally rest with his soprano beside him.

A soft bell sounded. His assistant entered and stopped at the edge of the room, silent as a shadow. The Maestro didn't look up at first. Then he spoke, measured.

"Alex Chambers has a fiancée." He paused. "She loves the opera. Emily Preen." The assistant waited; pen poised.

"Discreetly," the Maestro continued, "I want a concierge package for Miss Preen. Two seats for a Sunday matinee. One for her." A beat. "One for her roses. No one else. Front row. Center."

"His name is not to appear anywhere," the Maestro said. "Make sure Sergio waits until after Chambers arrives home tonight."

"Sì, Maestro." *Yes, Maestro.* The Maestro slid a second envelope across the desk. "This goes to Sergio for Lucia." He repeated, "Sergio's hands only."

"Senza errori," the Maestro added. *No mistakes.* The assistant tucked the envelope into a leather pouch and remained still.

"For Lucia," the Maestro said, "she will host a stage dinner after Sunday's performance. Everything will take place on the stage. One light. One table. A chef who serves." His eyes narrowed. "I do not need another performer on that stage."

He cracked his neck, then spoke in Italian with quiet precision. "Tieni Lucia in luce, non incatenata." *Keep Lucia in the light, do not chain her.*

He stepped closer to the assistant. Distinction mattered. "Proteggi la musica." *Protect the music.* Then, colder: "Miss Preen is our bait. Make sure Chambers is fuming." He lifted his chin. "Go." Only then did the assistant leave.

The Maestro pulled out his chair, opened his laptop, and searched his files until he found footage he would deny watching. Lucia and Marina, old footage in a rehearsal room. Two young women in their early twenties, still young enough to believe the future was only a well-sung note away. They laughed at a missed entrance, then corrected each other without mercy but with love.

He'd put them together because each had what the other lacked. Lucia's steel. Marina's light. He paused the frame where their heads rested together. That softness had always been dangerous to him. It made them stronger. And strong women were hard to control.

So he wrote their bond into the mission, gave it a purpose, a narrative, a holy reason. He let them believe their closeness served him, knowing full well he would cut it the moment it didn't.

Marina had been slipping. Lucia, by contrast, had hardened into something that made him proud but not unafraid. He sent Lucia to save Marina, his best soprano, from the stage, off for an entire season. He had hoped Lucia could fix what was wrong, but no progress had been made. He reassigned Lucia. If Marina could not be saved, there would be a curtain call. He would file it under necessity and call it mercy.

The Maestro slid his chair back toward the opera feeds and brought Lucia up again. He watched her performance a second time, carefully, like a man studying evidence. He paused. Looked past the monitors to the dark line of Cypress beyond the veranda. Then back to the screen.

He saw something he hadn't caught before. Her pitch was perfect. Her craft remained unchanged. But her choice had shifted. She wore the roughness he gave her like jewelry. She threaded pleasure into pain and turned obedience into art.

The Maestro let the fantasy rise, thin and dazzling. Ten years older. Ten years truer. Lucia could retire. He could keep her at last, not as an instrument, but as a partner.

They could stop. He could stop.

His hand drifted toward the baton again, as if to anchor himself. He struck the same tender skin on his forearm. "Svegliati," he told himself. *Wake up.*

He pushed away from the desk and crossed the room, flinging open the doors to the veranda. Tuscany glowed below as if someone under the hills had lit a fire and forgotten to put it out. He pressed his forehead to the railing and exhaled something between a growl and a prayer.

"Il mio cuore è tuo." *My heart is yours.*

He imagined Lucia laughing at him for such a novice mistake. He imagined her believing him. He imagined himself, human, for once, inside that belief. He smiled, tired. Then he turned back into the room and let discipline reclaim him.

With a flick of a switch, the screens brightened: sopranos across the world. Athens, one singer smiling at an ambassador in a way that would cost him his ministry. Buenos Aires, a mezzo threading a banker into a scandal that would teach a paper how to print consequence. Seoul, a coloratura laughing at a billionaire who mistook attention for affection.

The Maestro wanted to believe he still did all of this for the reason he'd begun, when the world seemed newly corrupt and still correctable. If he were honest, he would admit he was not as far as he'd hoped. People were learning that the truth didn't matter if pride was bruised in the process. He turned Lucia's volume up slightly and let her voice warm his blood for a moment, then turned it down again.

"Ricordati," he said. *Remember.* "You were not taught to feel. You were taught to perform."

A red pulse appeared on his phone. Berlin. He let it flash once. Twice.

Berlin meant his perfect machine was cracking, something he could not fix with music alone. If Marina could be brought back into tune, the handler wouldn't be calling. The Maestro closed his fist around the edge of his desk until his knuckles whitened, then forced his hand to soften.

He looked at Lucia on the screen and bowed his head. "You will understand," he said quietly. "You will forgive me."

Then he picked up the phone. He listened to the handler's voice. And with his eyes lowered, he turned Lucia's image off and began issuing instructions.

Chapter Three
The Salon

The applause still lived under Lucia's skin when the door opened.

"Lucia," the Director said, smiling carefully, the way men smile when they want something more than a woman is willing to give. "Just a few minutes in the Guild salon? Our founding patron is over the moon. Mrs. March."

Sergio answered before Lucia could. "Fifteen minutes," he said. "No liquids. Minimal talking. 'È il rito." *It's the ritual.*

Lucia slid on a black silk wrap that matched nothing and everything. In the mirror, she pressed two fingers to the base of her throat, found the easy rise of breath, and left them there until her pulse remembered who it belonged to.

The Guild salon glittered the way money does when it wants to be thanked. Low lamps. Too much velvet. A tower of champagne flutes arranged like a castle. Mrs. March stood in pearls as if she'd never known rough water. Her hair was the color of snow at a distance, her lipstick a shade that did not exist in nature. She offered her hands, and Lucia took them lightly.

"Signora March," Lucia said, kissing the widow's cheek. "La vostra generosità mantiene vivo il teatro." *Your generosity keeps the theatre alive.*

“My dear,” Mrs. March breathed, old money softened by European summers. “You made the ceiling breathe. I swear I saw the chandeliers lift.”

“You are generous,” Lucia said. “It is the house. It remembers how to hold sound.” Mrs. March beamed as if she’d personally taught the chandeliers to rise. Then she shifted slightly, deliberately, and made space beside her.

“And this,” she said brightly, “is Mr. Alex Chambers. He’s done so much for the city’s future. He is on the way to being our next mayor.”

Alex stepped forward with a smile that looked effortless because it had been practiced into his face. Lucia’s own smile arrived slower. She knew immediately, intimately, that he had not heard of her before tonight. Not really. Not in the way the opera world meant knowing. Her eyes lingered on him, amused.

Mrs. March continued, pleased with herself. “And his dearest Emily is an absolute fan of yours. She speaks of you constantly.” Her gaze flicked between them with the satisfied malice of a matchmaker. “He should know your name by heart.”

Lucia kept her expression soft, almost kind. “He doesn’t,” she said, as if stating a fact anyone could observe. Then she tilted her head. “Do you, Mr. Chambers?”

Alex’s smile held, barely. “Of course,” he said too quickly. A fraction of a pause, just long enough to be a crack. He recovered. “I mean, yes. My fiancée is a devoted admirer. I’ve heard plenty.”

Lucia’s brows lifted in polite disbelief. “Plenty,” she repeated, tasting the word. “And yet you watched me tonight like a man seeing a storm for the first time.” Mrs. March made an eager little sound. Lucia turned her head slightly, voice sweet as polished marble. "So you haven't heard of me, really, even though your fiancée has. Perhaps you are only tone-deaf." Her smile sharpened. "Ma anche mezzo sordo." *But also half-deaf.*

Alex exhaled a laugh, smooth and controlled, because that was what men like him did when challenged in public. "That's fair," he said. "I deserve that." He said it charmingly. Almost convincingly. Almost. "My fiancée has mentioned you," he added, and his eyes flicked quickly to Mrs. March, then back to Lucia. "And I'd be honored to bring her a memento."

Sergio stepped in from the shadows with the impossibly soft tread of a man who once wore different boots. "No autographs," he said. Not harsh. Just final.

Lucia didn't look at Sergio when she softened it. "Rituali," she said lightly. *Rituals.* "I keep my hands for music."

Mrs. March rushed in to keep the room pleasant. "Of course, of course. And tell me, cara, will the Maestro be visiting this season? We all know you are his favorite." Her eyes gleamed. "My circle would simply adore a private audience. Mask optional."

A small pain pinpricked along Lucia's ribs, fine as lace, invisible as restraint. Her answer was perfect, polished, and true enough to survive a headline. "The mask has always been gossip, madam. His talent is in his nature. He hides behind nothing except the music he gives us."

The Director laughed too loudly, relieved, and drifted away to charm a new cluster of donors. Mrs. March was delighted as she mingled her way around the room. Alex remained beside her, as if loyalty were a posture.

Lucia felt him watching her the way he watched numbers, collecting data for leverage. After a beat, Alex angled closer, only enough to speak without performing for the room.

"I should have led with 'congratulations on your opening night'," he said. His smile arrived a fraction late, like it had to clear security first. "That was... impressive."

Lucia didn't accept the compliment right away. She let it hang between them until he felt the silence.

"You were right," he added, and the admission cost him a little. "This was my first opera."

"Grazie." *Thank you.* Lucia inclined her head. "And yet you look unconvinced by the magic," she added, watching him.

"I'm more of a metrics person," he said, as if confessing a flaw. "Opera's hard to quantify."

"Capisco." *I understand.* Her smile touched only one eye. "Some things prefer to be measured by pulse."

A small spark lit behind his composure, competitive. He liked the rules even while pretending he didn't. "Mrs. March tells me you'll be the face of the season," he said. "That's good for the city."

"The city is good for the city," Lucia replied. "We borrow its breath and return it flavored with something useful."

"Useful," he repeated, amused. "Is that what we call it?"

"It depends on the throat," Lucia said simply.

Mrs. March returned, beaming. "We are all so thrilled to bring Alex closer to the arts," she announced, words tapping like pearls on porcelain. "He's very busy, but a future mayor should understand culture, don't you think?"

"Of course." Lucia offered a small bow that was real enough to be polite, mocking enough to make Alex wonder.

Alex's gaze flicked once to Sergio. "You have rules," he said.

"Rituals," Lucia corrected softly. "Mr. Chambers." Her voice did something deliberate on his name, warmth laid over threat like velvet on steel.

"Rituals protect the music," Sergio said. "La musica prima di tutto." *Music before everything.*

Alex nodded as if he respected it. Lucia could tell he was measuring the room, figuring out what would win, what would cost, what would be noticed. "It isn't that I don't appreciate it," Alex said, lowering his voice. "It's just... not my language."

"Then someone should translate," Lucia replied. "Piano piano." *Slowly, slowly.* He held her gaze. He didn't retreat. Good.

A tray of champagne drifted toward them on a perfect white glove. Lucia didn't touch it. "No liquids," she reminded gently, and Mrs. March laughed, embarrassed at herself for forgetting.

Alex took a flute anyway, like a man proving he couldn't be managed.

Lucia watched the unbroken bubbles in his glass, then looked up at him, deciding, precise as a downbeat. She stepped closer, close enough that he had to choose what to do with his breath. Then she extended her hand. Not a demand. An invitation disguised as courtesy.

Alex's gaze dropped to her hand, then lifted to

her face. He knew. He knew she was doing this on purpose. His smile shifted, almost honest. "You're enjoying this," he murmured.

Lucia's expression stayed serene. "For Emily," she said softly, letting the name fall like silk between them.

That did it.

Alex set the champagne aside without breaking eye contact. He took Lucia's hand with careful elegance, as if cameras existed even when he couldn't see them. Then he bent, no drama, no show. Refined. Correct. His lips brushed the back of her hand, just below her knuckles. Warm. Brief. Controlled. He felt her breath waver. Alex saw it register in his throat before it reached his eyes. He lifted his head, still holding her hand. "You're toying with me," he said quietly, not accusing. Naming it.

Lucia smiled as if she approved of his intelligence. "And you're still here."

A beat.

His mouth twitched. He released her hand like it mattered. He didn't step back. He didn't step closer. He held the line.

Around them, questions bloomed and died. Photographs were staged and dissolved. Lucia did what she'd learned to do when rooms demanded charm. She gave them the exact size of a story they could carry home and place on a mantel.

When fifteen minutes were nearly fifteen, Sergio touched the inside of Lucia's elbow. "Basta," he said. *Enough.*

Lucia turned first to Mrs. March. "Next Friday," she said. "Con piacere." *With pleasure.*

"To Friday," Mrs. March chimed, delighted.

Lucia turned to Alex last, a courtesy that felt like a decision. “Buona notte, Signor Chambers.” *Good night, Mr. Chambers.*

“Good night,” he said, voice betraying nothing except that he would be thinking about the way she’d offered her hand and the way she’d breathed.

Sergio guided her out through a side door into the corridor. The quiet there was the kind that happens after rough weather. Lucia breathed once, deep and even, and let the Queen fall from her shoulders like a cloak. Behind her, the salon’s velvet conversations resumed their planned trajectories. Ahead, her dressing room waited.

And somewhere between exactly where she liked to live stood a mark she had not claimed, and a man who knew he was being played and did not yet know whether he wanted to win or surrender.

Outside, rain stitched the night. A black car waited for someone else.

On another block, another car opened its door, and a candidate who did not yet have a language for hunger slid into the back seat.

The city inhaled. The city exhaled.

Chapter Four
The Candidate

The first thing Alex Chambers thought in the cab was how goddamn boring opera was. City lights smeared against the rain-streaked window as the black car wound back through Pacific Heights. His tux collar itched. He tugged at it with the same impatience he gave anything that couldn't be monetized, managed, or measured in a poll.

Boring. All of it. The gilded ceilings, the bowing orchestra, the donors laughing like they'd bought Mozart by the ounce. He'd endured galas and banquets and "culture" events his whole adult life. Opera was just another performance, another room where everyone pretended to be impressed.

Until she walked onstage. Lucia Conti.

He hadn't bothered to learn her name until Emily said it weeks ago, background noise about a soprano flown in to open the season. Another excuse for the Opera Guild to squeeze millions from people with more money than sense. But when the lights fell and she appeared, midnight gown, crown wired with thorns, eyes bright green like emeralds from the stage, something in him shifted.

Not reverence. Not wonder. Heat.

He didn't know anything about technique. He didn't care about vowel placement or breath support or whatever professors wrote on chalkboards. But he understood the effect, and Lucia's was undeniable. The way she pulled a room into silence as if silence belonged to her. It wasn't the aria that got him. It was her control, the way she made beauty feel like a threat.

And later, after the applause, after the donors and the velvet salon, he couldn't stop hearing it. That quiet, involuntary inhale she tried to disguise when he kissed the back of her hand. Not loud. Not dramatic. A small betrayal of breath she couldn't quite swallow. It had been so subtle he could've pretended he imagined it.

He didn't. He replayed it anyway.

The socialite hosting him, a widow in a fur stole who smelled of gin and grief, had tossed a million-dollar check onto the campaign like it was foreplay. She'd leaned too close, fingers brushing Alex's sleeve with a familiarity that made his skin crawl. Alex had smiled. Of course, he had. He always smiled.

Promise access. Endure the ick. Take the money. Politics was theater. You wore the mask, played the part, and cashed the check.

The cab slowed at his block. Pacific Heights: townhouses carved like miniature palaces, iron balconies dripping with vines, windows glowing warm against the mist. Alex paid the driver and stepped out. The air was sharp with ocean and money. He hated this neighborhood.

Emily was exactly where he knew she'd be, curled on the couch, bare feet tucked beneath her, a plate of manchego and figs on the coffee table beside a half-drained glass of pinot. Gray sweats. Loose T-shirt. Hair in a messy bun that still somehow looked wholesome and approachable in the way voters liked and donors trusted.

The Opera Channel flickered on the television. A rerun of The Magic Flute. Of course.

"Hey, babe." Emily looked up, smiling with the soft earnestness that made donors' wives call her refreshing. "You're late."

"Donors." Alex loosened his tie, shrugged out of the tux jacket, and hung it on the chair. "You know how it is."

Her eyes brightened immediately. "From the Guild?"

He poured himself a whiskey before he answered. The first sip burned clean through performance and rain and the memory of Lucia's skin under his mouth.

"Widow," he said. "Big check. Boring conversation."

Emily wrinkled her nose. "But the opera—" Her face lit like someone had turned up her voltage. "How was it? You saw Lucia, right? First time singing in the States. Everyone's talking about it. Did she—was she—?"

"She was... good," he said, and hated that he couldn't make the word sound like nothing.

Emily laughed, delighted and offended on Lucia's behalf. "Good? Alex. She's the Queen of the Night. Do you know how impossible those arias are? People train their whole lives just to—"

"It's opera," he cut in, too quickly. Then he softened his tone a fraction, as if tenderness could be negotiated. "Maybe I'll take you. Soon."

Her smile thinned. Then steadied. Emily swallowed whatever she'd wanted to say and took a sip of wine. Still, she couldn't help herself.

"You know Lucia trained in Tuscany, right?" Emily leaned forward. "I've listened to all her recordings. We're almost the same age. I mean, I assume she's a little older—" She got brighter as she spoke, the way she always did when music took the wheel. "There's even a rumor she auditioned at La Scala at eighteen, and the panel argued for days over whether to bend the rules. She's been called the most promising pupil of the Maestro."

Alex paused mid-sip. Mrs. March's question flashed in his mind, Lucia's eyes resetting so fast it was almost invisible. He kept his tone casual. "Who's the Maestro?"

Emily stared at him like he'd said he didn't know what Thanksgiving was. Then she put a hand to her chest, as if steadying herself. "You cannot be serious."

"Humor me."

"The Maestro is..." She searched for a word big enough and didn't find one. "He's a legend. A conductor. A trainer. Some people say it's all rumor, others swear he's the reason sopranos sound like weapons now."

Weapons. Alex's mouth twitched, almost a smile.

"He takes a handful of singers," she continued, "hides them in villas and rehearsal rooms, and what comes back isn't just a voice. It's... an instrument with a will."

Alex smirked. "And he's handsome, I assume. Otherwise, this sounds very illegal."

Emily colored, caught, and then made herself laugh. "He's Italian," she said, as if that absolved everything. "There are photos from years ago. Not many. And he wears a mask sometimes. It's a whole thing." Her laugh turned smaller, then softer. "When I was in college," she admitted, "I used to joke that if the Maestro ever heard me—*really heard me*—he'd call and ask me to come sing." Her eyes went distant, not sad exactly, but full. "I would've gone anywhere. Anywhere."

"But he didn't call," Alex said. The words came out flatter than he meant them to.

Emily smiled anyway, as if smoothing a wrinkle in her own story. "He didn't." She shrugged, gentle with herself. "And it's okay. I love my kids. I do. When one of them finds the center of a note and holds it, when they look up like they've caught a star in their throat..." Her eyes glassed, not from sorrow but from love. "It's enough."

Alex held her gaze a beat too long. Pretty enough. Marketable enough. The good woman he needed beside him when cameras turned, and voters listened. He didn't ask if she loved him. They didn't do that. They had an agreement. She made him look good, and he gave her the big-city life she wanted. Love was useful if it appeared. Unnecessary if it didn't.

He lifted his glass slightly. "To catching stars," he said.

Emily clinked her wine to the air. "To stars."

The knock came sharply. Three raps against the door.

Alex frowned. Midnight visitors in Pacific Heights weren't common. He crossed the living room and opened it.

Sergio stood there in a sharp suit, expression unreadable. Italian. Controlled. Eyes like flint. Alex recognized him instantly, the man who'd been shadowing Lucia, the one who spoke rules like prayers. Sergio held a bouquet of red roses, a chilled bottle of champagne, and an envelope sealed with black-and-red lace.

"For Miss Preen," he said, accent deliberate.

Emily gasped softly and hurried to the doorway. She took the envelope like it might crumble in her hands. Her fingers trembled as she broke the seal. Alex watched the color rise in her face as she read, pure joy, unguarded.

"An invitation to Sunday's matinee performance of The Magic Flute, featuring Lucia Conti as the Queen of the Night," Emily read aloud, voice shaking. "After the performance, an early dinner for two. And a nightcap on the stage of the San Francisco Opera House..." She looked up like she couldn't believe the ceiling hadn't opened. "So that Miss Preen might feel the power of standing where only the greatest voices have stood," she finished, barely able to breathe.

Alex's jaw tightened. "Looks like I made an impression," he said, voice dry.

Sergio's expression didn't move. "No, Signore." A clean pause. "This invitation is from the soprano herself." Then, precise as a blade: "You are not requested."

For a fraction of a second, Alex didn't hear the rest of the room. He heard only that sentence. Not requested. Not wanted. Not even worth the courtesy of inclusion.

It wasn't embarrassment that hit him. Alex didn't embarrass. It was something hotter. Something that made his pride stand up like hackles. The kind of anger that came when a door closed and you realized, too late, you'd assumed it would open for you.

Emily made a sound between a laugh and a sob, clutching the roses to her chest. "Alex, did you hear? Me. She invited me."

Sergio gave a small nod, all business. "Buona notte." *Good night.*

Alex closed the door before the silence could become a performance. The frame thudded. When the latch caught, Alex stood very still, hand still on the knob, until his face remembered what it was supposed to look like. Then he turned.

Emily was glowing, moving too fast, already talking about what to wear, what to bring, what to say, how she'd never dreamed Lucia Conti would know her name.

Alex watched her, watched how much this meant to her. Then he softened. Not into joy. Into something quieter. Practical. Gentle. The kind of kindness a man uses to manage guilt or control a narrative.

"That's... incredible," he said, and meant it.

Emily froze like she'd been waiting for that exact permission to feel everything at once. "Right?" Her voice cracked. "Alex, I—"

He crossed the room and took the roses from her arms so she didn't crush them. Found a vase. Filled it with water. Set them on the table like they deserved a place.

"You should go," he said evenly. "You'll love it."

Emily stared. "You're not mad?"

He kept his voice controlled. "No." It wasn't a lie. It just wasn't the whole truth.

He reached out and tucked a loose strand of hair behind her ear, small, familiar, something that looked like love from the outside. Then, softer: "You will text me when you're seated."

Emily blinked. “Really?”

“Yes,” he said, as if it were only practical. “Front row. Center. Take a photo of the view.

Her smile broke wider, bright and grateful. “Okay. I will.”

“Pick something simple,” he added. “Something you feel good in.”

Emily laughed through her happiness. “I’m going to try on everything I own.”

“I know,” he said, and his mouth almost smiled.

She hugged him quickly and earnestly. He let it happen. He even held her back, briefly, correctly, before easing away. “Go be excited,” he said. “I’ll pour you another glass.”

Emily nodded, wiping her cheeks, and disappeared toward the bedroom, already talking to herself about shoes.

The townhome filled with drawers opening and hangers clacking like castanets. Alex stayed in the living room. He poured another whiskey. The good stuff. He didn’t drink it right away. On the table, the black-and-red lace seal stared up at him like an eye. Lucia’s eye.

He stepped out onto the balcony and lit a cigarette he didn’t need. Fog hid the Golden Gate Bridge except for its red spine rising through the night like a cathedral arch. The bay shimmered below, black and silver, endless. This city would be his.

He’d paid his dues. Built the companies. Made the money. Played the part of the charming tech visionary until people stopped asking where he’d come from. In Silicon Valley, no one asked for birth certificates. They asked for balance sheets. But on nights like this, the mask felt heavier.

He came from nothing, an inland town no one visited, where jobs dried up and people cracked under the weight of survival. He'd lied his way out. Invented a past glossy enough to satisfy investors. And the persona had worked so well it became the truth.

Almost.

Beneath it, he was still the boy who watched his mother die because a mistake on her insurance paperwork delayed treatment long enough to make it useless. Still the boy who learned, young and furious and helpless, that "coverage" didn't mean care. That executives could call it policy while people called it a loss. Still the boy who watched his father grind himself flat on a factory line and then collapse under grief and exhaustion.

That was what made him. Not books. Not speeches. Not ideology. Just death, the kind of death rich people never had to understand.

He hated them. The donors. The people who toasted "healthcare innovation" while families begged on hold. The men who signed policies in glass towers and never once stood in a hospital hallway listening to someone, they loved struggle to breathe.

He smiled for them anyway. He promised them access. And one day, soon, he would betray them.

Emily thought he was building a campaign for power. She had no idea he was building a campaign for revenge. He would tell her someday, free her from the mask she wore for him. But not yet. She was too useful. Too perfect as a political ornament. And he wasn't done using her.

Alex took a drag and watched the smoke vanish into the fog. Then, because his mind had turned into a traitor, he let himself replay the evening. The donor suite. The widow's gin-slick breath. The Director's nervous voice. Lucia stepping into the light. He'd expected lust and boredom, nothing more.

But when Lucia spoke, the room changed. Donors set down their glasses without meaning to. The chandeliers seemed to still. Even Alex, who treated art like an accessory for important men, felt something shift behind his ribs, like a door he'd bricked up long ago taking one unpermitted breath.

He watched her mouth form daggers of sound. Watched the muscles in her throat flex like something tempered.

Beauty, yes. But beneath it, discipline so absolute it bordered on violence. And then that moment in the salon, her hand offered like an invitation, her gaze daring him to behave. His mouth on her skin. Her breath catching, small, involuntary.

And then the invitation. Not to him.

He'd expected jealousy. He'd expected irritation. What he hadn't expected was the humiliation of being excluded. The calculated insult of it. A woman he hadn't known existed four hours ago had just proven she could reach into his life and rearrange it with one envelope, and he could do nothing but watch.

It made her more dangerous. It made him want her more. He ground out the cigarette and leaned on the balcony rail, staring at the bridge.

"This city will change," he told the fog. "And I'll be the one to do it."

Chapter Five
The Prima Donna's Reflection

Morning came softly through the curtains. Lucia's suite overlooked the bay, windows washed in fog. San Francisco's gray was a new habit she was slowly learning not just to tolerate, but to love. The opera house slept behind her, exhausted from a week of packed houses, bright lights, and smiles that lined up to praise her as if praise were currency.

Praise had weight. It waited for her on the low table by the window: newspapers folded open to the arts pages, her tablet glowing with messages from directors she barely remembered, emails from critics who'd ignored her last season and had suddenly found vocabulary for her talent.

She rose slowly, slid into slippers, and reached for her robe. Her tea was already prepared, set out earlier by the housemaid, steam still curling from the cup like a small confession. Lucia pulled back the armchair and opened the first review.

She read it aloud, as if the room were an audience. It was a habit from the old rehearsal dormitory in Tuscany, where Marina and the other pupils had pretended to read rapturous reviews of performances that hadn't happened yet, flawless futures rehearsed like scales.

"A voice like cold starfire... coloratura that slices the ceiling and leaves the air glittering... an entrance that made the audience forget to breathe."

Lucia smiled without showing teeth. Night-blooming flowers left pollen; praise left residue. The paper crackled as she folded it and set it down. A knock followed, three precise taps. She didn't turn.

"Avanti," she called. *Come in.*

Sergio entered in a measured silhouette, moving with the quiet patience of a man who took pride in being unnoticed. In his hand was an envelope she'd been waiting for.

"Maestro," Sergio said simply.

Lucia made a small, casual gesture for him to sit. He remained standing anyway, as if chairs were permissions he no longer granted himself.

She broke the seal and read three words written in a clean, familiar hand.

"Brava, mia regina." *Bravo, my queen.*

For an instant, it warmed something in her, a part she hated to admit could still be warmed. She imagined the ink drying beneath his hand, the mask set aside on the desk, the villa holding its breath like a throat trained for silence.

Once, she would have kissed those words.

Now she placed the note on top of the review like it belonged there, another critic's praise, no more sacred than print.

She took a sip of tea. "Any letters, Sergio?" The question was light on the surface, careful enough to pass as routine. "From the others. Anya in Vienna. Leila in Paris. Sora in Seoul." She watched him over the rim of her cup. "From Berlin."

Sergio's fingers tapped once against his knee. Quiet. Controlled. He did not sit. He did not answer.

Instead, he stood straighter, as if he could physically block the question from traveling further into the room.

"I'll ask for more tea and breakfast," he said.

Lucia didn't stop him. She watched him choose silence the way other men chose lies.

At the door, Sergio hesitated, hand on the handle. When he finally spoke, his voice belonged to the walls.

"Berlin is not quiet," he said. "It's watched." Then he left.

Lucia stayed still, cup suspended halfway to her mouth, listening to the suite settle back into itself. Outside, fog made the bay look like erased ink. She held the memory of Marina's last note like a pressed flower between her ribs.

Do not stop singing because of me. I will find you once more.

Lucia knew the Maestro had seen it. What she didn't know, what she couldn't know, was how hard Marina had pushed him, and how close that silence was to becoming a sentence.

The maid returned with breakfast, setting the tray down with careful softness. Lucia ate little. She had work to do. Tonight would be her seventh performance and her most watched one yet. And it wasn't merely for an adoring audience. Tonight, she would sing for Emily Preen.

From beneath the stack of reviews, Lucia pulled out a black manila folder. She slid a photograph free and felt something in her chest tighten with the wrong kind of attention.

This was new. Not the mark, but the reflection.

The Maestro didn't usually waste time on reflections. He struck the target clean. He didn't pluck at the soft edges unless he wanted the wound to spread, unless he wanted the target to bleed from a place no headline could cauterize.

Emily's face didn't belong among passport scans and flight schedules. It belonged on a mantel, in the hallway of a home where love lived openly. She wore a soft cardigan, hair pulled into a practical bun, eyes unguarded.

Pretty in the way sunlight was pretty on a garden. Not sharp. Not glittering. Honest.

Lucia turned the photo over. Sergio's block handwriting listed facts like notes:

Utah-born. Public school music teacher. Volunteer program coordinator. Fiancée of Alexander Chambers, tech founder, mayoral candidate.

Lucia leaned back, letting the shape of it settle into place. The Maestro wanted a chord with dissonance hidden at the center. Humiliate the candidate without touching him. Humiliate his reflection, the woman who made him palatable. Let Emily step into the light and choose something else. Let goodness become negative space around the ruin of his pride. Cruel perfection. Emily was the path. Alex was the ruin.

Lucia flipped through the rest. Emily with children on a dilapidated school stage. Emily outside a food bank. Emily smiling at a modest holiday party. The opposite of the glitter Lucia had been drowning in all week.

Then the photos of Alex. Lucia had learned a great deal about men over the years. Something in his face didn't feel like simple arrogance or simple ambition. There was a seam in him, a pressure point.

A place he guarded too hard.

And the Maestro had found it.

Lucia didn't ask questions out of disobedience. She asked because if she was to sing this particular duet, she needed to know the other voice.

The answer came the way answers often did: not as logic, but as music. Emily loved art not for power, but for what it gave children. She would come to Lucia not because a Queen summoned her, but because a woman's voice had once saved her on a gray afternoon and might again.

And Alex? Lucia pressed her lips together.

The Maestro must have concluded Alex would bleed more from being deserted by goodness than from any scandal Lucia could orchestrate on her own. Not destruction by force. Destruction by contrast.

Lucia rose, moved into the bathroom, and shut the door behind her. She dropped her robe in front of the mirror and studied herself. Silk skin. Collarbones like a question. The disciplined softness of a body trained into obedience and made dangerous by it. She grazed her hands over herself, not to worship, simply to remember the difference between body and instrument.

She did not define herself by sex. The world would try. It always had. But if the world insisted on turning the body into a weapon, Lucia had learned where to aim it. Lucia loved making love not as conquest, but as liturgy. To men and to women. To voices quiet in ways some were too afraid to show. She loved the miracle of recognition, the way touch could translate a person back into themselves.

There were nights after certain seductions when

she sank into a bath and let the water decide whether she was light or heavy, whether the voice that rose belonged to the stage or the woman beneath it. She'd learned to carry ache like a charm hidden in the pocket of her gown.

She turned on the shower and stepped into the steam. Emily again, her photo returning like a refrain.

American girls were different. Not worse. Not better. They moralized desire even as they sold it. They treated sex like a dare that had to be shouted to be real. In Europe, desire was a language as old as bread. In America, it was a confession made in a parked car, breath fogging the windshield.

Emily would require patience. Emily would require permission.

Lucia would make the room soft, the light kind, the first touch plausible as an accident. Something that could be mistaken for nothing until it became undeniable.

Not performance. Revelation.

The words from the Maestro followed her into the water. "Brava, mia regina." *Bravo, my queen.*

Once, she'd wanted more than praise. She turned her back to the water and let it fall against the place where marks used to bloom, where memory still lived under skin.

Tuscany returned, sharp as scent. The veranda. Cicadas practicing relentless scales. The villa's stone drinking sun. They'd finished a rehearsal that scraped her throat raw, and the air outside tasted like reprieve. She stood beside him not as pupil but as woman, still trembling with breathlessness.

"The world is on fire. We will nourish it with

water." He spoke gently.

Lucia turned toward him. He turned with her. And for one fragile moment, there was nothing between their mouths but wanting. When his lips met hers, she believed, like a fool, that he had chosen her. Not just her voice. Her.

She'd cupped his jaw with both hands and offered him something that wasn't discipline but invitation. "Be a man with me. Come apart with me, just once. Let music be a bridge and not a cage."

He kissed her back. The universe felt safe. Then he corrected it. Punishment was never a surprise; punishment was the grammar of their world. Still, its fervor reached into her like betrayal of the air they'd just shared.

Hours later, she sang the same lines he demanded, blood in the vowels. He didn't look at her mouth. He listened only for obedience and nodded when satisfied.

After that, she didn't try to reach inside him again. She mourned something she never named, then hardened the grief into weaponry.

If he could not be pierced by love, she would not attempt to pierce him with it. Her body would be an instrument. Her heart would be a private garden where no batons were allowed.

A knock pulled her back into the present.

"Signorina," Sergio called through the door. "We have a schedule."

Lucia shut off the water, dried herself, and wrapped herself in a terry robe. When she returned to the living area, Sergio sat with his folio open, posture careful as a man standing on a narrow ledge.

Lucia's eyes went to the table, to Emily's photo, then back to Sergio. "What has the Maestro planned?"

"Today," Sergio said, "the stage will be transformed. An early dinner. After the show."

"She'll be cold," Lucia said immediately.

Sergio's gaze held hers. "Then you will keep her warm."

A beat.

Lucia's voice lowered. "She is not a pawn."

Sergio's jaw tightened. "To him, everyone is." His eyes flicked to the folder on the table. "Even you."

The words landed harder than he intended, and still he didn't soften them.

Lucia didn't look away. "Then I'll stop behaving like one."

Sergio's mouth pressed into a line. He didn't argue. He didn't have to. They both knew what it meant to cross the Maestro. They both knew how quickly "correction" could turn inward when it wasn't controlled.

"The crew will dress the stage," Sergio continued. "One light. One table. A chef modest, but revered. He will treat her like a queen." He paused, weighing his next words. "But you must not let that become a promise you cannot keep."

Lucia moved closer, voice gentler now. "She is not bait to me."

"The Maestro believes she is," Sergio said, and the sentence sounded less like accusation than warning.

Lucia's gaze sharpened. "I don't."

Sergio studied her the way a man studies a fuse. "Approachable," he said at last. "No crown. No thorns. She is a teacher."

Lucia nodded, already composing the night like a score. "Soft red," she agreed. "Hair down. A loose braid, maybe."

"I will bring her to the wing," Sergio said. "We will wait for you. You will give her the stage."

Lucia's gaze softened, then steadied into something more dangerous than softness. "She will lead," she said, as if stating a principle. "I will follow her pace. I will not take what she hasn't offered."

Sergio's expression flickered with approval, or relief. "Bene," he said. *Good.*

Lucia picked up the folio as if it were hers now. "No clutter on the table," she said, certainty settling into her voice. "Candles low. Warm plates. Champagne to greet her, nothing too sharp."

She thought for a moment, tasting the menu as if she could already hear it.

"Stone fruit and goat cheese with basil. Hand-cut pasta. Shaved truffle. Dungeness crab, something of the bay, something that belongs to this city."

Sergio's mouth twitched. "Dessert, Signora?"

"Dark chocolate and fig," Lucia said. "Portable." She nodded toward the suite. "We finish it in here. After."

Sergio held up a small, careful warning without accusation. "Lucia. This is... a lot of detail."

Lucia met his eyes. "Because it matters."

His voice lowered. "You are flying too close to the sun."

Lucia pretended not to hear the caution beneath it. She thought of Marina's silence. How it had expanded, day by day, into something that felt like a threat. How Sergio had said Berlin was watched.

This would not be a seduction of ruin for Emily.

Lucia would handle the Maestro and Alex another way. Tonight, would be a lesson in pleasure. She would not break Emily to use her. She would raise her.

One word of praise. One slow breath. One kiss offered only when asked, until the woman who arrived bashful at the stage door left Lucia's suite knowing her own divinity.

Lucia picked up Emily's photo one last time and felt what she always felt before a performance: the dilation of the world, the slight tremor under her ribs as air became choice.

If he wants humiliation, she thought, he will have it. Then another thought wrote itself quietly beneath that one, steadier and truer.

"If a woman comes to me on a night she might regret in the morning, it is my job to make sure she doesn't."

Sergio watched her a moment longer, as if deciding which version of her would survive this. Finally, he closed the folio. "We leave in two hours," he said. "And Lucia?" She looked up. His voice was very soft. "If Marina calls, you answer. Even if the Maestro is watching."

Lucia's throat tightened once, controlled. She nodded. "I always answer Marina," she said. And for the first time all morning, the truth felt like a vow.

Chapter Six
The Matinee

Alex woke to the sound of hair dryers and the smell of heat-protectant mist, chemical jasmine, and singed silk drifting down the hall like a promise. Sunday. By noon, the light felt clean and untheatrical, perfect for a two o'clock matinee.

He lay still and listened. Brushes clinked in glass jars. Someone laughed, Emily, high and breathless, and a stylist answered in the soothing sing-song professionals use to keep excitement from tipping into tears. His home had become a backstage: garment bags unzipped, mirrors circled with light, a narrow procession of women arriving with rolling kits and competence.

His phone sat face down on the nightstand. He'd meant to sleep. Instead, sometime after midnight, he'd done what he always did when he couldn't control the room: he'd tried to control the information. He watched Lucia in other cities, other gowns, other lights. He read the profiles, the breathless praise, the rumors dressed up as journalism. Photos too. Lucia on Mediterranean beaches he couldn't name, arms of men he didn't recognize at her waist, a prince here, a financier there, the kind of company that made headlines without ever needing to be introduced. She sang for royals, for governments, for rooms that could make or break a person with a smile.

So how had she noticed him? And why, of all people, had she chosen Emily?

Enemies came for him all the time. That was the cost of being visible. Alex knew how to take a hit, how to bleed in private and smile in public. Emily didn't.

He pushed himself up and stared down the hall, listening to her laughter drift through the townhouse like proof she still didn't know what kind of games could be played with a person. He never wanted anything bad to happen to her. That was the truth, even if he'd built his life on other kinds of truth.

Emily had barely slept. He knew it from the way she padded out at three a.m. to make chamomile, then slid back into bed still murmuring facts to the dark: Lucia's conservatories, aria names, some anecdote about a rehearsal in Vienna where the lights went out and the soprano kept singing because the hall itself knew the cue. He'd offered mm-hmm at the appropriate places and willed his mind blank.

Now he watched from the doorway as Emily turned, eyes closed, while a makeup artist feathered light into her face. Her skin took glow without protest; she was the kind of pretty that didn't need marketing. A stylist teased her hair into something soft and theatrical, not the schoolteacher twist she wore when she came home with clef stamps on her fingers. On the armchair waited a tea-length dress he'd never seen, ice-blue silk crepe that skimmed rather than shouted, paired with a soft cashmere wrap and delicate heels. The outfit looked like courage made wearable.

"Too much?" Emily asked the room, though her eyes stayed on the mirror, not on him.

"Perfect," the stylist said. "Classic. Not trying too hard."

Alex swallowed the small nerve that pricked his pride. He didn't like being irrelevant in his own home, and this morning he was a prop between two professionals and a woman turning toward a kind of light he didn't own.

His phone buzzed with the morning's campaign choreography: graphs, a screenshot of last night's total ("$1.3M confirmed"), a link to the podcast he'd recorded earlier in the week ("Top of the feed; trending upward; you sound like the adult in the room"), a clipped message from policy reminding him to retweet the housing plan thread by noon. He tapped through them with the practiced split-screen of a man who could campaign while staring through his own windows at a life he might never get to inhabit.

San Francisco will be a working city again. Fair. Honest. An ecosystem that rewards contribution, not just capital. He typed a thank-you to the finance chair and deleted the smiley face twice before sending.

By the time he pocketed the phone, Emily had become a version of herself he'd never met. The dress, the glow, the careful artifice of mascara made the joy on her face look almost cinematic. She stepped down from the stool and touched her earlobe, as if the small pearl there could keep her from floating up toward the ceiling.

"Wow," he said, and meant it in spite of himself.

Her smile broke open. "You think so? It's not too...? I mean, it is a lot, but she—" Again that detonation gesture. She reached for her clutch and fumbled, nervous electricity spilling out of her. "I can't believe she invited me."

He could. He believed it so fiercely his teeth ached. He'd never seen Emily look like this for him.

"You should enjoy it," he said, and meant it. Then he stepped closer, close enough to really see her: the careful shimmer on her cheekbones, the way her throat moved when she swallowed, the courage disguised as excitement. "But, Emily..." His voice lowered. "With your permission, I'd like to come with you." Emily's eyes flew up to the mirror. "Not to take away your day," he added quickly. "I'll grab the cheap seats. I'll be invisible."

She studied him, a little suspicious of his sudden gentleness. "Alex," she sighed, "you're letting the dramatics of the opera mess with your reality."

"Maybe." He lifted her hand, slow and deliberate, and pressed his mouth to her knuckles, soft, old-fashioned, almost reverent. When he looked up, his charm had seams showing. "Would you laugh at me if I said something feels off about all of this?"

Emily hesitated. "Off how?"

"I don't know. I read things I shouldn't have read." He kept his tone light, but his eyes weren't. "I just know you're my fiancée, and if anything happened to you because of me, I wouldn't forgive myself."

He didn't say I love you. The word sat behind his teeth, too risky to offer when he wasn't sure she'd believe it wasn't another performance.

Emily blinked, as if she hadn't expected him to say the right thing without being prompted. "Okay," she whispered, grateful and a little shaken. "You can come."

Alex nodded once, as if he'd just sealed a decision. He picked up her lipstick from the counter and slipped it into her clutch without comment, an ordinary gesture that felt like a vow he wasn't ready to name.

"You won't even know I'm there," he said, and tried to make it sound light.

He went to his closet and pulled a suit. Not tuxedo formal. Not casual. Dark, lean, the kind of cloth that turned you into a line drawing. When he came out, knotting his tie, Emily's reflection caught him.

"You look nice," she said softly.

He made a small sound of gratitude and discomfort and finished his cuff links with manufactured steadiness.

The buzzer sounded. Sergio had arrived.

When Alex opened the door, the man was already extending an arm toward Emily, palm up, as if escorting royalty. Roses again, this time a profusion so red they carried their own gravity.

"Miss Preen," Sergio said, bowing the exact amount courtesy requires when it knows it will be obeyed. "The car is ready."

He turned his head slightly toward Alex without moving the rest of his body. "Signore. You are not invited."

Alex smiled as if listening to a charming superstition. "We can share the car. Drop me at the public entrance. I got some cheap seats in the back."

Sergio's mouth performed something that, in a kinder man, would have been a frown. "This is a personal invitation," he repeated, accent curling around personal like a velvet rope. "From the soprano herself."

"It's fine," Emily said quickly, placing a gentle hand on Sergio's sleeve. "He can ride with us.

Please." She glanced at Alex with something between apology and appeal. "It'll save time."

Sergio weighed the request the way a jeweler weighs gold. Then he inclined his head once, clipped. "As you wish."

Outside the townhouse, a limousine waited at the curb, black and obedient, paint so glossy it made reflections behave. A driver held the rear door as Sergio slid into the back first, taking the small rear-facing seat, posture immaculate. Alex followed, then Emily, gathered into the center like the reason the car existed.

Emily's breath caught. The back seat was a small mythology: more roses laid like a low tide; a silver bucket sweating cold around a chilled bottle of champagne engraved with a crest Alex didn't recognize; and, absurdly, a bouquet of cotton candy spiraled into a confectionery sculpture, cellophane rustling like opera tulle.

Alex almost laughed. Then didn't.

"Childhood favorite," Sergio said, watching Emily's face the way a conductor watches a soloist. "The soprano wants only to indulge Miss Emily's wishes today, and is honored to host her."

Emily put a hand to her mouth and then to her heart. "How does she even know—" She looked at Alex, flushed, pleading with him to be happy with her. "My grandfather took me to the fair every summer. Cotton candy before fireworks. I..." She shook her head, overwhelmed. "This is silly. I'm sorry."

"It isn't silly," Sergio said, and for the first time his voice gentled. "It is specific."

He leaned forward, steadying the bucket with one hand as the car began to roll. With the other, he popped the cork, a soft, polite sound that belonged to rooms with better manners than most people. He poured a single glass and offered it to Emily. She tugged a pink pillow of sugar from the bouquet and let it melt on the rim; foam threaded into the champagne like a blush.

Alex watched her take a sip, eyes closing as if permission were a flavor. He wanted to be irritated at the theatrics, the curated indulgence, the way every detail conspired to make him an extra in a scene designed for her. But another part of him, quieter and more dangerous, took notes.

This is how you disarm people: you make them feel seen down to the silliest, sweetest corner of their childhood. You build altars to their small joys.

Traffic folded away for them. The driver took wider streets as if the city were a ballroom and prosperity had the right of way. Outside, Sunday moved in its usual choreography: strollers, brunch, joggers negotiating with their better selves. Inside the car, the air thickened into ceremony. Emily kept glancing between the roses and the window, as if the world were competing with the gift for her attention.

"Miss Preen," Sergio said, "the Queen is honored you accepted. She looks forward to hearing you breathe the hall."

Emily laughed that soft, breathless laugh again. "I won't be singing."

"Everyone sings," Sergio replied. "Some remember."

Alex pinched the bridge of his nose and hid the shape of a smile. The man annoyed him, but the lines sounded rehearsed; deliberate, aphoristic, the kind of thing people forgave because it sounded profound.

Emily tucked a strand of hair behind her ear and looked at Alex. "You sure about the cheap seats?"

"Positive," he said automatically, then corrected himself, gentler. "I'll be nearby." He tapped the inside pocket where his confirmation warmed his sternum. Row P. Not the back. Close enough to see. Close enough to move. "You go," he added, searching for a word that didn't snag in his throat. "Be... adored."

Emily held his gaze a heartbeat longer than he expected, as if memorizing the rare moment when he didn't make a joke at the expense of the things that made her heart bigger. Then she looked away, and he was released.

They turned onto the avenue that led to the opera house. The building rose from the block like a white commandment. Banners snapped; tourists posed with arms flung wide before history. Alex felt the same uneasy pull in his chest he'd felt in the donor suite, the old door in his rib cage creaking open against his will.

It will be different from Row P, he told himself. And the voice that argued back said: It doesn't matter where you sit when the knife comes from the stage.

As the limousine slowed under the portico, Sergio spoke. "Signore, the public lobby is through the main doors on your right."

Alex could hear satisfaction in the last word.

Emily set the cotton candy bouquet in her lap like a sleeping animal and took one more small sip of blushing champagne. Then she reached for Alex's hand, squeezed it with gratitude, apology, joy layered thin as vellum, and let go.

"Text me where you are after?" she asked.

"I will," he said, and meant it.

A red-coated attendant appeared as if conjured and opened Emily's door. Emily stepped into the light the way people step into a cathedral: awed, self-conscious, braver than a minute ago. Sergio followed, offered his arm, and she took it, letting him escort her up onto the marble as if the building itself had been waiting for her.

"Miss Preen," Sergio murmured, "welcome."

Emily turned back once before the lobby swallowed her, eyes bright, clutch held tight, roses and sugar and champagne making her look like someone else's story. Alex lifted his fingers in a half-wave that felt like surrender. Then the door shut between them, and the limo continued toward the entrance he had no intention of using quietly.

The public lobby was full of daylight Sunday matinee crowds in tasteful neutrals, linen and pearls, the murmur of subscribers who knew where to stand and how to look like they belonged. No gala peacocks from opening night. This was a different constellation of eyes. Alex kept to the pillars and watched.

Emily didn't come through the main crush. An usher lifted a velvet rope at a side vestibule and said her name as if it carried rank. Roses preceded her like a procession; a staffer cradled the cotton candy bouquet so it wouldn't brush the marble. Heads turned, curious, appraising.

A board member's spouse glanced, then glanced again, expression rearranging itself into interest. Heat rose under Alex's collar. The opening night gala's donors had been courted. Today, Emily was being paraded.

Small courtesies unfurled around her that attention invents on short notice: a folded program ready in an usher's hand, a glass of water appearing the moment her throat moved, a whisper at her shoulder.

How?

Alex's mind picked at it with the precision of a thief. This wasn't Emily pulling strings. This was someone else arranging the world around her, someone who wanted her to feel special enough to forget to be careful. He slid his hands into his pockets to cage the urge to ball them.

Fine. Enjoy the coronation.

He would take his seat and mark the exits. He would be close enough to see the edges of whatever this was. Close enough to interrupt if it turned sharp.

Row P carried a hush of its own, close enough to read the conductor's breath, far enough to see the stage as a drawn bow. Afternoon light slanted through the high glass, thinning as the house lights fell in gentle degrees. The ceiling's gilt softened to honey; a thousand small conversations closed like books. A violin offered an A, pure as a thread pulled taut. The orchestra tuned in a brief storm of agreement. The conductor walked on to decorous applause, bowed, and turned his back to the room.

Alex felt the pulse in his wrist settle into the downbeat before a single note was played. He found Emily across the orchestra: two sections over, three rows ahead, flowers tucked neatly under her seat by an usher who'd anticipated the problem. Even from here he could see the way she held herself upright, a tremor at the throat, first-time awe.

The overture began brisk, crystalline, clockwork joy pretending not to know what darkness waits in fairy tales. Alex tried to think about policy, about the tweet thread he had to post at intermission, about donors who might be in this crowd wearing subtler masks. Instead, his gaze kept sliding to the empty slice of stage where he knew she would appear.

When the Queen entered, the room's temperature changed. Lucia didn't so much step into the light as bend it. The gown was midnight; the corset was armor; the crown threw cold fire onto the proscenium. Even the dust in the spotlight seemed to tighten, as if the air itself knew to behave.

It wasn't the costume that tightened Alex's chest. It was her stillness. The way she owned the square of air around her, as if gravity had taken her name. He told himself to breathe, once, evenly.

The first note was gorgeous in the way a threat is gorgeous. It stole his breath, then returned it on its own terms. And for a treacherous heartbeat, his mind supplied a different stage: Lucia's hand offered, his mouth lowering, her breath catching, that small gasp she tried to hide. Then the next note struck, clean and cold, and the vision shattered.

The audience leaned forward as one organism, as if proximity could keep them safe. Alex didn't lean. He sat very still and let the sound arrive like a verdict. He'd wanted to be immune. He wasn't. Beneath the brilliance, he could hear something else: discipline trained past kindness, iron under glass. It felt familiar in a way that made his teeth ache.

Lucia's eyes swept the house. He was nowhere special, Row P, a man among men. Still, idiot that he was, he braced. If she found him, he wasn't sure whether he wanted to be seen or spared.

The aria crested. Applause broke like surf and retreated just as quickly when she lifted a hand in authority without effort. Alex's jealousy performed a small, private tantrum, then sat down to take notes.

Intermission was twenty minutes, just enough time to move without looking like he was moving. To investigate this invitation and interest this Queen of the Night had with Emily. He watched. He looked and found nothing. After the bows, he assumed they would hold Emily at her seat and take her through the North Stage Door. Alex mapped the aisles. From his row, he could cut left, skim the back of the orchestra, and reach the side corridor before the lobby clogged. He turned his phone to silent and slid it into his breast pocket like a promise.

Back onstage, Lucia sank the last dagger of sound into silence and gave the audience her stillness again. It felt like a dare. It felt like recognition. It felt disastrously like fate's idea of a joke. He applauded with everyone else and did not smile. If this were a game, he was done letting other people decide who the pieces were.

When the curtain fell and the house breathed out, he would already be moving. Aisle left, along the back of the orchestra, shadow to the North Door.

Let them parade Emily. Let them crown her.

He would follow the procession to the edge of whatever door opened next and make sure Emily didn't pay for someone else's power.

Chapter Seven
The Onstage Dinner

Steam still clung to Lucia's shoulders as the dresser eased the gown away. Silk, pins, a hush. Powder lifted in pale clouds when the makeup artist brushed beneath her eyes. Another set of hands unhooked the corset with the reverence of someone closing a reliquary. The matinee had come down like a tide. Applause still shimmered somewhere high in the rafters, an echo returning to itself.

"Careful," the dresser murmured.

Lucia had been born careful, careful enough to bleed beauty without spilling.

The door clicked open. Sergio appeared at the threshold. Two assistants moved to intercept him. No men in here, not during disrobing. Lucia lifted a hand.

"È a posto," Lucia said. *It's fine*. "He's seen me in worse states than this."

The nearest stylist blanched. Sergio's mouth performed the smallest, private smile. He did not cross the threshold. He extended a phone wrapped in a linen handkerchief, as if it were something sacred.

"Per te," he said. *For you*.

Lucia's neck prickled. Unusual. The Maestro lived in directives and notes. He did not call.

She turned to the staff. "Grazie. Enough for now."

They hesitated, looking to Sergio for confirmation despite themselves. Then they filed out with an armful of silk and pins, the last door-softening clack leaving Lucia alone with the mirror.

The phone felt heavier than its size.

"Pronta," Sergio said. *Ready*. He withdrew, closing the door so gently the latch made no sound.

Lucia brought the receiver to her ear with a hesitation that felt like confession. She was still bare, skin flushed from scrubbing, hair damp and dark down her back. The mirror offered her the indecency of truth. She did not reach for a robe. If he wanted to speak to the instrument, he could speak to it unadorned.

The line opened into breath.

"Brava," the Maestro said. "Mia regina." *My queen*. "No one holds the square of air the way you do."

Her mouth went dry. Even across distance, his voice penetrated like a tuning fork tapped against bone. Memory lit her skin. Balcony. Baton. The veranda's kiss and its correction. She was a map of places he had already claimed.

He said nothing for a moment. The silence worked like pressure. Without thinking, Lucia's hand drifted to her chest, fingers resting over her sternum as if steadying a note. His exhale grazed the line.

"Non ti ho detto di farlo," he said. *I didn't tell you to do that*.

Her hand fell, obedient as a curtain. She could hear the recalibration. The exactness of it. The way he could place a thought on a half-beat.

"Do you want to prepare yourself for Miss Preen?" he asked softly. "Are you ready to bend her to your will, Lucia?"

Heat moved through her, then ache, then the practiced mastery that turns heat and ache into art. Sitting felt like yielding, so she stood. Even standing felt like the beginning of a bow.

"I am ready to perform," she said.

"You have performed," he murmured. "Are you ready to ruin?" Then, because indulgence always wore restraint in his mouth, he spent praise he rarely spent. "When you entered, you were carved in fire. The line of your back. The stillness. The way your breath makes a house shake." A pause. "Your beauty is not decoration. It is structured. Soft features, sì, but power under glass. Men forget the names they brought with them."

Praise. A dangerous sugar. It rots if you keep it under your tongue too long. Marina's name burned the back of Lucia's throat. The silences in Berlin bruised her thoughts. She did not let her voice show the bruise.

"I work to remain worthy," she answered, measured. "Miss Preen will be a delight." A beat. "An education."

"Dimostramelo," he said. *Show me.*

"Sempre," Lucia replied. *Always.*

And because her spine remembered the veranda and refused to yield to shame, she added carefully, "Sono la tua soprano, Maestro." *I am your soprano, Maestro.*

The line clicked clean, final, as if he could not allow certain words to live too long in the air.

The door opened at once. Sergio took the phone with two fingers and his handkerchief, as if absolving them both of fingerprints. His gaze swept the room, saw her nakedness without hunger or prudery, only inventory, then flicked to the wardrobe.

"Rosso?" he asked. *Red?*

"Rosso," Lucia said. *Red.*

The room resumed its choreography. The corset stayed gone. A silk chemise slid over Lucia's skin. Then a satin red dress, moving like a thought. Her hair was unbraided and re-braided over one shoulder. Skin polished, not powdered. Mouth in rouge, not gloss. Nails lacquered carmine, warning and promise in equal measure.

"Red is not a costume," Lucia told the junior stylist, whose hands trembled with the privilege of being this close to myth. "It's a key."

In the doorway, Sergio spoke in a low voice to a security captain. Lucia caught fragments. "North corridor." "Keep clear." Then, quieter: "Chambers."

Her mouth went still. Not surprise. Confirmation.

"Bene," Lucia said. *Good.* "The sooner the better."

The donors' suite held a particular kind of air. Perfume that had never belonged to skin. Fruit bowls arranged to look accidental. Glass that made the city behave. The Director turned from a cluster of patrons mid-sentence, relief and rapture sharing his face.

"Divina," he breathed. "They will talk about this season for years."

Then Emily came into view, framed by the window, champagne trembling near the bodice of her tea-length dress. At the sight of Lucia, she gasped. A small, involuntary intake. The sound a hall makes when a miracle shows up in daylight.

The glass tipped. Two pin-bright drops leapt for satin.

Lucia caught the stem with one hand and, with the other, reached into Sergio's breast pocket without looking. She found his handkerchief as if she'd placed it there herself. She dabbed, not rubbed. She kept her face close enough to Emily's that the world narrowed to breath and lashes.

"Non vergognarti," Lucia whispered. *Don't be embarrassed.* "Don't be embarrassed, Miss Preen."

Emily swallowed, color blooming at her throat. "I'm sorry."

"Shh." Lucia smiled, soft and exact. "I am a woman like you." Her gaze held Emily's long enough to make the statement true. "I'm pleased you're here," Lucia added. "Truly."

Emily's eyes went glossy. "I've been looking forward to meeting you my whole life."

The Director cleared his throat, the briskness of a man trying to schedule a miracle. "The hall is being dressed for dinner. If you'd like a tour while we wait..."

Lucia did not look away from Emily.

"Con il tuo permesso," Lucia said. *With your permission. She offered her hand.* Emily's fingers landed in Lucia's palm as if they'd rehearsed the gesture in sleep.

They moved through private corridors where the opera keeps its memory. Props asleep under muslin. Faded posters declaring seasons won and weathered. A rehearsal room smelling faintly of rosin and warmed varnish. The handler ghosted behind at a tactful distance, speaking into his cuff now and then in a language of doors and timing.

Lucia did not talk about herself. She animated the house. A corner where a diva once laughed so hard a costume split. Battered chairs where chorus tenors solved crosswords between entrances. The trick of the great hall where a whisper at center returns to you like an answer.

Emily drank every word like someone who'd been thirsty in public and had finally found a private well.

"Water?" Lucia asked, the single syllable holding kindness and a question about breath.

Emily nodded. Lucia handed her a glass and watched her swallow, watched her throat work. Only then did Lucia place her palm, visible and askable, at the small of Emily's back.

"Così?" Lucia murmured. *Like this?*

"Yes," Emily breathed, relief threading the sound.

"Va bene," Lucia said. *Good.* Her hand remained. Protective. Steady. Nothing stolen.

Onstage, the crew had made a room out of emptiness. A small table waited at the center under a single stand light, linen like a low cloud. Silver breathed cold beside a bottle turned to discretion. The curtain lounged like a crimson animal. The hall beyond was quiet enough that dust motes looked like constellations auditioning for relevance.

Emily stopped short. "Oh." She pressed the back of her free hand to her lips, as if holding in a word too large to say.

"This is yours," Lucia said, and heard the defiance in her own voice. Defiance against the man who had asked for a pawn. "For this evening. All of it."

Sergio cleared his throat softly. In the wing, a chef in whites waited with priestly precision. Lucia inclined her head.

He approached the table and set the first plate down with tenderness.

"Tomales Bay oysters," he murmured to Emily, not Lucia. "Lemon. A breath of mignonette. If you close your eyes, you'll taste salt and eucalyptus."

Emily laughed through something close to tears and did as she was told. When she opened her eyes, they were glossier than the sea.

They sat. Lucia waited until Emily took the first chair before she took the second.

"Tell me about your students," Lucia said, and the question opened a door.

Emily spoke, not in the breathless fan's language, but in the private glow of vocation. Names, stories. A child who only found pitch when no one watched. Another who insisted a bassoon sounded like a haunted closet. A fifth-grader whose bravery arrived in increments. Lucia listened with the attention she usually reserved for scores.

Courses arrived with the gentleness Lucia had ordered. Stone fruit with basil and goat cheese. Hand-cut pasta finished in butter. Crab bright as a bell. Wine that listened, then forgave. The chef narrated with affectionate pedagogy, as if teaching a duet between hunger and grace.

As plates changed, Lucia narrowed the world to the space between them.

"Ms. Conti—"

"Lucia," she corrected gently. "Please." A beat, and then, soft, certain: "We're sisters." The last word landed like a rule. Lucia surprised herself with it. She felt the shift in the room, the way she felt a tempo change in her bones. In the stand light, looking at Emily's open face, her eagerness, her careful reverence, the way she tried so hard to do everything right, Lucia saw it with a sudden sting.

Not Emily Preen.

Marina.

For a heartbeat, she couldn't breathe. The light in Emily's eyes was the old Marina-bright, earnest, desperate to be worthy. Lucia steadied herself. Changed the score back into something the audience could survive.

Emily swallowed. "This has all been... wonderful." Her fingers tightened around the stem of her glass. "But I have to ask. Why?"

Lucia's smile warmed, too warm, because it was trying not to break. "Why not, signora?"

Emily's laugh came out small. "Because it feels too good to be true."

"How do you mean?"

Lucia rose, carrying her sparkling water as if it were part of the staging. She moved to Emily's side, not looming, not cornering, simply present.

Emily's voice lowered. "You have a vendetta against Alex. My fiancé. This is to get under his skin."

Lucia let out a laugh, full and sudden, almost musical. It startled Emily into a blush.

"My dear," Lucia said, tenderness deliberate, "if you think that is why you're here, then you've been trained to see yourself as someone who needs a man, instead of someone a man should be terrified to lose."

Emily blinked. "I—"

Lucia extended her hand. Palm up. A choice offered, not demanded.

"I have no vendetta against your fiancé," Lucia said softly. "I have only a question for you."

Emily's fingers landed in Lucia's palm, tentative.

Lucia lifted Emily's hand and kissed the back of it, slow, courtly, intimate. Then she inhaled lightly against Emily's skin, the way a lover does right before taking.

Emily's breath caught.

"Why don't you exist without him?" Lucia asked softly.

"I don't understand."

"You will." Lucia's thumb stroked once over Emily's knuckles, gentle, anchoring. "Come with me."

Onstage, the hall waited empty, enormous, listening. Lucia guided Emily to the center, the mark where the boards tell the truth.

"I knew of you before my plane landed," Lucia said.

Emily's eyes widened. "How?"

"The music world is small." Lucia held her gaze. "We know who applies. Who gets rejected. Who keeps showing up anyway." A careful pause, then she stepped around the word she shouldn't say. "When I'm assigned to a new house," Lucia continued, "I learn who is protecting the music."

Emily's throat moved. "The Maestro—"

Lucia didn't deny it. She simply softened her voice.

"Sì," Lucia said. Yes. "And you, my love, are protecting it more than you realize."

Emily's eyes glossed. She looked overwhelmed by the attention, by the intimacy threaded into it. "I had... I didn't..."

"You remind me of one of my sisters," Lucia said quietly. "Marina." The name flickered and was gone, swallowed before it could become grief. Lucia stepped behind Emily, close enough that her breath could be felt but not used as force. "Tell me, Emily..." Lucia let the name roll slowly off her tongue as her lips hovered near Emily's ear. "Can you sing like her?"

"No," Emily whispered.

"Why?" Lucia's hands settled lightly at Emily's waist, visible and askable, turning her toward the empty seats as if the audience were there. "Tell them why you cannot."

Emily's voice shook at first, then steadied. "When I was little, I thought opera was only for women who had something to prove. That the gowns and crowns were shields." She lifted her eyes to the chandelier's patient glitter. "But when you sang, I..." She faltered. "I felt like I'd been very brave once. And then I forgot." A pause. "This isn't for me."

Lucia's hand warmed at Emily's spine. "You're brave now," she said. "Bravery isn't noise."

She guided Emily to the mark again. "Here. Breathe." Then, gently: "Say your name."

Emily laughed, embarrassed. "Emily?"

"Say it," Lucia urged, smiling.

"Emily," she whispered.

The hall returned it a heartbeat later, larger, kinder, as if the building had decided she mattered. Tears came and didn't fall. Emily exhaled, astonished.

"It's like—"

"A cathedral," Lucia supplied. "And it belongs to you." Lucia didn't step away.

"May I touch you?" she asked, clean, exact.

"Yes," Emily said, and the yes landed steady.

"Here," Lucia murmured, coming behind her. "Crown long. Shoulders released." She hovered, then placed her palms at the tops of Emily's arms, easing them back until the sternum rose. "Let the ribs open. Appoggio." *Support.*

Emily exhaled. A small shiver moved through her. "Like this?"

"Almost." Lucia set two fingers at Emily's side ribs, then low back, the place where breath turns into sound. "Don't lift your chest to be seen. Let breath do it for you."

She stepped to Emily's side, close enough that their sleeves whispered. "Say your name again."

"Emily," Emily breathed.

Lucia hummed softly a third above, then in unison, building a scaffold of sound for Emily to climb. "Feel where it lives," she whispered, guiding Emily's hand to the high belly, then the side ribs. "Here... and here."

Emily pressed lightly through silk. "I can feel it," she said, surprised and delighted.

Lucia faced her now, so close Emily could count the beats in Lucia's throat.

"May I?" Lucia traced the hinge of Emily's jaw, encouraging slack. "The mouth is an opening, not a gate."

Emily's lips parted on instinct. Lucia's breath caught, one involuntary note, then steadied.

"Brava," Lucia murmured. *Well done.*

Emily's gaze dropped to Lucia's mouth and stayed there.

"Emily," Lucia said, the name a vow more than a question.

"Yes," Emily breathed.

Lucia kissed her slow, shown before taken. The first press of mouths was tender and exact. When Emily answered, Lucia deepened, tasting lemon and sea and the faint sweetness of champagne. She caught Emily's lower lip, released it with a breath, and let the smallest stroke of tongue feel like a bow on a string.

Emily made a quiet sound, more breath than voice.

Lucia drew back just enough to keep everything visible. "Again?" she asked, not command, choice.

Emily nodded. "Again."

Lucia didn't hurry the second kiss. She let Emily rise to meet it. Consent held between them like ribbon taut, beautiful, unbroken. Lucia's hand settled at Emily's waist, open and declarative: you are held.

Emily's fingers came to Lucia's dress, trembling at the satin like a question.

Lucia guided the hand gently up to where her own breath moved beneath the fabric. "Listen," she whispered. "This isn't stagecraft. It's consequence."

Emily's palm paused, then stayed. Lucia exhaled through her nose, a quiet surrender she didn't offer easily.

Somewhere beyond the wing, a foot scuffed. A man's voice, muffled and startled, broke on a half syllable, then was swallowed at once by quiet, as if someone had pressed a hand over it.

The disturbance crossed them like a shadow and disappeared. Lucia didn't turn. She only tightened her hand at Emily's waist, protective, present.

"Still okay?" she asked softly.

"Yes," Emily whispered, steadier now. Trust learning its posture.

Lucia kissed her once more, slower, deeper, until the hall itself seemed to lean toward them. When they parted, the air felt tuned.

"Shall we continue the lesson somewhere quieter?" Lucia asked, voice low, leaving the door open.

"Dessert in my suite. I want to hear you again."

Emily's smile was shy and brave. "Yes."

Lucia lifted her hand toward the wing. Sergio answered with a single nod. The stand light dimmed a shade, as if the stage itself took a breath.

They crossed the boards unhurriedly, sovereign and guest, and slipped into the private corridor where the opera keeps its secrets.

At the end of that corridor, a door waited. When it closed behind them, it did so softly, as if marking the downbeat for the next movement.

Chapter Eight
The North Door

Alex had always believed a room could change a man, if you could get into it. Boardrooms sharpened him. Ballrooms bored him. Kitchens reminded him he had once been poor. Opera houses, he was learning, could make him feel both invincible and very small in the same breath.

The bows had thundered and thinned. The matinee crowd spilled into sunlight and marble like a tide of linen and pearls. He kept his cool by habit and by strategy. Paranoia had him by the throat; discipline loosened its grip. He would not make a scene. Not with this crowd. Not when the city's eye was a thousand phones and a hundred whispers deep. So he worked the lobby instead.

A woman with a rigid bun and an emerald the size of a sugar cube smiled like a cat discovering cream. "Mr. Chambers! How lovely to see you here on a Sunday. We were just saying how important it is for civic leaders to support the arts."

"Couldn't agree more," Alex said, smooth as a door closing. "The arts make a city worth saving."

She purred approval. "And that Lucia Conti, good God. The attack in those high notes. I haven't heard a Queen like that since..." She let the sentence trail off, inviting him to fill it with reverence.

He filled it with a nod. "Astonishing." The word

cost him nothing and bought him time.

He slid left, caught the sleeve of a tech founder whose fund had written him a check with enough zeros to choke a horse. "Saw you at CityLights," Alex said, as if the man were everywhere Alex needed him to be. "How's the new incubator?"

"Cooking," the founder said, displaying dental work. "Nice to see you slumming it with the rest of us Philistines. Lucia made me feel like I had a soul for forty minutes. Must be witchcraft."

Alex smiled. "Or training."

"Same thing," the man said, delighted with his own cynicism.

Alex moved again. He made jokes, offered two-sentence analyses about culture being a flywheel for urban vitality, and asked small questions that made important people hear themselves. Each micro-conversation clothed him in belonging. Each one took the edge off his certainty that something was happening to Emily that he could not control.

Near the grand stair, a silver-haired man in a navy suit that fit like a confession was telling a ring of listeners about Italy.

"You think you can buy anything with money?" the man said, amused and wistful in equal measure. "I took a jet to Milan, gentlemen. Twice. Still couldn't get in to see him."

"Him who?" Alex asked, before he could stop himself.

"The Maestro," the man said, savoring the definite article. He lowered his voice slightly. "There are rooms he fills where the tickets are stories. No one admits they were there, but everyone claims they were."

"You've never heard him conduct?" someone asked.

"Only from a stairwell, with a guard telling me to move on." The man laughed at himself. "Ridiculous, I know. I've bought art older than the country, and I still couldn't buy that. But I saw her tonight. One of his, how do you say, protégées. It's something, boys. It's something."

Alex let the idea turn over in his mind. A man in a mask felt stupid to picture. Private rooms and private power felt less stupid.

"You knew she was one of his?" he asked lightly.

"Everyone knows. The way she stands at the mark. The way she holds silence like a blade. It's his signature." The man's smile darkened. "I've heard he can make a soprano disappear and come back sharpened into a weapon."

Alex's mouth shaped gratitude while his brain wrote a note to itself. Maestro meant access to money that couldn't be bought. Power that didn't need a podium.

He didn't like it.

He liked it less because he understood it. He peeled away and followed the undertow of people toward the bar.

The opera bar had two speeds: intermission frenzy, and afterglow drift. The matinee's afterglow left room for elbows. Alex took a stool like a man who belonged on every stool in the world. He set his phone face-down on the mahogany.

The bartender clocked him and smiled, the kind of smile that knew how to stay a little too long. She was young, late twenties. Glossy hair pinned loosely. A mouth that looked like it laughed during other people's stories.

Name tag: TIFFANY.

She poured rye, and made it a heavy pour. Heavy pours bought minutes.

"Busy day?" he asked.

"You'd think so," she said, snapping a neat lemon twist over the next guest's gin and ignoring it for his. "Sunday matinee tips are a myth. Wealthy people are stingier in daylight. But hey, it's a job."

He let his gaze take her in, then look away. It was a trick for making interest look like taste. "You're making it look better."

Tiffany blushed, reflex and choice. "You politicians. Flattery is a service industry, too." She leaned in until their shadows met on the bar. "Do you want this neat, or do you want to stand around with a rocks glass and look like a man thinking about great art?"

"Neat," he said. "I already did my thinking."

She slid the glass over and, in a small sleight of hand, kept her fingers on it a beat after he took it. "So what's your verdict, thinking man?"

He swirled the rye, swallowed the heat. "On the Queen?"

"On Lucia." Tiffany rolled her eyes, affectionate and envious. "We're supposed to call her by her last name, but everyone whispers the first like it's a password."

"What do you think?" he asked, deflecting.

Tiffany made a face that said she would never admit how much she felt. "She's a god in a city that loves gods. The whole house treats her like a miracle with a rider that would make Mariah Carey blush."

"Rider?" he asked, amused.

“Don’t look at me like that. It’s not diva nonsense. It’s care.” She shrugged. “They move walls for her. They bring gardenias because she likes the air to feel like a memory. The stand light has to hum at a certain pitch. The tea gets measured like gold. You can roll your eyes, or you can look at her and understand why. One note and your whole body…” She cut herself off, suddenly shy. “If I did go that way,” she added, lowering her voice, “I’d try with her.”

Jealousy pooled in Alex, then turned into a sharper fuel. He smiled. “Do you feel anything when you look at me?”

Tiffany glanced at the line of his tie, the sternum his tailor had taught him to lead with, the eyes that could do crowds and corners both. She moved closer until he could smell citrus and something warmer, skin or perfume, or both.

“Enough to keep pouring,” she said, and stole a sip from his glass without asking. “Enough to wonder what you look like when you stop acting like a candidate.”

“So,” he said, amused at how quickly his body was willing to forget the lobby and remember that he was an animal. “Curious.”

“Hungry,” she said, then laughed at herself. “God. I sound like the posters.”

He leaned in. “Tell me what the posters don’t know.”

She mirrored him, hip to the wood, arm braced, mouth close. “There are quiet corners in this building. And there’s a door that sticks, if you want to see some magic.” She let the hook hang.

He took it. “Show me.”

They moved the way people move when they’ve

decided to be a little stupid in a building with rules. Casual first, then quick, then careful.

Tiffany led him along a service corridor painted so many times that the corners looked soft. She knew which doors needed a knuckle and which needed an open palm. She knew where to stop and kiss him so he'd forget to ask where they were going.

The first kiss was the kind people give against a wall when the world outside is trying to be good. She tasted like rye and lemon oil, and her breath held one beat too long. He cupped the angle of her jaw and let her lean into his hand. It was something he did to be kind and to give his body permission to want.

"Here," she said into his mouth, backing him into a darker turn. The corridor swallowed them. "One of my spots."

He laughed quietly against her lower lip. "You have spots?"

"Everyone has to be good somewhere," she said, amusement slipping into defiance.

She kissed him again, deeper. Then, because she understood leverage, she drew his hand down the curve of her hip and let him find the zipper's edge, where a dress becomes a possibility. His breath changed. She heard it and smiled.

He pulled back, breathing like he'd been running. "Can you get me into the theater?" he murmured. "Just for a minute."

Tiffany's smile turned wicked. "So this is the part where I'm supposed to risk my job for you?"

"Maybe." His mouth grazed her ear. "I want to hear my name in that room. Say it once. Let it echo back."

He checked his watch without meaning to. He'd

been circling the opera house for nearly an hour. Emily would be finishing dessert by now if they'd kept her on schedule.

A shiver went through Tiffany, half performance, half real. "God," she whispered, amused. "You're going to make me an accomplice in a theater." She took his hand. "Come on."

A freight door. A side stair that spiraled like a secret. Tiffany moved fast, then slowed at a corridor where the air changed. Cooler, charged.

"This is the edge," she whispered. "We don't go past the drop unless we're invited. Union rules. Malevolent ghosts. Pick your superstition." She winked. At the end of the corridor was a narrow door. She pressed her palm flat, then breathed on the latch. It gave. "Told you."

"Wait here," Alex said. The candidate returned long enough to give an order and get consent. "Let me check the coast is clear."

Tiffany leaned against the wall, mouth redder than before, hair a little less obedient. "Don't make me wait long," she said, touching his sleeve with two fingers. "Or at least make it worth it."

He smiled like a man with time on his side and stepped through.

The house was half-dark, the way rooms are when they're holding their breath. From where he stood, the stage opened sideways. No proscenium grandeur, just boards and scrim and the shape of what a stage is when it isn't pretending to be a palace.

He heard voices. Two of them, low, braided together. A woman's laugh sounded like relief. Another woman murmured something that didn't need words.

He moved farther in. The view sharpened.

Lucia. Red dress, hair with a black ribbon over her shoulder.

Emily. Tea-length blue, flushed, a look on her face like a door had opened in her ribs and let air into rooms she didn't know she had.

They were close, closer than friends.

Alex caught the flash of a hand and knew it was Lucia's before his mind named it. It rested with calm possession at the small of Emily's back. Emily leaned into it.

Lucia tilted her mouth and took Emily's lower lip like she was learning a line she wanted to remember.

For a second, Alex forgot jealousy and felt only a bright, clean wonder. Two people being exactly what they meant to be. The purity of it shamed him.

Then wonder turned into no.

He took a step. The floor scuffed under his shoe. Two shadows moved in the wing.

Sergio arrived with the indifference of gravity. "Signore," Sergio said, conversational, as if noticing a stranger in his kitchen. His hand closed around Alex's elbow. It wasn't violent, but it wasn't negotiable either. "This is not your room."

"It's a public building," Alex said, too late and too calm.

"Not from this door," Sergio replied. His other hand relieved Alex of the problem of standing there.

Alex caught one last sight. Lucia lifted her head, not startled, never startled, just aware. She did not look at him long enough to give him the honor of meaning anything.

Emily turned, dazed and beautiful, and in the

half-light she did not see him at all.

Sergio walked him out. Past the door that yielded to breath. Past the freight stair.

Past the corridor, where Tiffany straightened her dress and became suddenly fascinated by the toe of her shoe.

Sergio did not speak to her.

She watched Alex go with a stomach-drop of embarrassment, and a stranger's tiny thrill at having kissed a man who was now being escorted like a shoplifter who'd pocketed communion wine.

"Careful," Sergio said mildly when they reached the final door. He gave Alex's balance a firm suggestion.

Alex stumbled into sunlight and noise. He did not fall. He did put a hand to the stone to make the world hold still.

A couple at the curb gasped. Someone's camera lifted, that reflex that makes headlines. A security guard appeared, then recognized his face and put his hands back where they belonged.

"Mr. Chambers," a voice began. Sergio had already closed the door.

Alex straightened, smoothed his jacket, and let the crowd see a man who had chosen to be exactly where he was. "Afternoon," he said to no one and everyone. He took the steps as if they belonged to him and offered a polite half-smile to a woman who might have been a reporter, or someone on her phone. "Enjoy the show?" he asked her, as if he were the host.

She blinked and said yes, because that is what the world says to men who sound like that.

He kept walking until the air belonged to traffic instead of culture. At the corner, he pressed his palm to the stone and let his pulse finish what it needed to finish. He had seen what he needed to see. He had been seen enough to be dangerous. Jealousy burned down to a smaller, cleaner flame he could cook with.

At home, the townhouse was too orderly for the way his head felt. He loosened his tie and poured a drink he didn't taste.

Messages accumulated like hail. Maya was first, his campaign manager.

MAYA (CM): call me.
MAYA: what happened at the Opera?!? The Opera, Alex!
MAYA: There's already a clip. Nothing bad yet, just you "leaving abruptly???"

OLIVER (FINANCE CHAIR): You okay? Saw a thing. Optics, man.

He set the phone face-down, then picked it up again. Drank and poured again. He opened the laptop and typed: *Lucia Conti & Maestro,* as if a search could turn a legend into something mortal.

Profiles with glossy photos and careful facts. European press in a language that made rumors sound like prayer. Forums that knew everything and nothing.

A mask. A villa. Students who vanished for a season and came back sharpened. A list of sopranos written like a constellation. It wasn't a list so much as a map of where power had walked lately.

He set alerts. He read until midnight, flattened into two a.m., then into three. He skimmed a thread that insisted the Maestro's notes traveled like contraband, single pages in elegant hand. No words, only music.

He thought of the lace-sealed envelope in his living room and felt the sting of it a second time.

In an old forum chain, nested twenty comments deep beneath a recap of European seasons, he found a single line in plain text:

do not trust the sopranos, they will ruin you

No punctuation. No context. Account deleted. Joke? Warning? He couldn't tell. He texted Emily twice: *Home soon? then, You okay?* No reply. Her read receipts were off. They were never off.

The drinks took the edge off his jaw, not the nerve firing behind his left eye. He wrote himself a note and buried it three directories deep:

Who is the Maestro, and why? Not where, not how. Why.

He closed the laptop and told himself to sleep. He didn't make it to bed. He went down on the couch with the empty glass, the city breathing beyond the windows like a creature deciding whether to keep him.

His phone woke him at 6:41 a.m. with a stack of notifications that felt like a fire alarm.

MAYA: call NOW
MAYA: This is everywhere.
MAYA: A burner account just posted a thread. Docs, emails. Looks like a back-channel with a sanitation vendor. The claim is pay-to-play contracts if you win. We are not confirming ANYTHING. Also, the opera clip is trending with dumb captions about you being "escorted."

KIM (PR): URGENT. Need line in 20 min.
ALERTS: @CityWatchSF, @AriaNeraSF, and three rumor blogs are amplifying.

He clicked the link Maya sent and scrolled. Redacted PDFs with his name spelled correctly. Screenshots of the calendar hold that looked real enough to hurt. Half-truths arranged to feel like a confession he didn't remember making.

He picked up the phone and typed: *On my way.*

Then, to himself, without ornament: *Survive the morning. Learn the music.*

He grabbed his jacket and went for the door. Behind him, the laptop screen still held the search terms he'd left burning. Ahead of him, the day opened like a curtain to a stage he hadn't built.

The overture had already started.

Chapter Nine
The Morning After

Dawn rinsed the city in pewter, and the opera house slept like a great animal that had finally eaten. In Lucia's suite, the light was quieter, honeyed by lamps and held down by heavy curtains. Gardenias drifted from a porcelain bowl, sweet and faint, as if the room had decided to be gentle.

On the bed, Emily lay half on her back, half on her side, the sheet tangled at her knees the way ribbons snarl after a long dance. Lucia watched her breathe.

The night unspooled behind Lucia's eyelids in bright, exact threads. The long dinner at center stage. Laughter that sounded like relief. The first time Emily let her name return from the hall and believed it. The slow shift from lesson to touch. The standing kiss that felt like music refusing to resolve. Then the corridor where the light turned warmer. Then the door. Then the room, transformed the way Lucia had asked for it.

Silk robes folded like clouds at the foot of the bed. Perfume bottles turned discreetly away. Sheets heavy as sea fog. Dessert abandoned on a tray, as if the sweeter thing had been chosen.

Emily had entered uncertain at the threshold, then braver with every step. She had allowed Lucia to unpin her dress, to loosen her hair, to learn the story of her body through breath, pace, and permission. She had opened not from hunger, but from recognition, as if someone had finally spoken her name in the language it had been missing.

They had not turned out all the lights. One lamp remained, a small moon on the dresser, and the chandelier kept the faintest glow. Crystals starved of night, still speaking. Lucia had let Emily see her: olive skin warmed by stage and wine, lips that could be vow and instrument, the long black braid drawn forward over one breast like a ribbon marking a page.

She had not performed. She had revealed.

Now, morning. Lucia curled closer without touching, studying the slack of Emily's mouth and the quiet radiance that sometimes follows being fully seen. In that radiance, Lucia caught a familiar flash that pinched her heart.

Marina. The ache of her absence pressed like a finger to a bruise.

The Maestro's note lay folded in a drawer across the room, but his voice from last night still lived in Lucia's ear. His call. His praise. His corrections disguised as tenderness. Did he know she would disobey him? Was it a test?

If it was, she was content to fail.

Lucia slipped from the bed with the care of someone leaving a sleeping animal. Bare feet on wool. Silk kissed the backs of her knees as she drew a robe around her. She stood at the mirror and tied the sash, simple as a bow on a gift she was giving only herself.

A soft knock came at the inner door.

Lucia lowered her voice. "Avanti." *Come in.*

The maid entered with a tray and a glance of quiet pride. Toast thin as paper. A small omelet folded like a letter. Fruit cut into moons. A pot of jasmine tea exhaling its pale ghost.

Behind the maid, Sergio hovered near the suite's small study with a shadow's patience. Lucia nodded.

The tray settled on the low table in the sitting room. The maid vanished. Sergio did not.

He didn't speak. He didn't need to. His stillness said everything. The orchestration had begun. Somewhere in the city, a thread had been pulled, and something was already unraveling in the shape of a candidate.

Lucia poured tea. The first sip was nearly tasteless. Her mouth was still full of last night.

She carried the cup to the threshold of the study and stood without crossing it. Sergio kept his hands folded behind his back, as if empty hands could be proof he'd done nothing but breathe. A folder lay shut on the desk.

"Buongiorno," she said. *Good morning*.

"Buongiorno," he replied. *Good morning*.

A clip was trending. A thread was blooming. Emails, calendars, rumors arranged with a calligrapher's precision. A picture from a corridor where lemon and rye still hung in the air. A bartender who would be useful or forgotten by noon. The city liked to be entertained. Today it would eat.

Lucia inclined her head, as if to a conductor she did not need. "Grazie." *Thank you*. She did not open the folder. She took her tea back to the bedroom and closed the French doors with a softness that made the latch part like lips. Sergio stayed where he was. The walls returned to warmth.

Emily slept on. A crease at the hinge of her mouth

deepened when she dreamed, then smoothed when she inhaled. Lucia set her cup on the nightstand and let the back of her fingers hover over Emily's temple without touching.

"You will wake a goddess," Lucia murmured to the air, to herself, to the morning. "Non spaventarti." *Don't be afraid.*

She sat at the edge of the bed and studied Emily's hands where they lay slack on the sheet. Teacher's hands, callused not by hard labor, but by repetition and devotion.

Lucia kissed Emily's knuckles, light as an annotation in the margin of a score. Emily shifted. The sheet sighed. Lucia drew a breath at the same pace Emily did and felt the old resonance catch between them, the way it had onstage when a single name came back larger and kinder than the mouth that spoke it.

She began to sing.

Not an aria. Nothing that would make Emily feel placed under a spotlight without consent. A folk song instead, minor and tender, the kind of melody women sing when windows are open and a neighbor might overhear and feel less alone.

"Ninna nanna, ninna oh..." *Lullaby, lullaby, oh...*

Barely more than air. Emily's lashes fluttered. Her breath lengthened. Her mouth softened into a half-smile, as if a remembered summer had found her in winter.

Lucia leaned down and let the song become a kiss at Emily's hairline, then the hinge of her jaw, then the corner of her mouth. Each one placed carefully, visible and chosen.

"Buongiorno, Emily," Lucia whispered between two notes. *Good morning, Emily.*

Emily's eyes opened slowly, unfocused at first. For half a second, panic looked for a place to stand. It didn't find one. Recognition landed and stayed.

"Hi," Emily breathed, the word shaped like a shy laugh.

Relief moved through Lucia's sternum and settled. Good. Now the work could continue. "How do you feel?" Lucia asked.

"Like there's a bigger room in my chest than there was yesterday," Emily said, then flushed as if she'd accidentally been poetic.

"Bene," Lucia murmured. *Good.* "Then we begin there."

She kissed the soft curve of Emily's shoulder. "You were gentle and brave last night," Lucia said. "You opened the way music opens when someone listens, not when someone demands."

Emily turned her face into the pillow and made a sound of gratitude that almost wasn't a sound. She rolled toward Lucia, the sheet slipping to her waist, and Lucia regarded the body she had learned in darkness, now drawn in morning.

Not worship. Recognition.

Lucia slid closer, settling along Emily without weight, mouth finding the angle of her collarbone, then the sternum, then lower to the tender rise of her belly.

"Qui," she whispered against skin. *Here.* Emily inhaled sharply, then steadied, learning herself again. "You deserve to be loved like you matter," Lucia said, choosing the simpler truth.

Emily laughed, embarrassed, delighted. The laugh turned into a small, involuntary arch. "I'm not used to being talked to like that."

"Then listen," Lucia said softly. "And believe me."

She waited. A teacher's patience disguised as a lover's calm. She let the quiet lengthen until Emily decided what to do with it. When Emily's hands came up to Lucia's shoulders, hesitant and then sure, Lucia let herself be held.

"Tell me something true," Lucia said. "Not for me. For you."

Silence quivered.

Emily swallowed, eyes moving to the ceiling, then back to Lucia, as if deciding whether the room could hold the word without breaking.

"I'm unhappy," Emily said, almost apologizing to the air. "I feel stuck. With him. With..." Her hand gestured vaguely, and somehow that gesture contained a kitchen, a schedule, a thousand small compromises. "He isn't a bad man, I don't think. He's just not..." She searched for the exact word and found the one that had lived under her tongue for a year. "For me."

Lucia bowed her head as if a prayer had passed. She kissed the place beneath Emily's breastbone where breath turns.

"Bravissima," Lucia murmured. *Very good*. "That was honest."

Tears gathered and did not fall. Emily smiled at herself for almost crying, rolled her eyes as if the ceiling were a friend who wouldn't judge. "God. I sound ridiculous."

"You sound alive," Lucia said. Then, gentle as a question, steady as a note: "Do you want to keep giving your life to a man who does not hear you?"

The yes rose and died, an obedient reflex. The no came slower, then sure. "No," Emily said.

"Bene," Lucia whispered. *Good*. She kissed the word where it had come from. "Then we practice a life where you are heard."

"Practice?" Emily smiled through it. "Always the teacher."

"Always," Lucia agreed. She kissed Emily's mouth, a kiss meant to rehearse yes. The second press was hungrier, and Emily's hands in Lucia's hair admitted it. Tenderness rose, and Lucia let it carry them until she felt the edge where kindness ends and strategy begins. Lucia lifted her head just enough to speak. "Posso dirti una cosa?" May I tell you something?

Emily nodded, content and curious, still warm with being seen. "I am more than a soprano," Lucia said quietly. "When I come to a city, I work all day, and at night, if I'm lucky, I'm not alone. But there are many nights that are only me and a window." She kept the tone light, a friend's mischief. "Sergio mi sgrida." *Sergio scolds me*.

Emily's eyes widened, then softened. "Like a spy?"

"Dio, no." *God, no*. Lucia laughed softly, easing the sting into play. "Only a woman who imagines happier endings for strangers." She touched the corner of Emily's mouth with her thumb. "I saw you near your school. I saw the way you watched the door after you texted. I saw how your face changed when he was late. I did not know you, but I knew your longing."

Emily exhaled, and the sound held relief. "Thank you."

Lucia let the gratitude sit. She would not turn this into a battlefield. But duty tugged at her sleeve, and duty has its own breath.

“There is one more thing,” Lucia said. She rose onto an elbow and reached into the nightstand drawer. Not the top one, but the second, where the maid had placed a leather pouch at dawn. Lucia opened it and slid three glossy photographs onto the sheet between them.

Emily’s gaze dropped, and Lucia felt the shift at once. Anything placed between two bodies becomes an instrument.

“This is from yesterday,” Lucia said quietly. “After the performance.”

The first photo caught a corridor at an angle, too bright for privacy. A woman in a black dress with a bartender’s loosened bun. Alex’s mouth at the hinge of her jaw.

The second: another angle, closer. The bartender’s hand at his tie, his fingers at her waist.

The third: his profile in a doorway, posture relaxed with the confidence of a man who believed no one was watching him be himself.

Emily made a sound that wasn’t quite a breath. “I thought…” Lucia didn’t rush to fill it. She let the hurt find its own pace. “I thought he went home,” Emily finished, the words thin with disbelief.

Lucia stayed still, gaze steady. She would not force pain to move faster than it could. Pain moved anyway. Emily’s face traveled through disbelief into comprehension, and when it reached comprehension, it didn’t become rage. It became recognition.

“Of course,” Emily whispered. “Of course he did.”

Lucia gathered the photos and stacked them neatly, as if order could keep the room from collapsing. “You do not owe him your life,” she said.

“Non gli devi niente.” *You don’t owe him anything.*

Emily stared at the wall for a long second, then looked back at Lucia as if waking in a different century. “I don’t want to be with him,” she said. “I just don’t know how to get out.” Her throat worked, trying to swallow what had lived there too long. “He has friends. He has plans. He has a way of making the whole world feel like it’s safest if you do what he wants.”

Lucia drew her closer, not as seduction now, but as vow. “Every cage calls itself safe,” Lucia murmured.

They lay that way a moment, Lucia on her side, Emily on her back, the sheet drawn for dignity more than warmth. Outside, the city cleared its throat into morning. Somewhere in the suite, a floorboard settled.

Lucia reached for the remote. “Perdonami.” *Forgive me.* She pressed power.

The screen bloomed into morning news. Anchors in bright colors. Graphics in crisis reds. A clip looped: Alex on the opera house steps yesterday, jacket smoothed, voice pleasant, the kind of pleasant that sells a lie.

The lower third scrolled: PAY-TO-PLAY? CHAMBERS CAMPAIGN FACES LEAKED DOCS.

Another station showed screenshots of emails and calendar holds, blurred names, the word VENDOR highlighted like a bruise. Then a shorter, uglier clip: the shove through a side door, the stumble, a phone camera catching a small humiliation and making it enormous.

Emily stared, then turned her face away as if light

itself had become too loud.

Lucia lowered the volume. Then lowered it again. Then turned it off. She reached for Emily's chin with two fingers, the same gentle precision she'd used the night before to free a note.

"Guardami." *Look at me.* Emily's eyes found hers. Lucia kissed her. No performance. No hunger. A kiss like water offered to someone who didn't know she was thirsty. "He will try to take you down with him," Lucia said softly. "Non lasciarlo." *Don't let him.*

Emily closed her eyes as if the words would settle better in the dark. When she opened them, something had shifted. Not the softness of being adored, but the angle at which her life met itself.

"What do I do?" she asked.

Lucia's voice stayed gentle and practical. "First, we eat. Then we act." Lucia tipped a slice of pear toward Emily's mouth until she smiled and took it. Lucia broke toast into clean halves and watched the small muscles at Emily's jaw organize themselves around a new future.

"By now your townhouse will be a storm," Lucia continued. "Campaign staff, cameras, neighbors who suddenly remember your name. You won't walk into that."

Emily set down her tea. "Then what?"

"You leave," Lucia said. "With Sergio."

Emily blinked. "Today?"

"Yes." Lucia kept her voice calm enough to be believable. "You pack one small bag. You keep your phone on, but you don't answer. Sergio stays with you until the aircraft door closes. You fly to your parents. You sleep in your old room. You eat food that remembers you. You do not watch the news."

Emily's breath hitched, then released. Practical fear, practical relief. "My students," she said quickly. "What about my kids?"

"Already handled," Lucia said. "A patron moved money quietly. A stand-in teacher will cover your classes until you're ready."

Emily's eyes widened, then sharpened. "A patron?"

Lucia didn't flinch. "Yes."

"The Maestro?" Emily whispered, half-wonder, half-disbelief. "I barely believed you were real, and now this?"

"He exists," Lucia said simply. "So do I."

"Why me?" Emily asked.

Lucia kissed the crown of her head. "Because you protect music without even knowing you are doing it. And because you deserve to be protected."

A soft knock at the inner door. Sergio's voice was quiet as always. "Signorina."

Lucia raised her voice just enough. "Service entrance. A nondescript coat. Sunglasses. Novanta minuti fino all'aeroporto." *Ninety minutes to the airfield.*

"Capito." *Understood.*

They finished the tea.

Lucia watched the exact moment a life reorganizes itself, the moment a woman's gaze changes because she has chosen a different verb. She helped Emily into the ivory robe meant for her, tied the sash, and kissed her forehead.

"When you are safe," Lucia said, "send me one word. Arrived."

Emily nodded. "Arrived," she promised. Lucia opened the French doors. The suite inhaled.

Sergio was already in motion, turning the day's machinery without noise. Emily squeezed Lucia's hand once, thank-you by pulse, and stepped into the corridor.

The door closed with the soft precision of a downbeat. Outside, a car idled toward the sky.

Lucia stood in the doorway a long moment after the latch settled. The room kept Emily's warmth the way a sheet keeps heat.

She crossed back to the bed and widened her palms on the linen as if grounding a chord. Act I was finished. Now came the storm and the counter-melody.

She turned her head to the travel clock on the nightstand. Mid-morning in San Francisco meant dinner in Tuscany. Sleep asked politely. For once, Lucia consented.

***

In Tuscany evening arrived with its usual confidence. The villa held its quiet, its stone, its discipline.

In the Maestro's study, the air was cool and controlled, lit by the pale glow of monitors. He stood before them without sitting.

He had watched Lucia's morning. He had watched the tenderness, the practical instructions, the way she made a plan for Emily with a softness that still carried authority. He had not instructed softness. He had instructed ruin.

Anger moved through him, clean and familiar. Anger was useful. Anger restored order.

He opened a blank message and began to write in precise Italian, each word placed like a note.

"Hai cambiato la partitura." *You changed the*

*score*He paused, then added a second line, slower now. Colder. “Non dimenticare a chi appartieni.” *Don’t forget who you belong to.*

His finger hovered over send. It did not press. Control was not impulse. Control was timing.

He stared at the unsent message until the screen dimmed slightly, as if even the device disapproved of longing. He erased nothing. He closed the laptop.

For a beat longer than necessary, he remained standing in the dark, listening to the metronome that no human hand had set.

Outside, the Cypress trees threw long shadows across the gravel. Inside, the Maestro decided what to do next. And this time, he did not look back.

Chapter Ten
Clean Break

PART I: WAR ROOM

By noon, the townhouse sounded like a command center pretending to be a home. Laptops blinked on every flat surface. The dining-alcove whiteboard bled timelines. Three TVs talked over one another, all of them hungry.

Being anywhere else felt too risky. By the time Alex reached his office, he didn't get out of the Uber. He texted his team from the back seat.

HQ would be home.

Maya Reyes, Campaign Manager, planted herself at the marble island with three Post-its lined up like rounds in a magazine: donor line, press line, legal line.

"We hold position," she said. "We do not litigate on air."

Oliver Jones, Finance, adjusted a cuff that looked engineered for impact. "Optics first. 'We're aware, we're reviewing, we're committed to transparency.' No specifics."

Sanjay Iyer, Policy, pinched the bridge of his nose. "If any of those emails are real, we can't contradict ourselves. We need one truth we can survive."

Kara Nguyen, Press, scrolled a media grid. "One friendly outlet for the first stand-up. Two questions, then we cut. Post the written statement everywhere at once."

Theo Felts, Comms, stuck his head in from the foyer. "We've got CityWatch, KRON, and a blogger with a drone. Do we have a drone plan?"

"Not getting sued' is the drone plan," Maya said.

On the mirrored screen, the leak thread looped: redacted PDFs with Alex's name left glaring, calendar holds that looked built to incriminate, email screenshots ugly in their plausibility. Below, a chyron tried on punchlines: PAY-TO-PLAY? CONTRACTS IN THE CHAMBER?

On another screen, the stage-door clip played on repeat: Alex redirected, a hand on his elbow. The same ten seconds, reposted with different soundtracks because the internet couldn't help itself.

"Stop," Alex said. Not loud. The room obeyed because it had been trained to. "Here's the hold," he continued. "We say the documents are doctored. Timing is political. We welcome a full investigation. Add: 'I understand people are angry. They deserve answers."

Sanjay looked at him. "Is that the truth you want?"

It would have been easy to say yes. Easier than admitting his stomach still remembered a dark corridor, and a door that didn't feel like his. His jaw ticked once.

"It's the truth we can live in today," Alex said.

Theo came back, cheeks wind-burned. "They're asking for Emily now. Also..." He hesitated, like he hated the sentence. "Women are DM'ing CityWatch. There's a bartender photo."

"No one talks to her," Alex said. "No one reaches

out. If she's in this, we keep her out of it."

Maya's composure cracked by a millimeter. "A bartender?"

"Caption says 'last night."

Maya turned on Alex. "Really? Literally yesterday?"

Alex's reply rose to his throat and died there. How did he explain a dark corridor, a kiss he barely owned, Sergio appearing like a ghost, and Lucia Conti deciding to detonate his life by touching his fiancée with reverence?

He hated that Maya was right. He hated more that, in the moment, it had been convenient to forget he was capable of damage.

Internal discipline won. "Focus," he said. "We don't spiral in here."

From the street came a new wave of sound. Not applause. Not boos. The white noise of a crowd turning as one.

Theo's face shifted. "She's here."

PART II: THE BEDROOM

Emily pulled a carry-on from the closet and unzipped it with the efficiency of habit.

"Where are you going?" Alex asked.

"Home," she said. "My parents."

"Emily, wait." He tried to keep his voice calm. "Just... wait. We can figure this out." She kept packing. "This is a political hit," he said. "It's not who I am."

Emily didn't look up. "It's who you've been."

His jaw tightened. "Then tell me what changed overnight."

She paused. Not long. Just enough to show it cost her. "A photo," she said. "You. In a corridor. With a bartender. Your hand on her."

He blinked once, like the words hit his body before his brain. "Where did you see it?"

"Over breakfast."

"Breakfast?" His voice rose, then he pulled it back down. "With Lucia?"

Emily zipped a side pocket. "Yes."

He stared at her. "So that's it? One day and you're... gone? You're trusting her over me?"

Emily turned then. Her eyes looked clean in a way that made him feel suddenly, unmistakably dirty.

"In one day," she said, "someone looked at me and didn't treat me like I was part of your brand."

He scoffed on instinct. "Come on."

"I mean it." Her voice stayed steady. "She asked me how I was breathing. Not whether I was ready to smile for strangers." Alex's mouth opened, then closed. "And that photo," she added, "was you. If you want to argue timestamps, fine. But it's still you. It's still the pattern."

"The pattern?" He let out a short laugh and looked around the room like the house itself might back him up. "You liked this life, Emily. You liked the donors. The parties. The future of it."

"I liked believing it meant something," she said. She shoved a sweater into the suitcase. "I liked believing we were doing something good. And I paid for that belief with pieces of myself."

His voice sharpened. "We had an arrangement."

Emily nodded once. "Exactly. We had an arrangement." Her eyes didn't blink. "I didn't ask questions.

You didn't answer them."

He stepped closer. "That's politics."

"No," she said. "That's you."

He swallowed. "I'm trying to take power from people who keep this city sick." He admitted for the first time out loud. "To do that, I sit at their tables. I smile. I play the role long enough to change the outcome."

Emily's hands stilled. "And you play people while you do it."

"That's not—"

"It is," she cut in. "You don't change the system by breaking the person next to you."

He gripped the edge of the dresser like it could steady him. "So you're leaving because of one night?"

Emily's laugh was small and exhausted. "No. I'm leaving because I've been lonely with you for a long time."

The sentence landed. He stared at her like she'd hit him. Then his pride scrambled for traction.

"Is this because of the opera?" he said. "Because I said it was just opera? Did she take offense and decide to make me a target?"

Emily shook her head, half disbelief, half pity. "Alex. Listen to yourself."

He pushed again, because pushing was what he did when he was scared. "You don't think it's convenient she picked you? This week? You don't think you're being used?"

Emily lifted the suitcase onto the floor. "I think you're desperate to make this someone else's fault."

He softened fast, reaching for the version of himself that could still be loved. "Emily..."

She looked at him, and something in her face almost gave. Almost. Then she said, quietly, "She made me feel seen."

He swallowed, fighting the instinct to mock it. "By seducing you."

"By listening," she corrected. "By treating me like I wasn't there to make a man look good." Emily moved toward the door.

"Emily," he said, and this time it came out smaller. She paused. He took a breath. "Please. Just don't do this today."

She turned back, eyes bright but steady. "I believe the city deserves better," she said. "I'm just done pretending you're the man who can give it to them."

PART III: THE THRESHOLD

Outside the bedroom, the campaign remembered how to breathe until Emily appeared, and then it didn't.

A black sedan idled at the curb, engine quiet. A driver waited with his hands at ten and two, eyes forward. Sergio stood by the door inside, hands lightly clasped, as if he'd been part of the house all along.

He took the suitcase from Emily with quiet ease.

Alex stopped, stripped down to the human underneath the candidate. "You'll take care of her," he said. It wasn't a command. He didn't have that right. It was a request.

Sergio inclined his head. "The flight leaves in an hour. I will stay until the airplane door is shut."

Alex's voice caught. "That's... your job? From Lucia?"

Sergio's mouth twitched, almost amused. "Non lavoro per una soprano." *I don't work for a soprano.*

“Lavoro per la musica.” *I work for music.* “Proteggo il respiro che la crea, e il silenzio che la custodisce.” *I protect the breath that makes it, and the silence that keeps it.*

No one answered. Not in English.

From the living room, Theo’s phone buzzed again. Kara glanced toward the front windows, where the daylight had a sharper edge. Cameras. The crowd noise. A neighbor’s door opening. Maya’s face hardened into calculation.

Maya stepped in, voice low. “Emily.” She spoke. “If you want to go, go now. If we make this a scene, they’ll film it. If anyone lays a hand on you, we’re finished.”

Emily’s chin lifted. “Then don’t.” Sergio opened the door. Cold air pushed in. Emily looked at Alex once. No triumph. No cruelty. Just finality. Then she stepped out and the door closed.

PART IV: THE HOLD LINE

Alex dressed in a clean shirt and a tie the color of calm.

Kara chose the foyer for light and scale: a neutral wall, no art to meme, nothing for the internet to turn into symbolism. She clipped a mic to his lapel while Maya set the rules in a voice that didn’t invite negotiation. Two questions. No speculation. No Emily. Whitaker, security, hovered just out of frame like a bodyguard for the narrative. Sanjay stood with his phone and a legal pad, building a quiet list of phrases that would kill them if Alex let them live.

At 12:40, Kara sent the written statement to every outlet that mattered and a few that didn’t but liked to pretend they did. Theo queued a tweet thread in the same language, timed to hit as soon as Alex opened his mouth.

At 12:41, Alex stepped onto the foyer rug as if it were a mark onstage. KRON got the clean feed. The blogger got distant B-roll. Theo muttered something about angles and optics, as if they were weather.

At 12:42, Alex delivered the opener without blinking. "The documents are doctored. The timing is political. I welcome a full investigation." He added Maya's empathy line, clean and practiced: "I understand people are angry. They deserve answers."

At 12:43, the first question came. Procurement emails. Alex didn't take the bait. "We'll cooperate fully. We won't litigate in public." The second question came faster, uglier. The stage-door clip. "I was redirected by staff," he said, and kept his tone bored. "Nothing more."

At 12:44, Kara cut it before anyone could pry a third question loose. Theo pushed the donor email, subject line already drafted, tone pre-softened: steady hand, clean process. Sanjay texted Legal. Whitaker started calling the donors who panicked loudest.

By 12:50, the Slack sentiment chart was still ugly, but it had shifted. Not better. Just less immediately fatal. Maya watched the numbers like they were vitals.

"We feed this everywhere," she said, ticking off boxes with a pen that had seen worse weeks, "and then we go dark. Survive the day."

Alex nodded once. He didn't feel calm. He only looked like the kind of man who could afford it.

PART V: AFTER

The house emptied one profession at a time. Finance to calls. Policy to a memo. Press to the curb. Comms to a thread that would keep him awake. The TVs kept talking because silence felt like guilt.

Maya lingered in the kitchen with her shoes off, ankles tucked under a barstool. "There's a charity benefit tonight," she said. "Children's Arts Fund. Hyatt at seven. If you can stomach it, showing up says you're unbothered and keeps donors from inventing stories. If you can't, we skip. I'll hold the line."

"If I go, I look arrogant," Alex said. "If I don't, I look guilty."

"Or you look like a person making a decision in a bad week." She slid a note across the counter: wardrobe options circled, driver on call, talking points pared to bone. "I need an answer in an hour."

"I'll let you know."

"Do that." She gathered her bag, then paused at the door. "Whatever you thought the plan was, right now the plan is tomorrow." When the door closed, the house exhaled.

Alex opened his laptop. In a folder called Noise sat a screenshot: *do not trust the sopranos, they will ruin you.* He dragged it into Keep. He opened a blank note and typed: *Who is the Maestro, and why?* He left the cursor blinking.

He stood at the window until the glass cooled his forehead and the city looked like something that might forgive him later. Outside, a reporter delivered a stand-up in a coat made for television. A man held a sign that read CLEAN HOUSE. A neighbor rolled his recycling bin to the curb with determined calm.

By evening, the townhouse felt too large. Voices had drained from it, and the bay filled the silence. Alex loosened his tie and set it beside the sink. The day was over, but nothing had resolved.

He knew only one thing with the clarity of a man who could not yet admit his own part in the fire: if there was a single person to blame for the beginning of his ruin, it was not the press, not the donors, not even his impatience. It was a woman in a red dress with a black braid who had looked at him from a stage and seen the seam in his mask.

"Lucia," he said to the empty room, as if a name could be a plan.

And for the first time in years, he wasn't sure whether he wanted punishment or truth.

Chapter Eleven
The Long Fall

Days turned into the kind of weeks that didn't keep their names. They slid past in a smear of meetings, statements, and small humiliations until time felt like a river he was trying to drink from with cupped hands. At first, Alex counted losses the way a surgeon counts sponges. One donor paused. One endorsement wavered. One friendly columnist wrote a neutral paragraph that felt like a sigh.

Then the pattern found its tempo. Pauses became exits. Wavering became press conferences. Neutral paragraphs became op-eds about character.

The leaks didn't stop. They shifted. Each new drop made the last one feel plausible, until the public ear got used to the dissonance and started calling it truth. A contract calendar. A forwarded email with too many CCs. A photo of Alex at a golf event beside a man everyone pretended not to recognize. A consultant's memo annotated in a hand that might as well have been a verdict: future access contingent on win.

Anonymous accounts seemed to know the layout of his days. @CityWatchSF posted before Kara could draft a response. A blog no one respected until yesterday ran a piece titled Chambers, Chambered, and everyone respectable shared it "ironically," which meant they shared it.

Staff began to peel away, as wallpaper does in

a damp house, from the corners first. Theo took a job on a congressional race "to help a friend," which meant to save his own name. Sanjay was asked to "return to policy consulting," which meant leaving before the Ethics Commission asked why his fingerprints appeared on three phrases in a slide deck. Whitaker stayed, counting checks and casualties, his shirts still white while his eyes went dull at the edges. Kara kept her voice composed on three hours of sleep a night because that's what professionals do. Maya stayed. Because she was a professional. And because she had once believed this could be a good story.

The Board of Supervisors rediscovered nouns like probe and oversight. A rival campaign leaked a poll shaped like a cliff. The Ethics Commission issued a letter that wasn't an accusation but dressed like one. Former partners returned calls and changed pronouns. We became they. People who had cheered for his past became careful stewards of their future distance.

At night, Alex lay awake and listened to the house breathe without him. He reran the plan that had felt so clean in the abstract: sit at the banquet, win, flip the table, expose the rot. In his head, it still sounded righteous. In reality, it sounded like hubris with a project plan.

He searched until the internet thought it knew his heart. Maestro mask rumor villa Tuscany pupils vanish season. The same glossy profiles. The same careful rumors. The same screenshots, the same thread titles resurfacing in a circle. He typed the note again: Who is the Maestro, and why? He didn't send it anywhere. He just watched the cursor blink, steady as a second heartbeat.

Before Alex could register it, phones stopped ringing as much. The silence was worse. It meant people had decided who he was. Relationships fell away quietly. A restaurateur who had flirted with naming a dish after him suddenly had "plumbing problems" whenever his team called for a table. A foundation director with a generous laugh postponed breakfast indefinitely.

Emily did not call.

Her number became a cold star on his screen. He looked at it the way sailors look at light they cannot have and tell themselves it's for navigation anyway. He told himself she was safer. He told himself she had chosen a good door. He told himself this because he did not want to picture her back in Utah, in an old bedroom with blinds the color of dust and a life that would now be discussed like a cautionary tale. And because he missed her in a way that made him ashamed: in the quiet, domestic ways. The way she asked, every morning, if he wanted coffee, and waited for the answer. The way she folded his shirts as if caring could be a habit instead of a feeling.

Once, near two a.m., he thought he saw Lucia's man—Sergio—at the corner of his street. Coat. Posture. That gravity that made passersby curve around him without knowing why.

When Alex looked again, the corner was empty. He told himself that was sanity returning.

The rivals stepped forward, rehearsing lines polished by other people's failures.

"I respect the process."

"San Francisco deserves transparency."

"This is not personal."

One went on the radio and said the word integrity five times in four minutes. Another smiled into a camera and thanked Alex for "raising important issues." Everyone sounded like they had learned the same song in different keys. He stopped checking the polls. He learned what it felt like to become a paragraph other people used to prove they were responsible adults.

The morning of the end, fog feathered the bay and the bridge refused to commit to a color. Maya arrived with coffee and sat without opening her laptop first. That's how he knew.

"We can hang on another week," she said, "but it won't be hanging on. It'll be bleeding out." Her voice didn't crack. Professionals don't crack. "I can get you a medium outlet where the anchor will treat you like a human being, not content. You can say what you need, then you can keep a future."

"A resignation," Alex said. The word sat between them like a tool that had been waiting.

"A suspension," Maya corrected, because she liked verbs with hinges. "We can say for now. We can say for the good of the city."

"The city deserves better," Alex said. He had practiced the line. He didn't hate it. He hated that he meant it.

The final interview wasn't big. It was deliberate. Five p.m. A studio in SOMA with a view of cranes and a palette of earnest blues. The anchor was a woman Alex had once had dinner with. She looked professional now, and her kindness was measured.

Her first question was, "How are you?"

Her second was, "Why now?" The others were less kind.

Alex told the city what he could survive living

with. "I am suspending my campaign," he said, and the phrasing made it sound like physics. "San Francisco deserves better than this circus. I refuse to make myself the story while the city's problems go unaddressed. I welcome any investigation. I have nothing to hide."

He almost added the sentence that lived behind his teeth: I have everything to show you if you let me keep going. But that was the old plan trying to resurrect itself in a room that had already been cleared of ghosts. He looked into the camera's glass eye and practiced a new skill: losing with grace.

He thanked his team, his supporters, and "especially the people who challenged me."

He did not say Emily's name. He did not say anyone's name. Names would have sounded like excuses. When it ended, the anchor turned off the concern and turned on whatever came next. They shook hands.

"Take care of yourself," she said, in the tone decent people use when they mean it and know it won't be heard.

Back at the townhouse, the house looked larger than it had in months. The war room had been put away. The whiteboard was wiped clean until it squeaked. The Post-its were stacked like a rescue mission that had failed quietly.

Maya stayed long enough to watch the replay once, then twice, as if repetition could trap a different ending. When she finally turned from the screen, her eyes were clear in a way that made him love and resent her at once.

"In all my years," she said, "I've never seen anything like it. Not political suicide. Surgical." She set the remote down and rested her hand on his shoulder, a human gesture that refused to become a performance. “I’m sorry, Alex. I thought we had it.” She didn’t cry. She had promised herself she wouldn’t. Then, practical again: “I hope I can rebound. Being attached to your name is... a lot.”

“People remember competence,” he said. “You’ll land before I do.”

“That’s not the point.” She squeezed his shoulder once. “Eat. Sleep. Don’t read the comments.” At the door she paused. “If you need a reference, don’t use me,” she said, and smiled a small, real smile. “I’m radioactive.” After she left, the room regained its echo.

The refrigerator hummed. Somewhere outside, a bus exhaled. Alex stood in the middle of the kitchen and realized he was making fists just to remember they were still his. He turned the TV on and let noise fill the air the way white paint covers stains. A segment about housing. A segment about an encampment “clean-up” that felt like moving rain from one street to another.

Then a familiar face: the Director of the Opera House, standing in front of a season poster. His suit fit like applause.

“Record ticket sales,” the man said. “A renaissance for the company.” He said renaissance like it had paid him to. “We owe so much to our incomparable Queen of the Night, Lucia Conti.”

The footage cut to Lucia: black dress, black braid, mouth open mid-note. Alex felt something in his chest shift, not jealousy exactly. Something colder.

He told himself he was being ridiculous. He told himself that blaming a singer was the kind of magical thinking that ruins adults. He told himself to turn the

TV off, call a friend, ask them to take his phone away.

He did not turn the TV off.

Lucia looked down from light into darkness and, even through a screen, Alex felt the same sensation he'd felt the first time: as if she could see the seam where his mask fit worst.

He stood so abruptly the chair scraped.

He went to the bedroom and put on a jacket without deciding to. He checked his wallet. He checked the time. He looked out the window as if the city might object.

It was a performance night. He didn't need a calendar to know. Certain evenings San Francisco held itself differently, as if waiting to be told when to clap.

And beneath all of it—beneath the speeches and the rage—there was a simpler want he hated: proof. Proof he hadn't imagined the hand on his elbow, the door that opened into the wrong room, the way his life had been guided like a body toward a mark.

He grabbed his keys. He grabbed nothing else.

He didn't try the front. He went to the alley that smelled like wet wood and old rosin, where the stage door had been painted a black that ate light. Rain slanted in fine sheets, like threads. Somewhere inside, an orchestra tuned: A after A after A, the note that means the body is about to be asked for something.

He waited.

Time flattened into water and footfalls. Stagehands ghosted in and out, black-clad and invisible by profession. A security guard with a clipboard asked for his name. Alex gave one that used to work and watched it fail. The guard had the courtesy to pretend he didn't recognize him, and the kindness to stop arguing when the weather made argument pointless.

The door coughed up sound: applause like surf, then the metallic hush that follows curtains.

A black sedan nosed backward into the mouth of the alley and idled. Wipers ticked the night into pieces. Headlights cut the rain into pale strands.

The stage door opened.

Sergio came out first, umbrella already raised, movement economical and deliberate. Then Lucia. A red coat that made the alley forget its own color. Her braid over one shoulder, neat as a line drawn with intention.

Alex stepped forward into the headlights and into his own ruin. Not fast. Hands open. Voice lifted over rain and engines.

"I just want to know why!" he shouted.

The syllable tore something he'd been using as armor. Sergio shifted, placing his body between Alex and the car with a calm that felt rehearsed.

"Indietro, signore," Sergio said. *Back, sir.*

Lucia paused with one foot inside the sedan. For a heartbeat, she was only a face framed in light: rain caught on her lashes, cheekbone sharp, expression unreadable. Then she turned her head slightly, and Alex saw something he hadn't seen before. Not pity. Not triumph. Recognition, maybe. Or curiosity.

Lucia slipped into the car, away from the rain, then lowered the window. The motor hummed. The umbrella held.

"Signor Chambers," she said softly.

Alex laughed once, rain salt in his mouth. "Tell me."

Sergio angled the umbrella to block sightlines

from the street, turning this into privacy by force.

"No," Sergio said, not to Alex exactly. To the situation.

Lucia didn't look away from Alex. Her voice dropped into the register of a decision. "Come sit," she said. In one swift motion, she pushed the door open from inside.

Sergio's jaw tightened. "È una pessima idea," he said. *It's a terrible idea.*

"Adesso," Lucia replied. *Now*. There was an edge in it. Not cruelty. Control.

Sergio exhaled through his nose, as if deciding whether a prayer could become a curse. He opened the rear door with two fingers and a warning.

"Cinque minuti. Senza telefoni," Sergio said. *Five minutes. No phones.*

Alex stared at the car's dark interior. Then he looked at Sergio, at the man who could break his wrist and make it look like an accident. He climbed in.

The door shut. Rain became architecture on the other side of glass. Inside, it smelled faintly of gardenia and cold leather.

Lucia sat a careful distance away. Her coat was unbuttoned enough to show a dress the color of certainty. Up close, her beauty felt less like seduction and more like a rule you couldn't ignore.

Sergio got in front, becoming a silhouette with ears. The city outside blurred into streaks.

For a moment, no one spoke.

Alex set his hands palm-down on his knees to keep them from becoming fists. He turned to Lucia. "Why me?" he asked, quieter now. The car demanded respect.

Lucia regarded him the way a musician regards a note they can hit but don't know if they should. "Because you were already breaking," she said. Then, after a breath, "Or because someone decided you should look like you were. Sometimes those are the same."

Anger rose in Alex, looking for a foothold. It couldn't find one. "What did I do?" he asked.

Lucia tilted her head. The braid shifted like punctuation. "You insulted the music," she said evenly. "You didn't love your woman. You used her the way you intended to use the city." Her mouth held the smallest smile, not unkind, just precise. "And you built a plan that believed beauty could be a means instead of an end."

A rough sound escaped him, almost a laugh in a different weather. "So this is punishment for bad taste? For being a bad fiancé?"

"No." Lucia's gaze flicked once to the mirror where Sergio watched the rain. Then back to Alex. "This is a lesson."

"From whom?" Alex asked.

Lucia didn't answer. Instead she said, "You came to ask me why. I'll ask you something easier." Her voice softened by a fraction. "Perché la città?" *Why the city?*

Alex opened his mouth and felt the donor speech rise automatically. He shut it down. He tried again. "Because I hate the way people who can fix things don't," he said. "Because my mother died from a form and a bureaucracy that made the rich richer on the bones of people like her." His throat tightened. He pushed through it. "And my father died on a shift while the owner was in Barbados with his mistress, even though that owner called himself a man of the people. Even as he sat in the front pew at church."

Lucia listened without interrupting. Her face didn't soften, but the air did.

"Bene," she said. *Good.* "Then perhaps you are not a ruin. Perhaps you have a chance to be yourself."

Sergio cleared his throat once, quiet but immovable. "Tre minuti," he said. *Three minutes.*

Alex leaned forward despite himself. "Did you do this to me?"

Lucia's smile vanished. "If I wanted to ruin you," she said, "we would not be sitting in a car."

Rain slid down the window in clean lines. "Then who?" Alex asked.

Lucia let the question sit, unanswered, like a glass of water neither of them would touch.

"When you are ready to hear the answer," she said at last, "you will stop asking the wrong person." She lifted one hand, palm up, offering nothing and something at the same time. "You have one more question," Lucia said. "Use it."

Alex looked at her like a man who had been underwater too long and found a window. He surprised himself. "What do I do now?" he asked.

Lucia considered him as if choosing a tempo. "Tell the truth you can bear," she said, "and none you cannot." Then, more quietly, "And listen. Cities are instruments. They sound like the hands that hold them."

Sergio spoke again, gentle and final. "Tempo." *Time.* The door unlocked with a soft click.

Lucia nodded once toward Sergio. "Accompagnalo fuori," she said. *See him out.*

Alex didn't move right away. "This isn't over,"

he said, and he didn't know whether he meant the conversation or his life.

Lucia held his gaze for one beat longer. "No," she said softly. "It never is."

The door opened. Rain reached in like cold hands. The alley took him back. Behind him, the sedan became a shape the night understood, and then it was gone.

Chapter Twelve
The Red Silence

The news did not arrive like a headline. It arrived like a wrong note that would not resolve.

Lucia woke to her phone's small light and a message with no preface. Just a link. A thumbnail. A few words in Italian, clipped into English by a machine that had never been in love:

Soprano found... accidental fall... no foul play suspected.

The photo did not match the language. It was old and wrong for the text: Marina laughing into a winter scarf, cheeks pink from rehearsal air, hair caught mid-motion, as if she were mid-sentence and would finish it any second.

For a full minute, Lucia forgot how to breathe. Then her body remembered. A thin sound broke loose inside her chest. Not a scream. Something smaller and worse, like the first crack in glass. She stood because standing was what you did when the floor shifted.

Sergio was already in the sitting room, dressed and composed, the morning arranged around him like proof of control. He rose the second he saw her face. He did not ask what happened.

Lucia crossed the room and struck him once, open-handed. The sound startled her into a second strike. Her palm burned. Her shoulder did too. She lifted her hand again, furious at her own trembling, and the blow went wide, catching the edge of the console table instead.

The vase tipped and shattered. Water slid across marble. Gardenias fell onto the floor, white bruises in an instant. Lucia stared at the broken porcelain as if it had insulted her. Then she went still.

Her breath came too fast. Her hands shook. Her eyes burned, but tears would not come. She turned on Sergio again, as if he were the only solid thing left. "Lo sapevi?" *Did you know?*

Sergio's voice stayed low. Careful. "No." Then, after a swallow that looked like restraint forcing itself down his throat, "Non così." *No. Not like this.* He didn't look away when he added, "Non oggi. Non così in fretta." *Not today. Not this fast.*

Lucia's throat tightened until her next word came out too small. "Chi?" *Who?*

Sergio's eyes flicked to the window, as if looking at it too long would make it real. "Quando ci ha creati," he said quietly. *When he 'created' us.* "Ci ha fatto giurare." *He made us swear.* "A qualunque costo." *At any cost.* He met her gaze. "Non a lui." *Not to him.* "A voi." *To you.* "Alle soprano. Alle allieve. Alla musica nei vostri corpi." *To the sopranos. To the pupils. To the music in your bodies.*

Lucia blinked. She wanted to call him a liar. She wanted someone to be lying.

Sergio's jaw flexed once. Betrayal showed itself, fast, then disciplined back into place. "Ho chiamato l'uomo di Marina," he said. *I called Marina's man.* "Da quando siamo usciti dalla Germania." *Since we left Germany.* "Silenzio." Silence. He went quieter, the words pushed through like splinters. "Il Maestro... silenzio." *The Maestro... silence.* "Le linee sono morte." *The lines are dead.* He lowered his voice again. "Temo il peggio." *I fear the worst.* "Non una caduta." *Not a fall.* "Non un incidente." *Not an accident.*

Lucia's mouth opened. Nothing came out.

Sergio stepped closer, one pace. Not to touch her. Only to make sure she didn't fall without anyone noticing. "Non oggi," he said. *Not today.* His voice softened into something that could pass for care. "Mangia qualcosa." *Eat something.*

Lucia did not answer.

Later, a tray arrived. Lucia shoved it away without looking at it. Tea cooled on its saucer until the surface filmed over. On the console, amid the spilled water and broken petals, a black-and-red lace envelope waited like a joke.

She stared at it as if it were breathing. She didn't touch it. Not because she was afraid of what it would say, but because she already knew. He always wrote the same way: praise was poison. She could picture him at his desk in Tuscany. The pen moving without hesitation. The small private smile as the wax cooled. The crest pressed down, firm, final. She hated that wax. She could feel the brand of it in her memory. Too many letters. Too many orders dressed up as elegance. Too many times being reminded that even paper could belong to him.

Lucia snatched the envelope up and slammed it against the console. Once. Twice. The seal cracked. Red wax scattered onto the wood like dried blood.

Her breath came sharp through her nose. She stared at the broken crest, at the pieces, as if she'd just watched something sacred die. Then she tore it open.

The paper inside was clean. Expensive. Calm. Cruel, in its restraint. At the bottom, in his hand:

Resta nella partitura. Stay in the score.

Lucia let the letter slip from her fingers. Her hands shook. Her face did not. She walked into the bedroom and sank to the floor beside the bed, knees up, palms flat on the wood. Grounding herself the way a singer grounds herself on a stage.

Sergio did not follow her in. He left. He came back. He left again. Hours thickened. Time stopped behaving like time. At some point he set a bowl of broth beside the doorway, not near enough to demand she eat it. At some point he moved her phone out of reach without asking.

Then, gently: "Mezz'ora." *Half an hour.*

It was the last performance before the break. Lucia stared at the wall and tried to imagine standing under light with Marina's name lodged like a stone in her throat. Her first instinct was to refuse. Not because she feared the audience, but because she feared the moment sound becomes visible. She feared the crack that would announce itself in the air and never stop. She rose anyway. Grief could be carried. Not cured. Carried.

At the opera house she let the women who loved her work more than they loved themselves zip her into the dress. She did not speak. They braided her hair the way they knew they liked. Then she looked at her hands. Red nails. Still obeying.

In the dressing room, she tested the voice on a quiet scale. Nothing theatrical. No aria. Just breath and placement. The sound came out thin. Not broken. Worse. Controlled and wrong, as if her ribs had forgotten the shape of mercy. She tried again. Her throat tightened on a pitch that had never frightened her. A small heat rose behind her eyes. Panic reached for her like a hand.

Lucia gripped the vanity edge until her knuckles paled. She dropped her chin by a fraction, rolled her shoulders back, and began to do the arithmetic of breath.

In. Low. Wide. Hold Release. Support. Not force. Not fear.

"Five minutes," someone called. "Places."

Lucia stood in her light and went on. She sang. Not beautifully by her measure. Not safely. She sang like a woman walking through fire without allowing the audience to smell smoke.

In the high passage she felt it: a seam widening where Marina would have floated. A bar tightening like a throat that remembered it contained a heart. Lucia did not flinch. She made the body do what it had been trained to do. She let technique carry grief the way a bridge carries weight without announcing it. The house did not hear her failures. The house heard only the Queen.

The applause at the end came loud enough to humiliate her. Lucia bowed because bows are what you do when you have survived. She kept her face composed and her mouth obedient and walked offstage as if nothing inside her had changed.

Backstage, she didn't let anyone speak. She let the crown come off. The lashes loosen. She moved through congratulations like a person walking through rain who refuses to admit she's wet.

Sergio appeared in the doorway, careful. "Car ready," he said in English.

Lucia nodded. She put on a red coat. Red like blood. Red like the only rule the Maestro had ever given her that she had chosen to keep, until now.

Back at the hotel, Lucia didn't remove the coat. She went straight to the drawer and pulled out everything she had, searching for Marina's last letter. Marina's last words on paper. Her hands trembled. She had been held together by the opera house and its rules. Now she was back in the room where her phone had shown her the message. For one breath, she thought: it's not real.

Marina is alive. This is a test. This is him. Lucia turned toward Sergio, standing at the bedroom door.

"Tell me this is a test," she said in English. The words came too steady, which made them worse. "Tell me she's alive."

Sergio's face went still. Not the stillness of control. The stillness of a man receiving a final blow. He didn't speak right away. He didn't soften it. He only shook his head once.

Lucia's expression emptied. Then she ripped the framed program off the table and flung it. Glass exploded. The sound finally invited her tears.

They came hard. Not delicate tears. Not pretty tears. Ugly, furious ones. She slammed the Maestro's letter to the floor and stepped on it like it had a throat.

Sergio moved fast. Not like a handler. Like a man crossing a line he had promised himself he wouldn't cross. He didn't hover. He didn't ask permission. He caught her shoulders, steadying her the way you steady someone at the edge of a ledge.

"Lucia," he said in English, because her mind was

slipping, and she needed something simple. "Look at me."

She shoved him. Not because she wanted him gone, but because grief has nowhere to go. Sergio took it, then pulled her in. Lucia hit his chest once, twice, fists useless. Then she collapsed against him, finally allowing her body to do what it had been refusing all day.

A sound tore out of her, raw and childlike. "Marina," she choked.

Sergio's voice cracked on the name. He made himself steady anyway. "Sì." *Yes.*

Lucia shook, breath coming in violent bursts. "L'ha fatto lui," she whispered. *He did it.*

Sergio went very still. Then his jaw flexed once, like an animal refusing to show its teeth. He didn't correct her. He didn't defend the Maestro. He didn't say we don't know. He only said, in Italian, "Ha tradito anche me." *He betrayed me too.* He swallowed, and the next words looked like they scraped him. "Mi ha tenuto con un guinzaglio." *He kept me on a leash.* His eyes held hers, steady and ugly with truth. "E oggi lo spezzo." *And today I break it.*

Lucia pulled back just enough to look at him. Her face was wrecked. Her eyes were furious and bright. "This isn't about a man anymore," she said in English, clear and sharp. "It's about what he thinks he can take." She gestured at the ruined room. At the broken glass. At the torn letter under her foot. "He took the best part of me that I didn't own," she said. "He changed the rules." She bent, snatched up the letter, and held it up like evidence. "So I will change the game."

Sergio stayed close. He didn't touch her again,

but he didn't move away either. "How?" he asked, not challenging. Practical. Hope disguised as logistics.

Lucia's breath steadied. Something frightening settled into place behind her eyes. "Not alone," she said. "Not this time."

She thought of Emily in Utah. Of Alex at his door. Of Tuscany, screens, and a man who believed distance was discipline. "I will make him step into the light," Lucia said. "Where sound can't be edited and power can't hide behind rumor."

Sergio watched her. For the first time, his expression wasn't only duty. It was devotion. Grief. Anger. "Dimmi cosa ti serve," he said. *Tell me what you need*. Then, carefully, because he needed her to understand the price: "Se attraversiamo questa linea, non si torna indietro." *If we cross this line, there is no going back*. He switched to English. "He will call it betrayal. I will call it an oath I should have kept sooner."

Lucia nodded once. "Time," she said. "Names. And distance between me and his letters." She pointed at the drawer. "You will not deliver them anymore."

The first real disobedience sat between them like a flame.

Sergio looked at it. Then he nodded. "Capito." *Understood*.

Lucia wiped her face with the back of her hand, almost angry at her own tears. "Tomorrow I plan."

Sergio's voice softened. "È il tuo intervallo." *It's your interval*.

Lucia turned off the remaining light as Sergio left her to rest. Darkness filled the room gently, as if the night itself knew not to make noise. In the dark, Marina laughed again in Lucia's memory. Scarves. Pink cheeks. That clean tone into hell.

Lucia closed her eyes around the sound and made a promise with her mouth, because vows spoken out loud are the ones gods can hear. "Per te," she whispered. For you.

For Marina. For herself. For the music he had tried to turn into a weapon.

The Maestro had changed the rules. She would finish the piece. And when she did, the final curtain would not be his to call.

***

Near midnight, Pacific Heights held its breath. The press vans were gone. Only streetlights kept vigil, turning fog into gauze.

The car stopped two blocks shy. Sergio cut the headlights. He said nothing.

Lucia tucked her braid into the collar of her red coat and stepped out into the cold that smells like salt and money. At the stoop, she pressed the bell once.

Inside, a house woke cautiously. Locks turned. The door opened the width of a decision. Alex stood in shirtsleeves, unshaven, the blue glow of a news crawl washing the room behind him. For a beat he looked at her like a man seeing a ghost he had accidentally prayed for.

"What do you want?" he asked, not hostile, just emptied.

Lucia met his stare. "To change the score," she said. Her voice was quiet enough to be believed. "Let me in, Alex."

Behind her, Sergio waited under a streetlamp, watchful but not hovering. “Sarò qui,” he said to the night. *I’ll be here.*

Alex stepped back.

Lucia crossed the threshold.

Chapter Thirteen
The Gambit

Alex's townhouse was not the ruin Lucia expected. The remnants of a war room had been reduced to a neat stack of legal pads on the marble island. The whiteboard was clean, except for a ghostly rectangle where timelines had been. A TV murmured a late-night panel to itself in the next room. The place smelled like rain on wool and expensive soap that tried, and failed, to be anonymous.

Lucia stepped in. The door clicked behind her, and the city fell away like a backdrop.

Alex watched her with wary curiosity, not nerves. He had the look of a man who had outlived a fire and still didn't trust the walls. Shortsleeves. Dark stubble. A loosened tie folded on the counter. Ruin shaved down to bone, still upright.

She said nothing at first. She slipped the red coat from her shoulders and let it drape along her arm. Beneath it, a whisper of black Italian silk answered the room like a low note. She didn't do it for him. She did it for the ghost in another country who had turned music into a leash.

"Will you not offer your guest a drink?" she asked, as if this were a visit and not a trespass.

His gaze snapped away like it had been struck. He crossed the space in two steps, caught the coat, and flung it back over her shoulders as if modesty could be a weapon.

"No," he said. Then, harsher: "No. You have to leave. Whatever this is, whatever I did, it's over. I'm out. You won." His voice broke into something raw. "There's nothing I have left."

Lucia lifted her brows, calm. She drew the coat off again, slower this time, and arranged it neatly over the back of a chair. She smoothed the sleeve as if correcting a crease in a score.

"I would like a drink, Alex."

A muscle in his jaw jumped. He turned to the kitchen because he needed somewhere else to look. Cupboards opened. Stemware chimed. He avoided her reflection in the stainless steel. He found the Barolo. He didn't ask whether she liked Barolo. He didn't ask her anything.

He poured with a steady hand and set the glass on the island.

Lucia didn't cross to it. After a moment, Alex picked it up and brought it to her, as if delivering a verdict.

She took the glass. The first sip was velvet on a bruise. She let the wine settle her throat, almost like a steadying hand.

"What did you mean," she asked, "when you said we ruined everything?"

He gave a short laugh without humor. "I'm not saying another word until you tell me who 'we' are. Why you're half-naked in my house. And why you destroyed me."

Lucia studied him. The set of his shoulders. The way grief could make a man look like he was wearing a suit borrowed from someone larger. She set the glass down.

"Answer," she said, not unkindly. "Then I will answer you."

"I don't want to be rewarded," he snapped. "I want my life back. I want none of the last months to have happened. I want to have won, and then taken those assholes down who took everything from me."

The volume startled even him. It rang off the marble like a dropped knife. He shut his eyes once, opened them, and tried again with quieter brutality.

"You want the line? Fine." His mouth tightened. "We ruined everything means we, the rich, the clever, the 'visionaries' and their pets built something so efficient at protecting itself that the only way to fix it was to break it from the inside." He swallowed. "That was the plan. Win. Flip the table. Show the rot. Prosecute."

He looked at her like he expected mockery. He braced for it.

None came.

"Who taught you the table could be flipped?" Lucia asked.

"My mother." His voice turned flat with memory. "In the car. I told you how she died. The wrong insurance." He dragged in a breath. "My father couldn't handle the grief. He died on the line." His eyes stayed dry. His honesty didn't. "I bounced couches, worked three jobs, did what I had to do."

He stared past Lucia, as if the room might show him the exact moment he became this man.

"I didn't forget where I came from," he said, slower now, as if he was correcting himself in real time. "I buried it. I had to. If I kept it on the surface, I wouldn't have survived." His throat tightened. "Then I made a life so polished that sometimes I could pretend it had always been mine." He looked at her again. "And the whole time, the only thing that was ever radical was paperwork and a funeral."

Lucia sat then, finally. The silk creased beneath her. The room felt like it creased with it.

"You were going to leak it all yourself."

"After I won." He hated how it sounded the moment it left him. "Because otherwise it dies in process and memos. Because otherwise they win."

"And someone decided your reveal should arrive before your victory." Lucia let the sentence land without ornament. "Someone who understands timing."

"Your Maestro," Alex said, turning the word into both accusation and question.

The name moved through her like a cold hand and a heat.

"He is not mine," Lucia said. She chose each word the way a surgeon chose instruments. "But he exists. And there are others like you who have fallen without ever seeing his face." Alex stared at her. "Ministers who never survived their own press conferences," she continued. "Billionaires who discovered the market doesn't forgive a man caught with a ghost. A judge who learned what mercy was only after his daughter forced him." Lucia's mouth tightened. "Patterns. A conductor without a program."

"You're asking me to believe in a man behind a curtain," Alex said. "A myth with a mailing list."

"I'm asking you to believe what you already do." Lucia's voice softened just enough to sound like tenderness if you didn't listen closely. "That some rooms are built to make outcomes feel inevitable. He builds rooms."

Alex reached for the Barolo and took a drink from

her glass without asking. It wasn't intimacy. It was the rudeness of a drowning man.

"This is a dream," he muttered. "I took something to sleep and you're in it. You're not here."

Lucia stood. Alex stepped back, and the pressure in the air changed. "Then let the dream have one true thing," she said.

And she kissed him.

Not a theft. An offering, slow enough that he could step away.

He didn't. His hands lifted like surrender and then found her waist on their way down. Palms discovering heat under silk. Fingers remembering the fact of a human body.

For four counts she let it be only that. Breath, warmth, and the ache of being seen. When she stepped back, his pupils were blown wide, the way a room looks after the lights go dark.

"Why are you here?" he whispered. No armor. No strategy. A man with nothing left to sell, asking for the receipt.

"Because I need another player," Lucia said. "Because if I'm going to bring him out of his villa, I need to stray in a way that undoes him." She kept her gaze on his mouth as she spoke, like she was testing whether he could handle being wanted and used at the same time. "He worships discipline," she continued. "He worships distance. He believes I cannot love. So I will." Her voice sharpened. "And he will come to collect what he thinks is his."

Alex's throat worked. "Use me," he said, trying to make it sound like agency instead of surrender. "What does it cost?"

"Everything," she said softly. "But not the way

you think."

His eyes flicked to her mouth again, furious at himself for it. "Tell me his name."

"I cannot," Lucia said. "Not because I fear him. Because long ago, he became nothing other than Maestro."

"Then tell me why Marina is dead," Alex said, and the name surprised both of them.

Lucia stilled. "How do you know her name?"

Alex exhaled. "When you spend a night reading every rumor about a mysterious Maestro and his dangerous sopranos, the algorithm decides you like opera." His voice dipped. "It pushed an alert to my phone this afternoon. A thumbnail. Accidental fall." He paused, as if the words were too intimate for his mouth. "I'm sorry for your loss."

Lucia's throat worked once. She sat down slowly, as if the chair had discovered gravity.

"Because music is dying in him," she said. "And power is winning." Her hands rested open on her knees, empty. "Because I didn't stop it when I might have. Because I believed the line between baton and blade was thicker than it was."

They sat in the quiet of a kitchen that had hosted ten thousand negotiations about breakfast and none about revolution. Outside, a car rolled past with a tire that needed air. Inside, the clock over the stove found its voice.

"I'm sorry," Alex said. He meant it. He didn't know which part he meant it for.

"So am I," Lucia said. "And I'm finished being sorry."

Alex breathed like a man learning to keep time again. "What happens to me if I say yes?"

"You become what you were pretending to be," Lucia said. "A man the city can believe. Without the mask." Her mouth softened. "It will hurt. You will lose the friends who loved your mask. You will gain enemies." She held his gaze. "You may also live."

"And if I say no?"

"You will still be ruined," Lucia said. "But without a chorus."

Alex let out a small, helpless laugh. "You talk in opera."

"It is the only language I am fluent in," she said. "I am trying to learn another." She reached across the island and took his hand, careful, like an instrument that had seen better days and could still tune true.

His hand did not flinch.

"Tell me the we," he said at last. "Back to the first question."

Lucia released his hand. "The we you need to know," she said, "is me, and the girl I was before he found me." Her voice tightened. "It is Marina. It is any woman who learned to breathe for a living and was told her breath belonged to a man." Her eyes lifted to Alex. "It is you, though I hate that it is you." A rest. "It is anyone who thinks beauty is currency, and then learns it is a country." She glanced toward the window. "It is the men who were told to guard our bodies and are now guarding our souls."

Alex followed her glance, as if he could see the dark shape under a streetlamp. "Your man," he said. "He'll tell on you."

"Tonight, and forward," Lucia said, "he will not."

Alex shook his head once, as if the sanity in him was trying to make a last stand. "It can't be this simple. We talk. We kiss. You kill a king."

"No," Lucia said. For the first time, she smiled like a woman and not a soprano. "It isn't simple." Her smile faded into something colder. "I have to make him angry enough to leave his mask. I have to make him believe he can still own what he never owned. I have to make him step toward me and forget the distance he teaches." Lucia lifted the glass and finished the Barolo he had stolen. "Desire has always been his weak note."

"And love?" Alex asked.

"That," Lucia said, eyes steady, "is mine."

Silence sat with them like a third person who had seen too much and promised not to tell.

"I don't have anything to offer you," Alex said finally. "I'm almost out of money. I don't hold power anymore. I just hold the truth I can bear."

"That," Lucia said, rising, "is precisely the currency I need."

Alex stood too. They were closer than the room should have allowed.

Lucia looked up at him and saw not a mark, not a mission, not a man to be used, but a human who had built a mask because the world taught him it was cheaper, and then discovered the debt.

"Lucia," he said. Her name in his mouth sounded like a chord resolving.

"If you kiss me again," she said softly, "it will be for comfort. Not strategy."

He nodded once. "Then not tonight." He stepped back as if she were a cliff he had almost walked off, and thanked himself for learning the map.

Lucia picked up the red coat. "Tomorrow," she said, "you will issue a statement. Not to win. To tell the truth you can bear." She met his eyes. "You will not perform strength. You will describe failure, simply and cleanly. And you will ask the city to hold you to what you do next."

"What do I say next?" he asked.

"That you will not run," Lucia said, "but you will still work. That you will name what you know, not for revenge, but for repair." She slid the coat over her arm. "That you will help anyone who wants to clean the room, whether they like you or not."

"And you?" Alex asked.

"I will make a spectacle he cannot ignore," Lucia said. "Then I will invite him into a room with no exits."

"Seems fair," Alex said.

"It is not," Lucia replied. "But it will do."

Lucia crossed to the door. Alex followed without deciding to. Her hand found the knob. She paused.

"You were right," she said, not looking back. "We did ruin everything. Now we'll see if we can make something worth hearing out of the wreck."

The door opened onto fog that had learned restraint.

"Good night, Alex," she said.

"Good night," he answered, and didn't add her name because some words were safer in the chest.

Lucia stepped out into the city. The red coat closed around her.

Alex closed the door on a silence that did not hurt. On the counter, the empty glass kept the shape of her mouth. He touched the rim, then wiped it clean, and found that his hands were steady.

Chapter Fourteen
The Second Baton

The villa kept time even when the Maestro refused it. Clocks did their quiet work. The Cypress trees held formation. Gravel waited for tires that would arrive on schedule, because everything arrived on schedule here, even when grief pretended it did not.

On the music room table, the black mask lay where he'd left it. The ribbon had loosened, patient. The Maestro checked the log again, not because it could change, but because ritual was what men used when they could not pray.

02:10 — Lucia: warm-up complete.
02:34 — Lucia: step to wing right.
03:59 — Lucia: curtain call.
04:17 — Sergio: escort to car.
— no room check
— no receipt opened
— no heartbeat ping from Lucia

Absence sat in the column like a rotten tooth.

A monitor on the far wall held a paused frame from San Francisco: rain carving silver diagonals through an alley, a sedan idling, a smear of red that had to be Lucia's coat. He did not press play. He already knew what it would show him. Choice.

A soft knock at the threshold.

"Avanti." *Come in.*

Matteo stepped in without apology. Dark coat. Clean shoes. No visible weapon. He carried himself like a man who had learned to be invisible in bright rooms. He had been Marina's handler, which meant he had once been trusted close to beauty and taught not to flinch.

He stopped one pace inside the doorway, head bowed. "Maestro."

The Maestro did not return it. He let the title hang the way he let silence hang before a downbeat. "You are late."

Matteo's mouth moved into something resembling regret. It did not reach his eyes. "I needed confirmation before I spoke."

The Maestro's fingers rested on the edge of the table. Still. Controlled. "Speak."

Matteo produced a slim folder and held it for a beat, waiting for permission, as if obedience were a gift. "It is holding," he said.

The Maestro's gaze sharpened. "Say it properly."

"The fall is holding," Matteo replied. "The story is holding. The word accidental is holding."

He set the folder down with careful respect. The Maestro did not open it. He wanted the shape, not the details.

"And Lucia?" the Maestro asked.

Matteo did not hesitate. "Cut off."

The Maestro's eyes flicked, small and sharp. "Explain."

"No contact from San Francisco. No contact from Sergio. The channels are dark." A beat. Then Matteo added, quiet and precise, as if he were reporting the weather: "The railing height was corrected before anyone measured it."

The Maestro's gaze held on him a fraction longer. Good. The line landed, clean and wrong-keyed, telling the truth without confessing it.

Matteo's posture remained perfect. He did not overplay his courage. He did not ask for praise. He simply continued. "Sergio will not remain dark for long," Matteo said. "He has gone soft."

The Maestro's expression did not change, but the air did. "You are certain."

"I spent time with him," Matteo said. "In Germany. I watched him with her."

"With Lucia," the Maestro said, tasting the name.

Matteo nodded once. "I watched him while she tended Marina." His voice stayed steady, but something hardened beneath it. "He stood at Lucia's shoulder as if he belonged there. He moved like... family."

The Maestro's mouth almost smiled. Almost.

Matteo went on, careful now, because he knew he was walking on a blade. "He understands your discipline. He respects your methods. But he is no longer loyal in the correct direction."

"Correct direction," the Maestro murmured.

Matteo met his gaze. "If you press him, Maestro, he will protect her before you."

Silence.

The Maestro let the sentence sit. He let it bruise him without showing where. "And Lucia will allow that?" he asked at last.

Matteo's voice softened into something intimate, conspiratorial. "In grief, she will want comfort. She will want somewhere to put the ache."

“And?” the Maestro said.

“And she will use the last available target,” Matteo replied. “Not for love. For leverage.” A pause, then the blade. “She will use Chambers.”

The name sat in the room like a stain.

Matteo continued, watching the Maestro’s face for the smallest slip. “She will use him to taunt you. She will put him where you can see him and pretend it is nothing. She will make you feel distant.”

The Maestro’s eyes narrowed.

“That,” Matteo said gently, and his gaze flicked once toward the mask before he disciplined it away, “is why you will send me. Send me to get them. Bring them home before the comfort turns into a habit. Before Sergio makes the wrong kind of vow. Before Lucia decides she can write her own score.”

The Maestro laughed. It was small. Not warm. The laugh of a man who had seen too many fantasies die to believe in this one.

“Lucia is incapable of love,” he said.

Matteo held still, accepting the correction like a servant.

The Maestro’s gaze drifted to the black mask, then back. “If that were even possible,” he went on, “I would bring myself to San Francisco.” He said it like a joke. But something caught in his throat. A line he did not fully speak aloud, because speaking it would make it true.

His fingers tightened once against the table edge. He smoothed the motion into elegance. “No one is to love her,” the Maestro said, voice clean again. “No one is to claim what I shaped.”

Matteo lowered his eyes, obedient, thrilled.

The Maestro’s face stayed composed, but the

thought moved behind it with frightening clarity, as if the solution had always been waiting. "Chambers," he said softly, almost tenderly, "will be broken." Matteo lifted his gaze. "In front of her," the Maestro continued. "So she learns what love costs. So she remembers what comfort becomes." His tone remained measured, almost instructional. "If she ever believed she could love, I will cure her of it."

Matteo bowed his head. "Come desidera, Maestro." *As you wish, Maestro.*

The Maestro turned away, as if dismissing the subject. "We will not retrieve her with force," he said. "We will retrieve her with music." Matteo waited. "A funeral," the Maestro added.

Matteo's voice was immediate. "Firenze." *Florence.*

"Not Venice," the Maestro said.

"Venezia perdona," Matteo replied. *Venice forgives.* "Firenze ricorda." *Florence remembers.*

The Maestro's eyes held on him. Approval, slight and lethal.

"We make it public," Matteo said. "Dignified. Worthy. Lucia must sing."

"Must," the Maestro echoed.

"If she refuses, she looks wrong to the world that worships her," Matteo continued. "If she goes, Sergio insists on escorting her. He will call it duty. He will call it closure."

"And when she arrives," the Maestro said, "she does not leave."

Matteo's mouth shaped devotion again. "Esattamente." *Exactly.*

The Maestro crossed to the sideboard where the black-and-red envelopes waited. One addressed. One blank. He slid the sealed one into a drawer. He left the blank on the table.

"No letters," he said, as if speaking to the house itself. "Not until Florence."

Matteo lowered his eyes. "Saggio." *Wise.*

The Maestro moved back toward the monitor. He pressed play.

Rain moved. The sedan idled. Lucia's red coat burned against the dark. The window slid down. Lucia paused, and for one intolerable beat, her face softened at something out of frame.

The Maestro turned the screen off. He did not allow himself to watch what came next.

"Chiama Firenze," he said. *Call Florence.* "Annuncia il memoriale." *Announce the memorial.*

Matteo bowed. "Immediatamente." *Immediately.*

"And Matteo," the Maestro added. Matteo stopped. "If you are wrong," the Maestro said, voice quiet, "you will learn what retirement truly means."

Matteo's smile did not waver. "Non mi sbaglierò." *I will not be wrong.*

The Maestro lifted the black mask, turned it once in his hands, then set it down again as if it had grown heavier.

Outside, the villa kept time. And across an ocean, a woman in a red coat began to change the score.

Chapter Fifteen
Winter Interlude

Two weeks is not long enough to change a life, everyone says. Lucia learned it was long enough to change a heartbeat.

San Francisco put on its winter costume: fog like gauze, lights strung along windows that didn't believe in curtains, wreaths that smelled a little too perfect to be real. Her break began the week after the rain-soaked alley accusation, the day Marina's name turned into a headline, the night Lucia made a vow with her mouth so the gods who listen only to spoken promises would have something to keep.

The company called it a hiatus. The gossip columns called it a mystery. The Maestro would call it disobedience the moment he understood its shape.

Sergio called it logistics.

He built her a small country out of routes and timing. A new place to sleep. A driver who didn't ask names. A set of exits that didn't look like exits. He walked ten paces behind her, or across the street, or posted himself where he could see the reflection of the door before the door opened. He taught the city how to treat her like a civilian.

Lucia didn't know how to be one. She had spent years above the common man—guarded, curated, concealed. Now she walked beside a man the city had decided it was allowed to punish. The looks weren't for her. They were for what she was choosing.

She had expected the stares to make her feel famous. They made her feel awake.

Alex learned to keep his voice low in public and his jaw unclenched when cameras appeared. He kept his kitchen clean because it gave his hands something to do. He didn't drink much. He didn't scroll at all unless she forced the phone out of his grip.

On the third morning, he said, "I'm going live."

Lucia watched him set his laptop on the marble island as if it were a simple object, not a stage. No backdrop. No ring light. No talking points taped to the screen. No Maya off-camera with a countdown. Just a cloudy window, bad overhead lighting, and a man who looked like he'd stopped asking to be saved.

He told the city where he was from and why he had lied about it. He said his mother's name. He said his father's job. He drew a straight line from paperwork to a funeral without asking for pity. He admitted he had built a persona because it got him into rooms, and that he had planned to burn those rooms down from the inside.

"For you," he said. "Not for them."

He said he had failed. He didn't blame timing or enemies. He didn't name Lucia. He didn't name Emily. He didn't ask forgiveness.

He asked to be held accountable.

"I won't run," he said. "But I'll still work. If you let me."

The feed filled with hearts and comments and angry paragraphs. It wasn't a strategy. That was why it worked.

Maya texted him five minutes later. *This is the only version of you that can live. If you want me back, I'll come.*

Alex stared at the message like it was a lifeline he didn't deserve. Then he typed: Yes.

By the end of the first week, the story had changed key. Not redeemed. Not forgiven. But altered. Old friends returned in cautious half-steps. Theo, contrite. Kara, pragmatic. Sanjay, exact and skeptical. They sat on the end of the couch like people visiting a convalescent and admitted the patient might walk again.

They spoke in verbs: file, notify, train, coordinate.

Whitaker arrived with a list of donors who didn't mind reputational risk as long as the spreadsheet behaved. He looked almost cheerful, which made Alex look briefly ill.

The gossip pages kept chewing their favorite mouthful: *the Italian prima donna on the arm of the fallen prince*. Lucia, in sunglasses at a coffee shop. Lucia, in a thrifted pea coat. Lucia, laughing at something Alex said that could not possibly have been funny. Lucia's hand at his elbow like an oath or a dare.

Headlines declared ARIE & ALIBI and meant it as a joke. The photos traveled farther than any aria.

On a quiet afternoon, Lucia ducked into a narrow nail shop where fluorescent lights buzzed like impatience and the air was thick with acetone, cuticle oil, and citrus disinfectant. No chandeliers. No velvet. A row of women in puffer coats, heads bowed over their phones, waiting their turn like it was nothing sacred at all.

Lucia sat anyway.

When the tech took her hands, Lucia didn't flinch. She watched the red polish come off in cotton swipes, watched the color lift away like a costume she had worn too long. The woman held up a strip of samples. Lucia chose a dark blue that almost looked like midnight glass, the kind of color you only notice when light catches it and insists.

Truce, disguised as depth.

Outside, Alex glanced down at her hands without meaning to. His attention snagged like a thread pulled from a sleeve. "You changed them," he said.

Lucia flexed her fingers as if she were testing new bones. "Yes," she said simply. "I wanted something that didn't belong to him."

Alex didn't speak for a beat, then nodded once like he understood the weight of that better than he should have. "It looks like you," he said, quiet.

Lucia didn't answer. She wasn't sure she knew what that meant yet.

The city gossiped, took photos. Lucia didn't mind the talk as much as she thought she would. It made her less lonely to know a city had made up a story about her and was busy living inside it.

The true story belonged to three people: herself, Sergio, and the man who had refused strategy when she offered it and chosen comfort instead.

On day eight, a message reached Sergio through a line he didn't trust.

Matteo. Marina's world. Marina's other shadow: *Florence. Service soon. You both should come.*

Sergio read it twice, then lowered the phone like it had weight.

"What is it?" Lucia asked.

"A funeral, a celebration," he said carefully, as if the word could break something in her throat. "It may be real. It may be bait."

Lucia's face went still. Her hands didn't shake. It

was worse when they didn't.

"We don't decide today," Sergio added. "Not until I know more."

Lucia nodded once and kept walking. Her calm looked like control. Alex saw it and didn't comment. He was learning the difference between silence and secrecy.

They walked the city, not the museum kind of walk where you pretend to be moved by what has been framed, but the kind where you learn a place by how it changes your feet. North Beach to the Presidio. Hayes Valley to a bakery that salted its chocolate as if sweetness needed an edge. A BART ride just to sit among strangers and remember what anonymity felt like.

At the Ferry Building, she tried a local pastry she'd never had before because the man behind the counter called her signorina and wouldn't let her flee. It was strange and perfect. At a Mission taqueria, she ate standing up and forgot to be elegant, juice running down her wrist. Alex handed her a napkin without making it a joke.

At a corner store, late, she bought a carton of milk like a normal person and felt human in the way only someone who has been watched for a living can when no one is watching.

Sometimes she sang. Quiet. For herself. Not arias. Scales. A folk melody her grandmother used for bread. Once, near midnight, she stood at the glass doors of his townhouse and held a straight tone into the dark until the room remembered it was a room and not a stage.

Alex sat on the floor with his back to the couch and let his breath learn the note.

He didn't touch her beyond what the city necessitated: a hand at the small of her back when someone didn't yield, a palm to steady her when a cable on the sidewalk tried to trip her. The restraint warmed the air between them until she could feel it without looking.

Then came dinner.

They chose a small restaurant with soft lighting and no music loud enough to compete with conversation. Sergio took the bar, back to the wall, eyes everywhere, hands empty.

Lucia and Alex sat across from each other like two people practicing something fragile.

Halfway through the first glass, a bottle of red appeared at their table, accompanied by a server wearing an apologetic smile.

"Compliments," the server said, and set it down.

Alex's shoulders tightened before he could stop them. Lucia lifted her eyes.

Across the room, Alex's mayoral challenger approached with a grin designed for cameras. He wore his confidence like cologne.

"Chambers," he said, as if saying Alex's name was a public service. His gaze slid to Lucia and lingered too long. "And Lucia Conti. A pleasure."

Lucia didn't offer her hand. She didn't have to. Her stillness made the gesture irrelevant.

"I wanted to apologize," the challenger continued. "For the way the city... indulged itself." He smiled like the city had been a silly child. "But it's nice to see you out. Both of you."

Alex kept his voice low. "We're trying to eat."

"Of course," the challenger said, and leaned in anyway, performing intimacy they hadn't granted him. "I sent you Barolo. Piedmont. Thought it fitting. I have a cellar you'd appreciate, Lucia. If you ever want to see what real Italian wine looks like outside the opera house."

Alex's jaw flexed hard enough to hurt.

Lucia set her fork down with slow precision. "You have a cellar," she repeated, as if she were translating. Her voice stayed polite. Her eyes did not. "In San Francisco."

The challenger chuckled. "Imported. The best. I'm sure you understand."

"I do," Lucia said. Then she smiled, small and surgical. "That is why I'm surprised you chose Barolo."

His grin faltered by a millimeter. "Surprised?"

Lucia turned the bottle slightly, reading the label as if it were a score. "This producer," she said, tapping the glass lightly, "is respectable. But you picked a vintage that is aggressive and young. It needs time or decanting, and you didn't decant it. Which means you wanted the name more than the taste."

The challenger blinked, caught between pride and irritation.

Lucia lifted her eyes to him. "That is a campaign problem."

Alex turned his face away fast, a laugh trying to escape.

"It was a gesture," the challenger said.

"It was a performance," Lucia corrected.

He tried again, voice brightening with desperation. "Perhaps you'd prefer something else. I can have the som—"

"No," Lucia said, gentle as a blade going in. "But thank you for confirming something for me."

"What's that?" he asked, too quickly.

She tilted her head. "That Alex Chambers is not the only man in this city who confuses power with entitlement."

The silence around them widened. Nearby diners pretended not to listen with heroic failure.

The challenger's cheeks colored. He forced a laugh and straightened. "Enjoy your meal."

Lucia nodded once. He retreated as if the room had turned on him.

Alex exhaled like he'd been holding his breath for years. His eyes found hers. "You didn't have to do that," he said.

Lucia lifted her wine. "Yes," she said simply, "I did."

"You're terrifying," Alex said.

Lucia's mouth softened. "I am learning to be human," she said. "It is slower than the training."

He held her gaze, then looked down as if the intensity had burned him. "It's nice," he admitted. "Being defended. I'm not used to it."

Lucia's fingers tightened around the stem of the glass. She didn't say what she felt. She didn't know what to name it yet.

They ate. They talked more than they had been. Alex told her about the first couch he slept on after his father died, and the woman who fed him without asking his last name. Lucia told him about her first teacher, the one who smelled like smoke and oranges and warned her that talent makes men greedy.

When they left, the fog had thickened. Sergio was already outside, watching the street as if it might lunge. In the car, Lucia stared out the window and felt the city slide past like a life she hadn't lived.

On the tenth day, Alex gave in to the smallest ritual, and it felt like breaking a law. He ordered pizza. A real greasy pizza. Lucia looked appalled until she tasted it, then laughed at herself, the pure, untrained laugh that belonged to the girl before Tuscany.

Alex froze for a second at the sound, as if he wanted to hold it in his hands.

He opened a bottle that didn't require decanting. He poured without worrying about pairing. They watched a movie in French, and Alex got up three times to look up a line and twice forgot to hit pause. Lucia corrected him without mercy. He refused to believe her translation until he didn't care as much anymore.

Somewhere after midnight, she fell asleep against his shoulder for exactly nine minutes and woke apologizing.

Alex shook his head. "I will always be proud to be slept on," he said, dead serious.

Lucia stared at him, then laughed again, smaller.

"Breathe," he said, like it was a reasonable request. "Without preparing the next breath."

She tried. One breath. Fear and relief fought inside her chest like an old duel.

"Again," he said. She did it again.

The rumors learned to feed themselves. *Is she moving in? Did they meet before the campaign? Will she sing at his wedding, funeral, indictment*?

Maya managed the worst of it with a half smile and a sharper email.

"Let them talk," she told Alex. "Noise makes cover. Use it."

Lucia didn't tell him what else she was using. The

quiet.

On the twelfth night, Sergio walked them to Alex's door and stopped at the stoop. Fog moved through the street like a slow animal. The streetlamp made a clean circle on the sidewalk.

Sergio didn't look at either of them for long, as if looking would make it a decision.

"Quando sei pronta," he said to Lucia. *When you're ready*. He switched to English, flat and clear. "I'll be outside."

Lucia's throat tightened. She nodded once.

Sergio stepped back into the fog and became what he always was: a line not to cross.

Inside, the townhouse was quiet in the way rooms are when they've learned to trust whoever is in them. No screens. No panels. The kitchen light a low gold.

Alex watched the door click shut, then turned back to her as if the room had changed temperature.

"Stay," he said. Not a command. A request.

Lucia's instinct rose fast, refusal already shaped.

Alex lifted a hand, gentle. "Just... say something," he added, quieter. "Tell me what you want. Tell me no. Tell me anything that's yours."

Lucia looked at him for a long moment. Her voice came out honest, not polished. "I do not sleep," she said. "I rehearse. I count. I wake."

"Then don't sleep," Alex said. "Rest, with me. That's all."

Lucia swallowed. No one asked her for small things. Small things were the beginning of large ones. She nodded once.

They didn't go to the bedroom. They sat on the rug by the glass doors, looking out onto a scrap of city. Alex put on a record quietly because the sound of a needle finding a groove felt like the opposite of surveillance.

Lucia tucked her feet under her, then out again, then under. A woman unlearning choreography.

"Tell me something true," she said, "that you have never said into a camera."

Alex's eyes went unfocused, like he was listening for an answer he didn't want. Then he said, "I wanted to win so I could be loved for how I lost."

Lucia's breath caught. It was a terrible sentence. It was an honest one. She kissed him for it. Slow. Offered, not taken. A kiss that asked permission simply by existing.

Alex didn't move away. His hands lifted like surrender, then found her waist. His palms met the heat under her clothes as if he'd been starving for something that wasn't power.

When she pulled back, his pupils were blown. His mouth parted like he'd forgotten language.

"Is this what you want?" he whispered.

"It is," Lucia said. Then, quieter, honest enough to scare her, "Not because I have to." She pressed her forehead to his. "Because I need you. And you need something that isn't a lie."

Alex swallowed, forcing himself to stay human. "Lucia," he said, and her name in his mouth sounded like a chord resolving.

She answered with his.

His hand found her jaw, careful at the hinge, the place where a singer keeps openness for sound. He didn't press. He let her open. He kissed her again, slower.

She felt her body respond like it had been waiting for permission for years. Heat. Pressure. Her spine lengthened without asking her.

Alex paused, forehead near hers. “Tell me to stop.”

Lucia’s mouth curved, brief and dangerous. “I am the one who stops things,” she said, and pulled him closer.

He lifted her only enough to move them away from the edge of the table and into the soft of the rug. Her laugh at being handled with such domestic care embarrassed them both and made them braver.

He took his time like time was a vow.

No theatrics. No performance. Just bodies learning what they were allowed to want.

When she came apart, it wasn’t an applause moment. It was a private, almost quiet thing. Relief more than triumph. A held note resolving into air. Alex stayed with her through it, one hand steady where her ribs met, counting breaths he couldn’t feel but could hear.

Afterward, she kissed his palm because it had told the truth about her body back to her.

Later, when his own breath finally broke, he said her name again.

Outside, under the streetlamp, Sergio stood with his hands lightly clasped, watchful but not hovering. He didn’t look up. He didn’t pray. He counted time the way he always had. Turning to the sedan to rest.

Inside, Lucia slept. Not rehearsal sleep Not vigilant sleep. Sleep that trusted the next note would come without her summoning it.

Alex did not sleep. He stared at the ceiling and made a list he would never write down of every room he would have to enter and every person he would have to apologize to in a language that did not taste like politics.

He wasn't planning. Not yet.

He was keeping time.

Two weeks, people say, cannot change a life. Perhaps not. But a body can learn a new rhythm in less time, and sometimes that is the same thing.

Chapter Sixteen
First Light

He woke before the city and, for once, didn't negotiate with the morning. The townhouse held a quiet that didn't ask for anything. No screens talking over each other. No calendar alarms. No voices in the next room trying to turn fear into a plan. Just the heat clicking on, soft and practical, and the fact of another person asleep beside him. Sergio's check-in had come at dawn, a single text from an unknown number Alex had learned to trust without liking.

"Sono fuori." *I'm outside.* Alex hadn't replied. He hadn't needed to. The message wasn't for conversation. It was proof of position.

Lucia lay on her side, hair spilled across his pillow like she'd forgotten she was supposed to keep it contained. The sheet had slipped to her waist. Nothing staged. Nothing precise. Just warmth and the faint ache of bodies that had stopped pretending they were made of only discipline.

Alex got up carefully. Habit had made him good at leaving without waking people. This time, he didn't want to leave. He just wanted the room to stay what it was.

He kissed her shoulder once, barely there, more promise than touch, then went to the kitchen.

He wasn't a natural in kitchens, but he knew how to try. Coffee first, ground coarse enough to smell like intention. He whisked eggs with cream and salt the way his mother used to. He burned the first piece of toast and stared at it like it had personal opinions. Bacon hissed. Potatoes took their time becoming edible, as if insisting on being taken seriously. He opened the fridge, found strawberries, and rinsed them under the tap with the kind of care that almost made him laugh at himself.

He plated everything without caring how it looked. Then his phone chimed itself into the world.

He stared at it. Didn't pick it up. The sound alone was enough to bring back the time he'd just survived: the comments, the threats dressed as concern, the kind of attention that makes air feel monitored. He flipped the phone face down and let it sulk on the counter. He was turning back to the stove when the floorboard creaked.

Lucia stood in the doorway wrapped in his robe, hair loose, face softer than he'd ever seen it. Sleep looked unfamiliar on her, like a luxury she hadn't been taught to accept.

She squinted at the kitchen. "What is that smell?"

"Bravery," he said. "And bacon."

She came closer, drawn by coffee and the honest ritual of someone trying. He poured her a mug and handed it to her with both hands, like he didn't trust himself not to ruin the moment with cleverness.

She took a sip. Her eyes closed, involuntary, and the expression on her face was so quietly pleased it almost hurt.

"Breakfast doesn't need to be a feast," she said, teasing. "An espresso. Fruit. A little cheese. This American insistence on... potatoes."

He speared one crisp potato and held it out like a

dare. Lucia accepted it with the solemnity of a woman agreeing to something small and dangerous. She chewed. Considered. Then, with obvious restraint, nodded once.

"I will not admit this is good," she said. "But it is not bad."

He laughed, softer than he meant to.

They ate standing up, close enough that neither of them had to decide what to do with their hands. Lucia stole a strip of bacon like she'd always been allowed to. Alex pretended not to notice how pleased he was that she did.

"Your live stream is still getting attention," she said after a while, careful with the subject as if it might bite. "They're calling your honesty a strategy."

"It wasn't," he said. "That's why it landed."

"And now?"

"And now people want a story. Some of them want me redeemed. Some of them want me punished. Most of them just want a reason to believe the city isn't fixed." He shrugged, and it looked like it cost him. "I don't know which part I owe."

Lucia set down her fork. "You owe the work."

He looked at her like she'd said something obvious that no one else had ever dared to say to him. "You sound like Maya," he said.

"I sound like someone who has spent her whole life being told what she owes," she replied. "If you're going to owe anything, let it be to something you can pay without bleeding."

He nodded once. Then, because he couldn't seem to stop himself, he said, "We could leave."

Lucia didn't flinch. She didn't smile either. She just watched him, calm in a way that made his impulse feel exposed. He tried to make it lighter and failed. "Italy. Somewhere quiet. Somewhere that doesn't know our names."

"You think I am a thing that can be moved," she said gently. "I am a person who has to finish a piece."

"I know," he said quickly. "I do." And he did. That was the problem. Wanting her to be safe wasn't the same thing as knowing how to keep her that way.

Lucia stepped closer, robe sleeve brushing his wrist. "You're not allowed to rescue me," she added, softer. "Not even from love."

He swallowed.

And then the line came out of him not like a speech, not like a romance line, but like the only honest sentence left. "I'm falling in love with you," he said. "Not because of the opera. Not because of any of this." His eyes flicked to her mug, the faint print of her lipstick on the rim. "Because you closed your eyes over coffee like you were allowed to be a person. Because you told me the truth without asking me to perform for it."

Lucia didn't look away. For a moment she seemed startled, as if the words had landed somewhere in her that had been locked for years and didn't know how to open quietly. Then she set her mug down, cupped his jaw with her palm, and kissed him. Simple, certain, like she believed in mornings.

The robe tie snagged when she stepped back. She frowned at it, irritated, and Alex laughed before he could stop himself. He leaned in to untangle it, fingers careful, and the smallness of it, its ridiculousness, made Lucia's mouth curve.

"Slow," she said. "We have hours before the world remembers our names."

He nodded, and for once, didn't try to fill the silence with a plan.

The second time they touched each other wasn't a repeat of the night before. It was quieter. More attentive. Less urgency, more trust. When Lucia's hair fell into her face, Alex tucked it behind her ear without thinking. When he kissed the inside of her wrist, she didn't turn it into something symbolic. She just let it be what it was: a place he wanted.

A plate slid off the edge of the bed at one point, clattering softly on the rug. Lucia froze, then burst into a short laugh, half embarrassed, half relieved.

"Your house is too honest," she said into his shoulder.

"My house is clean," he corrected.

She lifted her head. "It is not."

He laughed again. "Fair."

After, the room felt like a room again. Radiator hiss. A bus exhaling somewhere outside. The same branch tapping the window like it had always been there. They lay still, tangled in sheets that didn't care who they were.

"If the crowd asks you to run," Lucia said, not looking at him, "say no until you can say yes without needing them to love you."

Alex turned toward her. "And you?"

Lucia's gaze went somewhere he couldn't follow for a second a distant place with Cypress trees and a letter drawer and a room that didn't forgive. Then she blinked back into the present.

"I will make a spectacle that isn't a lie," she said. "And then maybe a life that doesn't require permission."

"Maybe," he echoed, and the word sounded like the first thing he'd said all week that didn't need defending.

A vibration from the phone against the counter cut through the quiet. Alex didn't reach for it. Not immediately. He looked at Lucia instead, like he was checking whether the world could wait.

When he finally flipped the phone over, he didn't open anything. Just read the top layer:

Maya: Town hall? 72 hours. Your rules.
Kara: Press will circle. We can starve them without feeding them. Call me.

He set the phone back down. "I don't want to leave this room," he admitted.

"Then don't," Lucia said. "Not yet."

They ate what was left of breakfast cold, sitting on the bed, laughing at the potatoes that had gone soft and pretending it wasn't perfect anyway. Lucia stole a strawberry and fed it to him with her fingers like she'd been doing it her whole life. Alex looked at her like he was trying to memorize something without making it a burden.

For an hour, they talked without planning, which turned out to be harder than anything he'd done in politics. They named small things. A street vendor he wanted her to meet. A bakery she wanted to revisit because the woman behind the counter had called her "honey" without knowing who she was. The hinge on the cabinet that squeaked every time the house tried to confess something.

Months of normal couples' time compressed into one morning of truth.

He didn't ask again to take her away. She didn't ask him to return to the race. They let wanting be a door they didn't have to open today.

Later, when they had to become people again, Alex showered and shaved and looked like a man with a future he hadn't decided on yet. Lucia braided her hair over one shoulder and looked briefly like herself.

At the doorway she paused. "Breakfast was too much," she said, which meant thank you.

"Breakfast wasn't enough," he replied, which meant stay.

Lucia's eyes softened. "I will," she said carefully. "Until I cannot."

He kissed her once more simple, clean, not trying to extract meaning from it. The day outside would be loud. The world would knock again.

But his hands weren't shaking. He didn't know what came next. He only knew this: the first light had come, and for once, he didn't try to outrun it.

Chapter Seventeen
The Spiral

The villa had always obeyed him.

Time moved differently in his rooms. Clocks stayed accurate. Doors never stuck. Even the Cypresses seemed trained to hold their breath when he passed.

Lately, the world outside had begun to seep into his walls: rumor, noise, a faint, stubborn sense that someone, somewhere, was moving without permission. The monitors confirmed it.

Lucia Conti was everywhere now, but not in the way he preferred. Not framed by velvet and footlights. Not held in the disciplined geometry of backstage corridors.

She was in daylight. In a thrifted coat. In a street-level life. And worse, she was beside Alex Chambers.

The private feeds from San Francisco had gone dark. No dressing-room ping. No room check. No clean, obedient proof of where she was and who she was with. He saw only what the world saw, and the world had begun to adore her disobedience. A crawl beneath one clip called it 'romance'.

He watched Lucia laugh at something Alex said and felt his throat tighten with a heat he refused to name. He didn't move. He didn't blink. Then he picked up the phone and made the only kind of call that mattered.

"Matteo," he said.

The line clicked once, and Matteo was already there in the sound of it. "Maestro."

"Bring me the status," the Maestro said, calm, simple, command dressed as conversation.

Matteo didn't waste breath. "It's as you wrote it." He had always been good at that, making obedience sound like devotion.

"All of them?" the Maestro asked.

"All," Matteo confirmed. "Vienna is packing. Tokyo is airborne. Buenos Aires has canceled. Paris has gone dark. Their houses are in mourning, and their boards are terrified of public grief."

"And Florence?"

"Prepared," Matteo said. "Every arrangement. Every room. Every car. Every flight. Every church detail approved through the channels you built." A beat, reverent, practiced. "They are coming home, Maestro. Whether they understand it or not."

Home. The Maestro let the word sit in his mouth, almost sweet, because it wasn't only home now. It was control.

"And Lucia?" he asked, finally.

Matteo's tone sharpened the way a blade does when it's pleased to be held. "San Francisco Opera announced Toscana." The Maestro's eyes flicked to the screens again. Lucia on American streets. Lucia in American gossip. Her name beside Alex's like an invitation.

"This isn't rumor," Matteo continued, careful to sound disgusted rather than intrigued. "This is defiance. This is her performing freedom from you. The handlers have said nothing but the houses talk. The sopranos talk. They call it courage."

Freedom. The Maestro exhaled through his nose once. Not anger. Not yet.

"Bring me the staff," he said.

Matteo didn't ask why. He never asked why. He only made things happen. Minutes later, the compound woke like a machine being reassembled: footsteps, soft voices, the press of purpose. Downstairs, staff prepared rooms that had not been used in months. Sheets aired out. Black clothing pressed. Security rotated. Cars aligned in the drive like quiet teeth.

The Maestro watched it all from the music room, his hands still, his face unreadable. The handlers could shape rumor. They couldn't shape bodies.

Then Matteo entered with the posture of a man who carried solutions. Behind him came two men who did not belong here. They weren't trained in breath and beauty. They didn't move like music people. They moved like money had taught them violence: close-cropped hair, clean shoes, eyes that did not drift to the art on the walls. They didn't bow. Matteo did it for them.

"These are the professionals," Matteo said. "Ex-military. Private contracting. Not sentimental. They don't speak in music, Maestro. They speak in outcomes."

The Maestro's gaze stayed on the men, then returned to Matteo. "And why are they here?"

Matteo's smile was small. Earned. Hungry. "Because your sopranos have been excellent," he said. "Your bait has worked. Your discipline has delivered." He took one careful step forward, reverence deepening. "But Marina proved something."

The Maestro didn't move. Matteo continued anyway.

"Even the finest instrument can be broken not because she failed, but because the world is clumsy with beautiful things." He let that settle, then offered the blade. "To ensure no more Marinas, the sopranos must remain what they are: seductive, untouchable, strategic." His tone hardened. "But the ending cannot be left to handlers and chance. Not anymore."

One of the men behind him shifted his weight, almost bored.

Matteo softened again, as if soothing the Maestro into the idea. "Your mission was never only to ruin," he said. "Ruin is slow. Ruin is messy." He lifted his chin. "Now it becomes something else."

The Maestro's eyes narrowed a fraction. Matteo smiled, pleased to have his attention.

"To end."

Silence.

The Maestro walked to the piano and placed his hand on the closed lid, fingers spread as if feeling for a pulse beneath the wood. "And you believe I should change the entire score," he said mildly, "because one soprano fell."

Matteo didn't flinch. "Because one soprano was allowed to be vulnerable," he corrected. "Because sentiment spreads. Because handlers grow soft." A pause, then the gift he'd been saving. "Because Sergio is no longer predictable," Matteo said, "and his soprano is not either."

The Maestro's hand didn't move. But the room did, just slightly, like air shifting before a storm decides it wants to be seen.

Matteo watched him with the attentive patience

of a man feeding an animal. "It's not one broken soprano, Maestro." He held the next line until it could cut. "It's two, and the second one is learning she can breathe without your permission." Then, quieter, devout, certain, vicious in its calm, Matteo said, "Sergio is allowing Lucia to betray you. He is allowing her to be loved and to feel love." His mouth barely moved around the truth he was selling. "He must retire. And I can bring her home to you."

The Maestro stepped toward Matteo until Matteo had to lift his chin to hold the gaze. "No one is to love her," the Maestro said quietly.

The two men behind Matteo stayed still, but the air changed. They understood that sentence the way they understood contracts.

"Only me." His fingertips pressed into the piano lid, then eased. A single, disciplined movement. A tell he would have denied if anyone had named it.

The room pretended not to hear the confession. Matteo lowered his eyes like devotion.

The Maestro's voice remained even. "Bring in the new one."

Matteo moved immediately.

Rosa arrived with her hair pinned too tightly and her hands too clean, like someone who still believed discipline could protect her. She didn't look like Lucia. Not truly. But she had the right bones. The right mouth. The kind of youth the world forgives.

"She is your replacement," Matteo said, not to Rosa, but to the room.

Rosa's eyes flicked to the Maestro, then down.

"Sing," the Maestro said.

Rosa sang. It was good. Clean. Young. Untouched by cruelty. Her tone had not yet learned fear. The

Maestro listened without expression. Then, after the phrase ended, he said, "Again."

Rosa sang again.

Matteo and his men watched her like investors watching a demonstration, evaluating, not reverent. When the lesson ended, Matteo escorted Rosa out as if she were already property that needed to be stored correctly.

At the doorway he paused. "Maestro."

The Maestro didn't look up.

Matteo gestured toward the television. "It's starting." The screen clicked, and sound filled the room. A town hall.

Alex Chambers stood under bright lights and clean angles, poised as if someone had coached him not just to survive but to win. He was polished. Controlled. Charming in a way that felt newly earned. The Maestro watched him with narrowing eyes.

"Trained," Matteo murmured, almost admiring despite himself. "As if inspired by..."

The Maestro didn't answer, because the camera panned. And there she was. Lucia. In the crowd. Close. Present. Real.

A subtext scrolled along the bottom: TRADING TITLES? PRIMA DONNA FOR FIRST LADY?

The Maestro felt something hot and violent move through his bloodstream.

Alex spoke into the microphone, calm and steady. "I'm not here to perform strength," he said. "I'm here to tell the truth, my truth."

A ripple of approval moved through the room on screen. The crowd leaned toward him like it wanted to believe.

Then Alex did something unexpected. He spoke

like a boy with foolish dreams who didn't understand how the world worked. He spoke to the people for the people, and the room answered with applause too large for the space.

The Maestro watched, jaw clenched.

Then Alex turned. He extended his hand. And Lucia stood.

The Maestro leaned forward without meaning to.

Alex drew Lucia onto the stage like it was the most natural thing in the world. Like she belonged there. They embraced one second too long. Then Alex leaned in toward her ear and said something the microphone didn't catch.

The Maestro's throat locked.

Matteo glanced at him, satisfied. The reaction was proof.

Reporters swarmed as soon as they stepped down.

One voice rose above the others. "Is she the reason for your comeback, Chambers?"

Lucia answered without hesitation, her tone perfect. "No," she said. "He is the reason. He decided to be honest. That is rare. That is his."

Another reporter pushed forward.

"And Marina Seaton, your esteemed late colleague, Lucia. Will you be attending the Florence service?"

Lucia's expression didn't crack, but her eyes sharpened into something that was not grief anymore. Not only grief. Steel.

"Yes," she said simply. "Of course." Alex blinked, surprise badly hidden. Lucia turned her face toward the camera, as if answering the world. But the Maestro knew who she was speaking to. Her voice lowered by half a step, the way singers drop into a register meant for confession and threat.

“Marina was not simple,” Lucia said. “She was a vow.” A breath, controlled, deliberate. “I will come to Florence,” she continued, “and I will sing her name into the stone. I will finish the score she never got to finish.” Her mouth curved. Not a smile. Not mercy. “And I will stay in the score.” A pause, sharpened to a blade. “But not yours.”

For a fraction of a second, the Maestro’s blood forgot it was supposed to move.

Sergio appeared then, cutting through the crowd like a blade with manners. He placed himself between Lucia and the cameras without touching her, and in the same motion guided them away. Protecting. Not owning.

The Maestro watched Sergio’s hand hover near Lucia’s back and felt something inside him split cleanly: rage and recognition.

He turned slowly toward Matteo. “She’s coming,” the Maestro said.

Matteo bowed. “Yes, Maestro.”

The Maestro’s gaze slid past him to the two men waiting in the shadows behind. “As soon as she is airborne,” the Maestro said, voice quiet and absolute, “bring Chambers to me.”

Matteo didn’t hesitate. He nodded once. Then he nodded to the men. They disappeared into the dark like an idea that had already been paid for.

The Maestro kept watching the screen, Lucia’s face still framed in light, still human beside the man she had chosen. His mouth shaped the word he’d been forcing himself not to say all week.

“Enough.”

Chapter Eighteen
The Summons

The high of the town hall died before the car reached Pacific Heights.

Maya talked the whole way, words tumbling out like confetti she refused to sweep up. "Trending in three categories. Three. Alex, do you understand what that means? It means America is bored and you are the cure. Also, your clip is on a teacher's account with a million followers, and she captioned it, 'he said his mother's name.' I'm crying. The internet is crying. Even the haters are crying."

Alex sat rigid in the back seat, jaw set, eyes forward. The city lights slid over his face and did not soften it. Sergio said nothing. Lucia watched the window as if the glass could teach her something. When they pulled up, Lucia was out first.

Sergio followed so fast his restraint snapped. "Dobbiamo parlare." *We need to talk*. His voice stayed too loud, too sharp, as if volume could bend fate. "Non dovevi minacciarlo." *You were not supposed to threaten him.*

"Così non posso proteggerti." *I cannot protect you like this.* "Non puoi andare al funerale." *You cannot go to the funeral.*

It was the first time Alex had seen him lose a thread. Sergio, always composed, always built from rules and silence, was suddenly a man on a sidewalk acting like urgency could rewrite what was coming.

Lucia let him spend the heat. She did not flinch. She did not defend herself. She stood with her hands folded in front of her while he scolded her in Italian like she was a girl, not a woman who had survived men with nicer voices and worse intentions.

Maya's voice slowed, then stopped. She and Alex watched from the steps, side by side, like strangers accidentally witnessing a private family fight.

Sergio finished with a final sentence that sounded like a curse disguised as devotion. He stood there breathing hard, furious with her and with himself.

Lucia blinked once.

"Sei finito?" *Are you done?* Sergio's mouth tightened. He gave the smallest nod. Lucia turned to Alex with a courtesy so calm it felt like a weapon. "May we go in? Sergio requires tea."

Sergio muttered, barely under his breath, "Mi serve qualcosa di più forte del tè." *I need something stronger than tea.*

Maya let out a startled laugh that broke the tension by exactly one notch, which was her gift.

Inside, Alex's townhouse smelled like coffee and marker ink and the faint, clean panic of a place that had been turned into a war room and then scrubbed back into a home.

Maya snapped back into motion as if she had a switch in her spine. "Okay. Great. We are inside. Everyone breathe. I have notes. I have next steps. I have a Google Doc called 'The Comeback' that you are all going to respect."

Alex threw his coat onto a chair with more force than necessary. The sound cracked the room open.

“When were you planning on telling me,” he said, voice low and sharp, “that you’re going to Italy? That you’re walking back into his arms?”

Lucia took her coat off slowly, like she was removing a costume. She moved through the kitchen as if she belonged there now, as if this life had been hers longer than two weeks. She reached for the kettle.

Without looking at Sergio, she asked, “Limone?” *Lemon?*

From the corner, Sergio scowled, embarrassed. “Sì.” *Yes.*

Lucia set the kettle on the stove. She poured water like nothing in the world had shifted. Alex stared at her, waiting for her to meet him where he was standing.

Maya, clutching her laptop like a shield, cleared her throat. “Okay. Town hall breakdown. Key wins. Audience sentiment. We have a sixty percent swing among undecideds in the—”

Alex cut her off without looking at her. “You will not go alone,” he said, eyes locked on Lucia. “I’m coming with you.”

Maya’s head snapped up. “No. Absolutely not. You cannot leave the country. You cannot even leave the zip code right now. Alex, you are winning. This is the comeback of a lifetime.”

“I agree with Maya,” Lucia said. Her voice was soft, but the sentence landed like a door locking. She opened a bottle of wine with a quiet click. She poured for herself, poured for Maya without asking, and then poured whiskey for Alex instead. A peace offering and a warning, both.

“Salute,” she said. Cheers.

Alex didn’t touch it. “You said you were leading

Toscana," he snapped. "You made commitments. To the city, to the opera house, to—"

"To you?" Lucia asked, and for the first time she let the implication breathe.

Maya closed her laptop slowly, as if she had just realized she was holding a live grenade. She glanced at Sergio, then made a decision and crossed into the living room with her wine.

"Well," she said brightly, too bright, "Sergio. Hi. You look like you need an anxiolytic and a therapist. I have neither. I do have memes, though."

Sergio exhaled through his nose, the closest he came to a laugh.

In the kitchen, Alex stepped closer to Lucia. The anger had started to fray. Under it was fear. "Tell me you're coming back," he said.

Lucia didn't answer.

The television in the other room looped the town hall clip, volume up just enough to give them privacy, not enough to keep sound from slipping through. Alex's voice. The crowd. Then the anchor, bright with manufactured awe.

"And joining him briefly on stage was opera star Lucia Conti..."

The camera panned. Lucia's face appeared on the screen, framed in bright American light. Beside her, a lower-third scrolled like a blade.

ROSA BELLINI, A RISING STAR TO SING WITH LUCIA CONTI.

Lucia went still. Rosa Bellini.

The name struck like a wrong note in a sacred room.

For a second she was not in Alex's kitchen. She was in hillside vowels, in a courtyard where old women shelled peas. She was in the memory of a girl with braids pulled too tight by hands that thought tightness was protection. Young enough to believe discipline could be love. Old enough to be used.

Lucia closed her eyes. Not one more, she thought. Not one more girl offered up as proof that the Maestro's work is righteous.

When she opened her eyes again, they were clear and cold.

"I must end this," Lucia said.

Alex's face changed. "Lucia—"

She turned toward the living room. Sergio had stopped humoring Maya. He was watching the front of the house like a man expecting it to explode.

"We need eyes on this townhouse," Lucia said. "Protection. The Maestro came for kin. He will come for Alex too."

Sergio's rage snapped into function. "This house is a circus I can choreograph," Sergio said. "We will have eyes here. Not only for him." His gaze moved, briefly, to Maya. "For the home."

Maya blinked. "Okay. Wow. I hate that sentence. I understand it. I hate it."

Sergio started listing logistics like prayers. Cameras. Exits. Drivers. Who gets followed. Who does not. Maya absorbed it with the grim focus of someone who has managed powerful people for years and has just learned what real danger looks like.

"I'll drive you home," Sergio told Maya, calm now.

Maya hesitated, then nodded like a woman choosing to be smart instead of proud.

At the door, Sergio looked at Lucia. "Partiamo domani," he said. *We leave tomorrow.* "Io ti preparo." *I will prepare for you.* Lucia gave a single nod. Sergio's gaze flicked once to Alex. Not warm. Not cruel. Only precise. Then he left.

The door clicked shut, and the townhouse felt suddenly too quiet. Lucia crossed to Alex and took his hands. She lifted them to her mouth. No words. No theater. Just a kiss against his knuckles that told him she was real, and that this was real, and that she did not know how to promise what he wanted.

Alex's throat worked. "Don't do this," he said, rough. "Just... stay."

Lucia pressed her forehead to his hand, then looked up at him. Her eyes were bright, but her voice was steady. "Tonight," she said. "Yes." Then, in Italian, softer than a vow and harder than one, "Domani, no." *Tomorrow, no.*

That night was not frantic. It was not desperate. It was the slow making of a memory meant to survive distance. Lucia touched him like she was learning a new language and refusing to lie in it. She held his face and made him look at her when his fear tried to turn him away.

Alex kissed her like a man who had spent too long being loved for a mask and had finally met a woman who did not ask him to wear it. When she fell asleep, it was not rehearsal sleep. It was trust. Alex watched her breathe and hated how much the sound controlled him.

By morning, his team arrived early.

The kitchen filled with the bright cruelty of productivity. Coffee. Sharpies. Phones. Maya in a tailored coat pretending she had slept, refusing to acknowledge that Sergio's warning had lodged under her skin.

Lucia was already awake when Alex rolled over. Her smile was soft. Her eyes were too bright.

"I am sorry to have ruined you," she murmured, as if the confession cost her, "but I am excited to watch you grow from it."

"Watch from afar," he said.

"Or close," she replied. "Operas do end, mi amore."

"I will come find you."

Lucia's smile faltered. "If I need to be found," she said quietly, "there will not be anything left of me to find."

He reached for her, urgent. "I'm coming with you."

"You do not know this world," Lucia said. "You are safest for me here." She moved over him, knees braced on either side of his hips, bare skin against bare skin. Not seductive. Anchoring. She kissed him between sentences, as if she needed her mouth to keep her brave.

"Stay," she said. She kissed him. "Here." Another kiss. "So I have this bed to come home to." Then, in Italian, softer than a vow, "Torno da te." *I will come back to you.* "Ma tu devi essere qui." *But you must be here.*

Alex made a sound that did not know whether it wanted to be a laugh or a break. "Lucia..."

"I will denounce him," she said. Clean. Direct. "Publicly. In his country. Under his God. I will say what he cannot afford for me to say."

Alex sat up fast, anger catching up to fear. "This is a trap. He killed Marina. He will—"

"He will try what he always tries," Lucia said, and her softness vanished. The woman left was not student, not courtesan, not soprano. Only survivor. "To turn grief into obedience. To make music into ownership. He will fail if I do not help him."

"Don't give him a stage," Alex said.

"I'm giving Marina a farewell," Lucia replied. She looked at him then, truly looked, and the tenderness in her face hurt more than any fight.

"If I do not come back," she said, "do not make my ghost useful to your plans. Make it kind to the girls who come after me."

Alex closed his eyes, opened them, and nodded once.

Maya knocked, waited exactly one professional beat, then opened the door just slightly. "Sergio is here," she said.

Alex left the bed, frustrated and raw, and followed Maya out.

Lucia stayed behind long enough to become steel again. She dressed slowly. Then she crossed into Alex's closet and hung her thrifted pea coat at the front, like a promise she was trying to believe.

She wanted to come back. She wrapped herself in her red coat and stepped into the hallway.

Maya stopped her. Her voice was low now, stripped of performance. "We'll keep him busy."

Lucia's throat tightened. "Keep him loved," Lucia said, and startled herself with the plea inside the instruction.

At the door, Lucia did not hug Alex. She did not kiss him. The room did not need theater. She adjusted her scarf. Tucked her braid over one shoulder, the way she did when she meant to get through something without being seen doing it.

"Eat," she told him. "Sleep when you can. Truth is

your music. Sing it loud."

"And you?" Alex asked.

Lucia held his gaze. "I will sing the truth I can live with," she said.

He reached for her hand. She let him have it for one beat. Then she took it back, because distance this time was love's armor. The door opened.

Lucia and Sergio moved through it together, not as handler and soprano, but as two people walking into the mouth of a storm they had named. At the front, the car waited with its lights off. The city performed indifference with style.

Lucia slid into the back seat. Sergio handed her a card that finally arrived. It wasn't an invitation.It was a summons.

"Pronta?" he asked. *Ready?*

"Sì," Lucia said. *Yes.* As the car pulled away, she touched the place at her throat where a necklace would have been if she believed in trinkets.

"Per te," she whispered. *For you.* For Marina.

Upstairs, Alex stood very still in a room that smelled like coffee and Sharpie and the kind of fear people only admit to in kitchens. His team filtered back in with faces that pretended they hadn't been listening at the door.

He looked at them and found they were waiting for him to become the mask again. His voice, when it came, did not shake. "Okay," he said. "From the top. What is the aftermath of the town hall?"

The city picked up its instruments.

Somewhere across an ocean, a man in a villa heard the downbeat and mistook it for control.

Chapter Nineteen
The Interruption

The day moved faster than Alex could hold. By nine, the town hall had already started turning into a story that belonged to everyone except him. Clips of his answers were stitched into montages with dramatic music. Old enemies pretended they'd always liked him. New supporters spoke about him like he was a cure. The challenger Lucia had humiliated two nights before did not vanish. He adjusted. He sharpened. By noon, polling emails were arriving with subject lines that read like warnings.

Maya was euphoric anyway. "This is the comeback that buys me a retirement plan," she said, pacing the kitchen with her phone in one hand and a legal pad in the other. "This is the kind of rebound that makes grown men call me ma'am."

Alex sat at the island and stared at a spreadsheet that looked like the city's bones. Revenue projections. Tax tiers. Budget lines that had been cut so often they looked like scars. His team filtered in and out of the townhouse in shifts, sleeping on couches and returning with coffees and new data, as if caffeine and competence could outrun consequence.

He kept thinking of Lucia in the hallway that morning. The way she had given him her hand for one beat and then taken it back. The way she had walked out without hugging, without kissing, because leaving clean is its own kind of mercy. He should have felt free. Instead, he felt exposed.

"Okay," Maya said, snapping him back. "We need initiatives. Not vibes. We need teeth."

He nodded once. "We have teeth."

He started building them out loud because saying the plan made it real, and because the room needed to hear him sound like a man who belonged in power without begging for it.

"First, housing. A vacancy tax that punished the kind of landlords who let buildings rot so the city would raise rents for them. A cap on rent increases tied to wage growth, not investor appetite. A fast-track court for eviction abuse. A city-backed fund that bought distressed units and flipped them into permanently affordable housing, not 'affordable for six months." He wanted community land trusts treated like infrastructure, not charity.

"Second, costs. A municipal grocery program that subsidized staples in neighborhoods where 'choice' meant one corner store and a lottery ticket machine. Permit reform for small businesses strangled by delays, not demand. A childcare credit that actually hit monthly, not once a year when people were already behind. Fare-free transit for youth and seniors, paid for by the people who profited from the city's labor but never rode its buses."

"Third, taxes. Corporate tax increases aimed at companies that treated San Francisco like a stage and its residents like crew. A luxury real estate transfer tax that made speculative flipping expensive again. An executive compensation surcharge. A public price for private excess. The kind of policy that forces boardrooms to notice their own math." And then the one he saved for last, because it was the one that made the room go quiet. "If a company relocates its headquarters to dodge these taxes," Alex said, "they pay anyway."

Kara's pen paused. Theo stopped tapping his laptop. Even Maya looked up.

"I want an exit levy," Alex continued, voice steady. "A penalty scaled to market cap, headcount, and the public resources they've used. Tax breaks. Infrastructure. City contracts. Talent pipelines. They took blood from this city. They do not get to leave without paying it back."

Sanjay blinked, slow. "They'll sue."

"Let them," Alex said. "They already own half the rules. I'm done being scared of the other half."

Maya stared at him for a beat. Then she smiled, sharp and a little proud. "So this is what you've been doing," she said quietly.

He didn't answer immediately. She leaned back against the counter, eyes narrowing like she was studying a crime scene. "You didn't build a mask just to win. You built it to get into rooms where the locks were kept."

Alex met her gaze. "You knew."

"I suspected," she said. "I saw the way you listened to donors. The way you never asked for their love. Only their access." Her mouth tightened, then softened. "I thought you were playing them. I didn't know if you were brave enough to play them all the way through."

He surprised himself by smiling, small and tired. "I am now."

Maya's expression shifted. Not sentiment. Recognition. A woman who had bet on the truth in a city built to punish it. “Good,” she said. “Then we’ll need guardrails. Because when you start moving like that, everyone decides you belong to them.”

He believed her.

By late afternoon, they had the outline. By evening, they had the first draft of a policy deck Maya could sell to a room full of skeptics without begging. The rest of the team was shooed into sleep or errands. The townhouse quieted into something almost domestic.

By the time the takeout arrived, it was just Alex and Maya. Paper bags. The smell of sesame and star anise. The kitchen light cast a low gold circle that felt almost kind. Alex sat with his elbows on the island, staring at nothing like the day had finally caught up to him.

“Why you?” he asked, quietly. “What set you on fire?”

Maya leaned against the counter. “A landlord who thought our door was a clock he could set. A bus line that stopped before my mother’s shift did. A counselor who told me college wasn’t ‘a cultural fit.” Her mouth went tight at the memory, then she exhaled. “I like it better when we win.”

He held her gaze for a beat. “We will.” It surprised him how little swagger the sentence required.

Maya nodded, satisfied, then turned toward the food like it was a reward they’d earned. “Please tell me they remembered the chili oil. I need spice or I will start tweeting threats.”

A knock.

Maya brightened instantly. “They heard my plea.” She opened the door. No one stood there. She frowned, leaned out slightly, and that’s when the cloth came from behind her in a practiced sweep. Not violence. Not spectacle. Just efficiency. A hand at the back of her head, a clean fold over her mouth and nose, a soft instructive murmur in an accent that knew theaters and airports.

"Sleep," the voice said. "You'll wake safe."

Maya struggled once, on principle. The world went velvet and then unhooked.

Alex had time to register surprise as a physical thing, the body's inability to route instructions fast enough, before two men stepped into the kitchen through the door that should have been chained. No guns, no shouting. Only the cool logistics of people who had done this in too many countries.

"Don't," Alex said, even before he knew what he was asking them not to do.

One of them met his eyes like he was offering customer service. "We will return her untouched," the man said. "We need you punctual."

Alex lunged forward on pure instinct. A needle kissed his skin with the false intimacy of a lover whose name you don't know. His vision narrowed. His mouth tried to form a threat. The room tipped.

The last thing he saw was Maya being carried onto the couch, her fingers twitching once, furious even in sleep.

Maya woke like a diver who knew exactly how much air was left. Her head hurt. Her mouth tasted chemical and cotton. The couch beneath her was familiar. The kitchen light was still low. The paper bags still sat on the island, sesame and star anise cooling into silence.

The front door was latched but not chained. They

hadn't been careless. They'd been polite. She hated the competence more than she would have hated a mess.

Maya sat up slowly and tested her body. No blood. No bruises. No duct tape. Only a faint ache behind the eyes and a scuff on the floor where a chair had been eased back, not thrown. Professionals. She hated the word.

"Alex?" she called, because she had to.

The house answered with nothing. Her phone was on the coffee table, face up, like someone had placed it there as a courtesy.

12:41 a.m.

She texted the group thread with fingers that refused to shake. *LOCKDOWN.*

Kara: On my way.
Theo: Pulling exterior feeds.
Sanjay: ISP tracer up in five.
Whitaker: I'll keep press blind for four hours. Use them after that or they'll use you.

Her throat tightened. She swallowed it down and opened her contacts. A number Sergio had given her. She called. The line connected on the first ring, like the phone had been waiting.

"Dimmi." *Tell me.* No surprise. No greeting.

"They took Alex," Maya said. Her voice stayed steady even as her body tried to revolt. "Two men. Efficient. I was incapacitated."

"Police?" the man asked.

"Not yet."

"Good." Keys clicked on his end, fast. "Send me the alley camera. The lobby. Not the front. The front is theater."

Maya exhaled once, sharp. "I need Sergio."

"You can't," the man said.

"Then who the hell are you?" Maya snapped. "Because I'm not taking orders from a mystery voice in the dark."

A beat. Not hesitation. Calculation.

"Enzo Ferri," he said. The name landed without decoration. "You have my number because Sergio trusts me."

Maya's jaw tightened. "What are you?"

Another beat.

"A door," Enzo said. "Send me what I asked for."

She sent the links, passcodes, timestamps. Her fingers shook and she hated herself for it, so she forced them steady.

"They're going to Italy," Maya said. It came out more statement than question.

"Yes," Enzo replied.

"And you can stop this?"

Silence, brief and honest.

"No," Enzo said. "But I can tell you where it's going." The line went dead with the efficiency of a man who did not tidy goodbyes.

Maya stood. Locked the gate. Checked the back door. Poured water with hands that shook only a little. She looked once at the couch where she had woken and let herself feel anger like heat with nowhere to go.

"Okay," she told the empty house. "We are okay." It wasn't reassurance. It was a command.

***

Alex woke to the hum that changes men, the sound a private cabin makes when air has been domesticated and altitude pretends to be optional. Leather. Recessed lights. The faint smell of citrus money believes counts as discretion.

His wrists were secured, not brutalized. Ankles too. A gag turned his mouth into a fact. Someone had thought to belt him in. The courtesy was an insult.

Opposite him, buckled into a facing seat, a small black screen waited politely on a folding table. A gloved hand reached into his field of vision, tapped play, and withdrew.

Lucia.

Not in the life he knew. In another. Younger by some years. Hair braided to one side. Red nails like courage or surrender, he couldn't tell. The room around her looked expensive and obedient, the kind of space that doesn't creak or apologize. A voice he didn't know yet and knew anyway.

"Hold."

Lucia's ribs expanded under skin the camera treated with an intimacy Alex despised. She held too long, like someone who had learned the punishment for failing to hold.

"Release." She released. The sound wasn't singing. It was air learning its future.

The footage cut. Same room. Different angle. The Maestro's hand reached into frame. Not grabbing. Placing. Two fingers under the hinge of her jaw. One palm over the flat muscle of her belly where breath learns discipline.

"Again." She obeyed.

Rage came in waves, not theatrical. Geological. Alex fought the restraints. Then he fought the uselessness of fighting them. He tried to find a place in the footage where she was safe, where she was somewhere else. The footage offered him only the room.

Another cut. The mask.

A Venetian face with a ribbon like punctuation. Not sex. Not theatrics. Profession. Desecration. A baton hovered in frame. It did not descend. It hovered where the body learns to trust wrong men.

"Again," the voice said, and Alex heard the smile under the instruction.

She sang this time. Not an aria. A thread of vowel that hit Alex's body before his mind made sense of it. He felt shame at that. He felt human.

The screen kept cutting. Lessons. Rooms. Sunset on a veranda. A kiss that was brief and not instruction.

That was what ruined him. Not the discipline. Not the cruelty. The implication that love had been offered like a reward, and then used like a knife.

He lost track of time. Once, the gloved hand reached in and wiped the screen with a cloth, as if fingerprints were another form of evidence.

At some point, Alex realized he had stopped straining against the restraints. At some point, he realized he had started listening for Lucia's breath. Where it shook. Where it steadied. Where it transcended the room that was trying to own her.

There was no vulgarity in it. Whoever had assembled this wanted him to feel something tidier than arousal. He felt rage. Jealousy. The particular male wound of comparing himself to a myth and losing.

Under all of it, he felt something he had not expected. Reverence. A woman had been built in that room, and she had survived it by turning herself into excellence sharp enough to cut the hands that held her.

When the screen finally went dark, Alex realized he was crying. Not the wet show of sorrow. The ugly, quiet kind that respects its own privacy. He breathed through his nose because the gag made him a student again.

A man's voice came from somewhere beyond his shoulder, careful English. "We land soon."

Alex swallowed. Tried to ask where. The gag turned the question into a sound not fit for language. The voice offered no pity.

Through a seam in the window shade he could see dawn. Water below. The descent measured itself in pressure behind the eyes. The cabin did not loosen. The restraints did not soften. The plane took a long, patient curve and committed to earth.

Someone lifted the window shade the rest of the way. Runway lights in an apricot dawn. A low building. A name his mind supplied before his eyes did.

Air that smelled like olive oil and ambition. Tuscany, or close enough for the Maestro's purposes.

The plane slowed. Stopped. The seatbelt light went off with a polite tone. The door did not open yet. Alex had never felt less free. He had never felt more certain of one clean truth.

This was not about politics. This was about possession. The device on the little table remained dark, waiting. So did Alex.

And somewhere, on the ground he had not chosen, a man named Enzo Ferri stepped into the hangar's shadow and watched two couriers bring him something precious.

Not a package. A person.

He did not smile. He did not flinch. He only reached into his coat, removed a phone, and sent a single line into a number that did not ring.

He's here.

Then Enzo looked up at Alex, long enough for Alex to understand one thing without words. There was an inside line. It just wasn't a rescue. Not yet.

Chapter Twenty
The Pietà

Florence in winter remembers how to hold sound. Stone does not amplify so much as cradle. Candles do not burn so much as teach light to behave.

Lucia stepped through a side door of the basilica, past sacristy incense and the hush of old wool, and felt the air correct her posture without asking.

Sergio walked half a pace behind her in a dark coat and a stillness made of decisions. He had gotten her here the way men move a priceless instrument through an untrustworthy city. A separate car to the airport. A separate boarding gate. A corridor that looked like storage until it became a shortcut. Small, ordinary lies that worked because they were too modest to question. New York had been a bruise they did not press. Florence felt older than fear, and just as familiar.

The main sanctuary was already full. Not crowded. Curated. A spectacle that pretended not to be one. Rows of dignitaries, donors who could make marble feel nouveau riche, critics who would call this a service because calling it a show would be to admit complicity. And there, the first six pews like a consecrated box inside the box: the sopranos.

His sopranos. The ones the world knew and the ones the world had never learned to name. Red nails like a private flag. Handlers at their shoulders like punctuation.

Lucia felt heat rise in her throat and told her body it was only the basilica's breath.

"Left aisle," Sergio murmured. "Fifth row, end. Sightline on the transept. We exit sacristy side the moment the recessional begins." His eyes moved without his head. "No greetings. If one approaches you, I answer. You keep your breath."

They moved when the mass moved. Processional under a long, patient organ line. Kyrie threading the stone with a plea older than any of them. Gloria withheld, because today did not deserve it.

Lucia tried not to count the beats between the incense swings and failed. Counting had saved her more than once. It would not betray her now.

She did not turn her head, but her periphery filled itself with faces and calculus. A girl she knew only from reviews, her mouth set like a bow string. An older woman who had taught Lucia what could be done with a pianissimo that did not apologize. A teenager who should have been in street clothes and school, but wore black like an adult who had already negotiated with men in rooms that smelled like this and won, for now.

The homily wound itself out in good Latin and better Italian. The priest said Marina's name like a man afraid of invoking something he could not handle, then surprised himself by not dying when nothing supernatural happened. He spoke of talent as loan, of breath as gift, of death as a rest in the score that was not the end of the phrase.

Lucia listened because religion had always been dangerous to singers. It knew too much about lungs.

She felt him before she saw him.

The Maestro stepped from the transept as if the basilica had yielded him up out of stone. No mask today. Not because he had changed, but because the room itself was his face. He wore black that made other men's black look noisy. He did not hurry. Attention came to him because it always had. If anyone saw Lucia's hand tighten on the pew ahead of her, they had the decency to pretend otherwise.

"My child," he said to the room that wanted him to say our, and somehow made it sound like we. His Italian was the Italy people pay for, the vowels of cities layered over the hills until the hills agree to be civilized. "Marina taught me humility as no man ever has. She took instruction with a fierceness that reminded me what discipline is for, not merely what it can do. We have lost a voice that could have taught churches how to pray again. We have lost a breath that refused to waste itself."

He let silence stand like a choir. He knew silence was the impresario's best instrument.

"To my sopranos," he continued, and believed himself as he spoke, which was always his most dangerous quality, "I say what I have not said in public for a decade. I love you. You are my work and my proof. You are the evidence that we can take this broken century and make it sing."

He looked down the first pew like a father at a table that terrified him.

"And to the one who has returned to us today," he said, and did not look directly at Lucia, which was worse than looking, "I say this: grief brings everyone home eventually. Even the ones who mistake distance for freedom." The sentence landed with the softness of a blessing and the precision of a collar closing. "In that spirit," the Maestro said, and the room bent the way rooms bend when they have been taught to, "I wish to present to you one who will carry a part of what we have lost. From the same hills that taught Lucia their vowels. Young, but not fragile. Devout, but not obedient." His gaze did not land on her. It circled her. "Rosa Bellini." He said the name with the satisfaction of a man who has kept a jewel safe from thieves.

A ripple went through the sopranos' pews. Recognition. Arithmetic. Those trained not to react, reacting anyway. Rosa walked from the choir gate as if she had rehearsed walking more than singing. She had. That is how these rooms worked.

She was young. Her braid too tight. The dress that tried to be invisible and therefore insisted on being seen. She did not look for Lucia. Lucia could not decide if that was good or bad.

"Offertory," the Maestro said to the choir master, and the old man with the new hearing aids nodded as if he had come up with it himself and was grateful to be understood.

The organ found a key that felt like weather. Rosa sang. It was clean and new. Unimproved by cynicism, therefore more dangerous than excellence. The vowel at the corner of the phrase that had always bothered Lucia did not bother Rosa. Rosa had not learned to be bothered by it.

Lucia felt a pettiness rise in her. I would have *shaded that*. She recognized the pettiness for what it was. Love misremembering itself as ownership. Marina's face, in her mind, refused to sit politely in the past.

No more, Lucia told herself. Then again, because the first time had not been loud enough.

The Maestro did not conduct with his hands. He conducted with breath. He watched Rosa the way a hawk watches a river, not for beauty but for the small distortions that betray a fish. When she came to the place where a lesser teacher would lift a finger, he did not move at all. She solved it on her own. Which meant he could later take credit for having allowed it.

Lucia felt the gaze before it arrived. She did not have to look up to know when it reached her. It was not lust. Not that. Nor was it paternal. It was a craftsman admiring his instrument through a shop window. It made her skin stipple. She hated her body for remembering his attention as safety.

"Arietta," she murmured, not as code but as private sacrament. *Little aria.*

Communion. Procession. The floor remembered how to take footsteps. White collars. Black coats. An ocean of hands that had never done manual work doing their best impression of humility. The recessional hymn threaded the air with a hope that could be mistaken for art.

"Now," Sergio said. They stood as one.

The corridor behind the front pews had been designed for nobility to flee scandals they might create. It worked equally well for sopranos who knew a different kind of scandal was approaching.

Lucia kept her face forward. She did not look at Rosa when the girl passed near enough to borrow perfume. Soap, sugar, new leather.

They reached the transept door. The sacristan moved to block them, then recognized Sergio's profession by the way he held space and stepped aside without the indignity of being told. The sacristy smelled like starch, candle ends, and a generosity with wine not always reserved for priests. The side door to the cloister was three steps beyond.

Marina's handler, Matteo, stood in it. Lucia's breath went cold.

Sergio's weight shifted onto his right foot. A detail Lucia had learned to recognize as the moment before force.

"Fratello," Matteo said. *Brother*. The word should have been a bridge. It arrived as a trap.

"We're leaving," Sergio said. "Another time."

Matteo lifted both hands, palms empty. His face looked like grief had practiced on it. "I will walk you to the car," he said. "It is chaos outside."

Sergio hesitated for the length of a heartbeat. Then, a mistake he would measure with his own body, he nodded.

"Ten steps," Sergio said. "No further."

They moved into the cloister. The light there knew how to be holy without effort. The door to the garden was open to air so clean Lucia wanted to drink it.

The knife arrived the way good knives do. Without announcement. A pressure below the ribs, Sergio's. Sergio's breath broke sideways. He took a step he had not ordered and sat where there was no chair.

For a second, Lucia could not make her mind accept what her eyes were seeing. The same posture. The same calm. The same hands that had once turned pages for the Maestro like turning pages was holy.

Matteo caught Sergio's shoulder as if he were helping him breathe.

"Mi dispiace," Matteo murmured, close to Sergio's ear. *I'm sorry*.

Lucia's voice came out low, controlled, lethal. "Chiama un medico," she said. *Call a doctor*. "Adesso," she added. *Now*.

Matteo's eyes met hers. Calm. Warning. Almost kind, which made it worse.

Lucia swallowed the instinct to scream. Not here. Not in the cloister. Not where the Maestro could turn her panic into proof. Not because she believed she was safe, but because panic was the only thing he could weaponize without touching her. Her voice sharpened. "If he dies," she said, "you will not get a soprano. You will get a scandal. You will get a body in a church. You will get headlines in every language. And I will be the one who sings them." She stepped forward, forcing the men around her to adjust.

For the first time, something flickered across Matteo's face. Annoyance. Respect. Calculation. He leaned toward her, close enough that only she could hear him.

"He will live," Matteo murmured. "If you do what you are told."

Lucia's mouth turned cold. "Then prove it," she said. "Bring him with me."

A pause. Then Matteo nodded once.

The black bag came down over her head anyway, fast and practiced. Cloth, dye, darkness. Hands guided her, not dragging. Escorting. Making force feel like ceremony.

She did not struggle. She saved air. But she did not go quietly. "Portatelo con noi," Lucia ordered. *Bring him with us*.

Weight shifted. Bodies repositioned. Sergio made

a sound that wasn't language. Then the car door opened. They placed Lucia in the back seat first. The bag stayed on until the lock clicked and the world narrowed to engine and leather and the shape of fear. Then the bag was pulled off. Lucia blinked against the sudden light and turned immediately.

Sergio was beside her, half collapsed against the seat, one hand pressed to his own side. Blood seeped between his fingers, too dark, too fast. His face was pale, lips parted around a breath that could not decide if it wanted to stay.

Lucia did not think. She moved. She caught his hand, peeled it back gently, and replaced it with her own, pressing down with the heel of her palm the way she had once learned to press on a singer's diaphragm. Except this was not breath. This was life.

"Guarda me," she said. *Look at me.*

Sergio's lashes fluttered. His eyes found her, unfocused, furious with pain.

"Respira," Lucia ordered. *Breathe.* He tried. Lucia leaned in, close enough that her hair brushed his cheek, and she began to sing. Not opera. Not performance.

A village song, old and plain, the kind her grandmother used to hum while kneading dough, while shelling peas, while telling Lucia that hunger and love sound the same if you listen long enough.

"Dormi, dormi, mio cuore..." *Sleep, sleep, my heart...* Her voice shook for one note, then steadied. She kept pressure on the wound. Kept singing anyway, because the body obeys rhythm even when it wants to surrender.

Sergio's breathing hitched, tried to match her.

The car moved. Lucia felt it before she saw it,

the way the road began to slope, the way the turns lengthened, the way the city fell away. Direction. Commitment.

South. Her stomach tightened. Tuscany. Of course it was Tuscany. She tasted iron and did not let it show. She sang the next line softer, like a secret she was trying to keep alive.

"Non andare via..." *Don't go away...*

Sergio's head lolled, then lifted by a fraction, as if her voice had given him something to hold. Lucia swallowed hard and spoke between phrases, not to the men in the front seat, not to Matteo, not even to Sergio.

To Marina. To God. To whatever kept breath in the body when the world tried to steal it.

"Marina," she whispered, voice breaking around the name. "Ti prego." *Please*. She pressed harder as the car hit a bump and Sergio made a sound that wasn't language. "Tienilo con me," she begged, silently, then out loud, because she needed the words to exist. *Keep him with me.*

Another turn. Another stretch of road. The city truly gone now. Lucia kept her hand on his blood. Kept her voice in his ear. Kept singing the same small song like a rope. And as the car pulled farther south, toward hills she had once called home and would now call a trap, Lucia lowered her forehead to Sergio's temple and made herself a promise that felt like prayer and threat in the same breath.

"Resta," she whispered. *Stay*. "Resta fino a casa," she added. *Stay until we get there.*

In the front seat, someone cleared their throat politely, as if to remind the world that manners still existed.

“Scusate,” a voice said. *Excuse me.*

The courtesy was almost obscene. Lucia did not look up. She sang to soothe and didn’t stop.

Chapter Twenty-One
The Curtain

They left Alex in the chair with the view.

Tuscany arranged itself like a lesson in obedience: domes behaving, roofs stacked in patient perspective, late light making a virtue of distance. Leather bit his wrists where the straps pretended to be medical. A thin line of blood had dried at the corner of his mouth. He was absurdly thirsty and tried to swallow against the gag.

The door clicked. He did not need to turn to know who it was. The air changed the way air changes when a man who believes in rooms enters one.

"Mr. Chambers," the Maestro said, not unkindly. "Your city makes such noise about you." A glass touched down on the small table beside the chaise. Water. Close enough to see. Not close enough to drink. "Welcome to a quieter one."

Alex stared forward. It was the only defiance left to him.

"You may look at me," the Maestro said, as if granting permission to a student. "It will not make you smaller than you already are in this story."

Alex turned his head a fraction. Maskless, the man looked like discipline executed upon a human face until the human learned to thank it. Nothing extravagant. Elegance that never apologized. Hands Alex recognized from the footage even when they were empty. Supple. Certain. The cruelty of precision.

"You have done well," the Maestro went on, conversational, as if discussing a concert. "A comeback. The love of a prima donna." His mouth curved. "Who knew a poor bastard could be rewarded so generously?"

Alex tried for speech. The gag turned it into a sound not suited to language.

The Maestro lifted one hand. "Allow me to do the talking. I am good at it, and you are not in a position to compete."

He moved to the stone balustrade and placed both hands on it like a man at prayer.

"Do you know what I do with my sopranos?" he asked, and did not wait for an answer. "I take talent, which is the wrong word for hunger, and I refine it until the world cannot pretend not to hear. I make instruments of women who would otherwise be told to be quiet beautifully instead of loud precisely."

He turned slightly, as if letting Alex earn the privilege of his profile.

"I have taken men down. Ministers. Bankers who lie with graphs. Judges who confuse robes with gods. They fall. Sometimes by scandal. Sometimes by fatigue. Sometimes by the smallest nudge at the exact right hour." His fingertip tapped the stone once, as if indicating a point on a map. "And nothing changes."

He looked at Alex and let the sentence sit like a failed aria.

"You imagine the problem is singular and therefore solvable. This donor. That law. Those blocks. Your mother. Your father. The one landlord. The three cops." His voice did not rise. It sharpened. "It comforts you. Arithmetic a child can learn." He took a step closer. "But the world is written in counterpoint. You strike one line, the others continue. You do not end music by tearing a page. You end it by breaking the hands that can play."

Alex held his gaze the way a man holds a heavy thing while deciding how to throw it.

The Maestro continued, almost gently. "So I built hands. I gave women technique. I asked obedience in exchange for excellence. They asked purpose in exchange for breath. We called it art. It served as justice for a while." A pause. Something like fatigue passed behind his eyes, quick and unwelcome. "And the bad keep winning. They grow more articulate. They learn our scales. They hire our students."

Marina. He said her name without saying it, as if the air already knew.

"Marina was the first I trusted beyond humiliation," he said at last. "Humiliation is cheap. Berlin, for example. You would have liked the Chancellor. A mouth that believed it owned a nation. In three months she would have rescinded protections her predecessors thought safe." He watched Alex's face with the calm of a man testing a blade. "Marina went to bed with her and could not ruin her."

Silence.

"I realized I had made a singer when the occasion demanded an executioner." A small shrug, nearly elegant. "So I corrected the lesson."

Alex's heart clenched into the shape it makes when it understands cloisters and knives. "Lucia was never meant for small fish," the Maestro said, and his voice warmed as if he were speaking of a favorite pupil. "When the lists began, you were not on them.

You were a domestic problem. A boy with good hair who made money the way boys make money now and thought that meant you deserved a city." He smiled. Private tenderness that made Alex want to break things. "Marina's failure made me redesign the score. I remembered Lucia."

The Maestro tilted his head, almost fond.

"With her, I built a cathedral. She is not the best because she obeys. She is the best because she knows when obedience becomes music." He leaned in slightly. "We have a chemistry that instruments envy."

The word sat filthy and proud in the air.

"You watched pieces of it," he went on. "The veranda. My error. A kiss that should not have been allowed on a night that should have remained wet with excellence."

Alex's vision edged with heat.

"I punished her because I punished myself more," the Maestro said simply. "We are not saints. We are professionals. We commit our sins in service to a grander sound." Then, kindly enough to be cruel, he looked at Alex. "You thought, briefly, that she loved you. It improved you. It made you attempt courage without cameras. I do not despise the experiment."

A rest.

"But you should know better than to believe a woman like Lucia could love a man like you."

Alex made a sound that might have been a laugh if knives were permitted to laugh. The Maestro watched him, amused.

"Do you know what she loves? The moment when breath becomes inevitable. That is the lover she returns to. I trained the rest."

He stepped closer. Alex felt him in the way you feel a shadow lean.

"You were meant to be a lesson," he said. "An elegant one, if you had had the grace to learn quietly. Instead, you made noise." The Maestro nodded toward the interior. "Now you serve a different purpose. Witness."

Footsteps sounded in the corridor: light, quick, eager. A young woman's gait. Careful weight placement. A soprano learning how floors forgive her. Rosa. The Maestro's eyes flicked toward the sound and changed. Not fear. Calculation. He reached to the side and drew a gauze curtain along its rail. Not a wall. A veil. It softened the light, blurred edges, turned the veranda into a listening booth.

"Silenzio," he said softly. Silence. "This will be instructive."

He did not look back as he stepped through the curtain, becoming a silhouette for a moment. A spine that had learned to be a baton. Then he vanished into the cooler light inside.

Alone with the view and the straps, Alex allowed himself one animal exhale. He counted in fours the way Lucia had taught him. In. Hold. Out. Hold. It did not calm him. It kept him intact in the way the Maestro wanted him broken.

Through the gauze veil, the house rearranged itself into sound. Rosa's voice, small but true, saying Maestro with a devotion that made Alex hate devotion.

Then Lucia's voice. Lower. Controlled. A warmth that did not belong to tenderness. A warmth set to a temperature she could raise or drop without flinching. He caught fragments of Italian he didn't fully understand, vowels that belonged to a country he did not know, consonants that landed like decisions. He understood the tone better than the words.

Command. Compliance. Performance.

His stomach tightened. Not jealousy. Not now. Something worse: the recognition that whatever was happening behind that veil was meant for him, built for him, calibrated to make him small.

He looked down at the straps that held his wrists and felt, sharply, how easy it would be to surrender. How neat it would be to decide none of this was his problem. He barely knew her. He barely knew her life. He could tell himself he was a victim of her world and leave her to it.

That was the story men like the Maestro counted on. Men like Alex had lived that story for years. Witnesses. Spectators. People who called themselves good because they did not make the knife move. Alex swallowed against the gag and chose something else.

Even if she had never loved him, even if he had been a role she wore for a city that needed a fairytale, he had seen enough to know one truth. Lucia Conti was not free in this house. She was brilliant inside it, but brilliance was not freedom. It was simply how you survived when you were not allowed to leave. He would not be another man who watched. He would not be another room.

A door clicked.

The slow slide of silk against wood. A soft laugh. Lucia's, maybe. Or the Maestro's. Alex could not tell, and that fact made his pulse spike. He listened harder, trying to turn sound into meaning, trying to learn what was happening to her in there without being able to stand, without being able to fight, without being able to do anything but endure.

Footsteps approached, closer than before. The gauze curtain shifted. A hand found the edge of it and pulled.

Light spilled across the veranda, bright and sudden. The veil drew back like a throat opening for confession.

And there she was.

Lucia in red, framed in the light, the Maestro half a step behind her like a shadow that believed it was a crown. Her face was composed. Her mouth arranged into something close to indifference. A mask so expensive it could pass for truth.

Alex's breath hitched anyway. Her eyes found him For one suspended beat, neither of them moved. No signals. No coded word. No reassurance.

Just the lock of recognition between a man who had finally decided not to be a spectator and a woman who had just been forced to perform as if she did not know him at all.

Chapter Twenty-Two
The Lesson Returned

She woke to the old room pretending it had never learned her name. Tuscan light, pearl and disciplined, slid through shutters angled to keep secrets. The ceiling beams still carried the weight of summers. The plaster held the memory of a winter she had once mistaken for love.

On the bedside table sat a low bowl of blood-orange wedges, a silver carafe sweating cold water, and a porcelain cup steaming violet with lavender and something bitter enough to wake the spine.

Lucia's hand went to her throat. Her next breath came too sharp, and the room tilted as if pleased to remind her who owned gravity here. Canvas. Leather. Engine. A cloister. A blade. Sergio's body folding as if the air had been taken from him.

She sat up too fast. Pain flared behind her eyes, a clean pulse that felt chemical. She swallowed it down and forced her breath into counts. Four in. Hold. Eight out. The way he taught her. The way she taught herself to survive.

"Sergio," she said aloud. The name came out wrong, scraped at the edges. No answer. Her feet hit the floor. The wood was cold enough to be honest. She reached the door and yanked it open.

A soft voice answered from the threshold, careful as a hand on a wounded animal. "Lucia?"

Rosa Bellini stood there holding a tray and the kind of hope that makes houses meaner. Her braid had been loosened since the basilica. Sleep had softened her into the youth the dress had tried to erase. Rosa hesitated, then lifted her chin as if bravery could be taught by posture.

"Posso?" *May I?*

Lucia's mouth opened and the truth tried to come out as a scream. Where is he. Is he alive. Did they leave him bleeding on stone. Instead, she forced the words through her teeth like a controlled note. "Sergio. Dov'è Sergio?" *Sergio. Where is Sergio?*

Rosa flinched at the sharpness, then recovered quickly, eager to soothe. "He is here," she said. "He is resting."

Lucia took one step forward. "Bring me to him."

"Soon," Rosa promised, too quickly, like a girl repeating a line she had been given. "They said you needed to wake first. They said the lesson begins in an hour."

Lucia's stomach knotted. She made her face smooth again because panic is a gift in this house. She softened her voice, not because Rosa deserved comfort, but because Lucia needed information, and girls like Rosa give it more freely when they believe they are safe.

"Rosa," Lucia said, almost kind. "Tell me the truth. Is he hurt?"

Rosa swallowed. "He was bleeding," she admitted. "But he is breathing. He is being treated." Her eyes darted away, then back, pleading. "Non ti mentirei." *I would not lie to you.*

Lucia exhaled once. It was not relief. It was calculation. Breathing meant time. Time meant options.

"Bene," Lucia said. *Good*. She stepped back into the room and let Rosa enter.

Rosa moved like a guest in a museum of saints. She set the tray down as if placing an offering. Fruit. Tea. Small comforts dressed as mercy. "I brought this," she said quietly. "They told me. They said you should eat."

Lucia sat on the edge of the bed and let the room stop spinning. The tea's steam rose like prayer.

"Grazie, piccola," Lucia said. *Thank you, little one.*

Rosa's eyes brightened at the endearment, as if Lucia had crowned her. Lucia hated how quickly the house turned kindness into a weapon and still, she used it.

She lifted the cup, sipped. Bitter. Useful. It gave her tongue a task. It gave her body a reason to stay in place instead of running barefoot into a corridor that would only lead her back into his hands.

Rosa hovered, then inched closer when Lucia patted the coverlet. She perched on the edge of the bed like a girl trying to be a woman.

"I saw you," Rosa said, and her voice shook with reverence she did not yet understand. "At the basilica. You did not look at me."

Lucia kept her gaze on Rosa's hands, on the faint tremor in the fingers. "It was right that I didn't."

Rosa's throat bobbed. "But I wanted you to."

Lucia let a smile appear. Small. Private. Controlled. "I heard you," she said. "I heard the room change when you sang. That is not nothing."

Rosa's cheeks flushed. "They said I will continue," she whispered. "That I am..."

She couldn't finish.

Lucia finished for her, gently enough that it sounded like a blessing. “Worthy.”

Rosa closed her eyes like she’d been touched by a holy thing. Lucia did not touch her. Not yet. Not in this house.

But she did something worse. Something that kept the girl tethered to her. “Listen to me,” Lucia said softly. “You sang clean. Not obedient. Keep it that way. Do not hurry. Do not apologize to the room. The room will not apologize to you.”

Rosa stared, hungry for the instruction. Somewhere deeper in the house, a bell rang. Three restrained notes. No more. The summons. Modest. Inarguable.

Rosa’s eyes flicked to the chair by the window. A robe lay folded there. Not black. Red. Sanguine silk, the color the Maestro always said belonged to Lucia when she was not performing under someone else’s score.

“He asked me to bring it,” Rosa said, voice thin. “He said you will wear it.”

Lucia’s pulse stayed steady because she made it. “It is beautiful,” Lucia said, and meant: weapon.

She stood, slow. Tested her legs. The sedative still lived in the joints like a quiet threat.

“Go dress,” Lucia told Rosa, voice gentle and precise. “Closed door. Water on your wrists. Do not hurry. Hurrying gives them music you didn’t mean to play.”

Rosa nodded, relief visible. “You will come?”

“I will be there,” Lucia said.

The promise had to be that small because larger ones were lies in this house.

Rosa slipped out.

When the door closed, Lucia finally let her face change. She crossed to the mirror and studied the woman staring back. The Maestro's work was in her posture. His discipline lived in her bones. Her defiance lived in the eyes.

She braided her hair to one side the way he liked, the way she wore it when she wanted her neck to belong to herself. She slid into the red silk and let it drape like surrender.

She found the polish, the only shade he ever wanted to see. She painted each nail with steady hands, restoring his preference like a mask. Then she lifted her chin.

"Per Marina," she whispered. *For Marina*. Then, quieter, because superstition is a craft: "Per me." *For me*.

The lesson room kept its temperature like a grudge.The piano lid was closed, a black mirror. The bench sat exactly where it had always been after he corrected it a finger's width. The metronome waited on the shelf, righteous as a priest.

Rosa stood already in place, too straight, hands relaxed by force.

Lucia entered and did not look around. Looking around is how the room climbs into you.

The Maestro arrived without the door needing to confess it. No mask. He did not need one.

"Discipline," he said, as if greeting. Then, softer and sharper: "Defiance." His eyes swept Lucia, then Rosa, and recorded the tremor in each body as if taking temperature. "I am owed an hour of truth," he said.

Lucia inclined her head. "You are owed excellence."

He permitted himself a smile that did not involve the mouth. "Begin with breath," he told Rosa.

Rosa obeyed. The room filled with the clean young sound of lungs remembering they were instruments before they were organs.

"Again," he said.

Rosa held longer, released sooner, corrected herself faster than a girl should, which meant she had been punished into precision.

Lucia watched Rosa's ribs expand and felt something hot and protective rise in her chest. She forced it down. This was not the time to feel like a savior. Savior is a role the Maestro enjoys crushing.

"Now you," he said to Lucia.

Lucia stepped forward and placed her palm under her ribs. The old gesture. The obedient one. She made air into something the room had to believe. It frightened her how easily it still fit.

He watched her like a craftsman deciding whether his instrument had warped.

"From 'Vissi d'arte," he said. *Tosca's prayer*. Not a request. An accusation.

Lucia sang one line. Not a plea. Not martyrdom. A blade. Clean. Controlled. Beautiful enough to be dangerous.

Rosa's head turned, eyes wide, then dropped in automatic apology for curiosity.

The Maestro moved closer. His hand hovered at Lucia's waist, never touching, closer than touch.

"You have made choices recently," he said. "You mistake choreography for freedom."

Lucia kept her eyes on a point past his shoulder, the way tightrope walkers pick a doorframe and refuse to let the room move them.

"I executed the piece you wrote," she said evenly. "If America misread the staging, that is America's vocabulary failing. Not mine."

The corner of his mouth lifted. A man pleased to have his language thrown back at him in the correct case.

"And the deviation in Florence?" he asked, soft as confession.

"The confusion was Sergio's," Lucia said. The sentence tasted like betrayal. She swallowed it anyway. "He is older," she continued, and made it sound like concern instead of strategy. "Age makes men sentimental. It makes them fearful. There was a lapse in communication between us. He panicked. He thought he was protecting me." She let her eyes lower for one beat. Shame, offered carefully. A woman remembering her place. "I thought," she added, "that I wanted something else. For a moment." The Maestro's gaze sharpened. Lucia leaned into it. "I was wrong," she said, and let her grief become proof. "Marina died, and I understood what I should have understood sooner." Her voice softened. Not weak. Intimate. "There is only one person in the world who has ever had room for me without asking me to shrink." The Maestro stilled, just slightly. Lucia pressed, as if she were confessing a love that hurt. "You."

Behind her, Rosa watched like a student watching a storm choose a direction. Lucia didn't turn. She didn't give the girl the burden of witnessing what this sentence cost.

"Go," Lucia said to Rosa gently. "Water. Ten minutes. Warm the 'Agnus Dei.' Alone."

Rosa hesitated and looked to the Maestro. He did not nod. He did not need to. She went.

The air changed when the door closed. Less oxygen. More history.

"You play with fire," the Maestro said.

"You taught me where to hold it," Lucia replied.

He stepped closer, the way men step closer to windows when they want to see if the storm is arriving or departing. "Tell me," he said, "what you think you are doing."

Lucia lifted her chin. "Advancing your work," she said. Truth and deception braided so tightly they could not be separated without blood. "We brought the cockroach down. He tried to crawl back up the wall. I came home to finish what you started." She lowered her voice, made it belong to a woman in love. "Or I come home for good," she murmured, "if you tell me the lesson has changed."

He studied her face like a score suspected of forgery.

Lucia let him see hunger. Shame. Rage repurposed as loyalty. She lifted her hand toward his jaw, not touching, tremble-close, and let her breath graze his mouth without giving him air. "You did not accept me on the veranda," she whispered. "It was my mistake to ask." Desire crossed his face like weather that does not seek permission. Lucia felt her stomach turn and kept smiling. "Let me correct it," she said. "Now."

His voice dropped, satisfied. "We have entered the next level." Lucia's pulse stayed steady because she made it. "Death is now on the line," he said. "Are you ready to cross that threshold with me?"

Lucia leaned in, lips a series of promises that

could be withdrawn before delivery. "You are my Maestro," she said, and gave him exactly the sentence his body needed to hear. "Io ti seguo." *I follow you.*

He laughed. The laugh of a man who has built a god and convinced himself it believes in him.

"Vieni," he said. *Come.*

He took her hand with the formality of a host showing a guest to the best view and led her down the corridor where oil portraits had learned to watch without blinking. Then he stopped at a curtain, as if unveiling art, and drew it back.

A chair. A man. A ruin.

Alex.

Strapped into the arms as if for medical care. Face swollen into colors the Renaissance never painted. Dried blood at the lip. Fresh at the hairline. Eyes open. Watching.

Alive.

Lucia did not let her breath change. Not one fraction. Not one betrayed note. She did not look at Alex the way a woman looks at the man she has chosen to love. She looked at him the way a professional looks at a problem she intends to solve.

The Maestro's hand closed over Alex's shoulder and squeezed, a parody of comfort.

"He has heard everything," the Maestro said conversationally, as if the dinner party had simply become interesting. "Your lessons. Your kiss. Your punishment."

Lucia let out a laugh. Brittle. Bored. Expensive. "This?" she said, tilting her head toward Alex like he was a broken chair. "Questo americano?" *This American?* She stepped closer to the Maestro and let her mouth hover near his throat without taking anything he did not give. “He was an assignment,” she murmured. “A cockroach you asked me to crush. You think I would trade paradise for drywall and campaign volunteers?”

Alex’s eyes found hers. Question. Plea. Accusation. Lucia gave him nothing.

Then everything. One blink, sharp as code, soft as promise.

The Maestro drew a knife from nowhere, the way some men produce a coin to charm a child. He set the blade gently beneath Alex’s jaw. Not enough to draw blood. Enough to mark the place where futures divide.

“Show me,” he said to Lucia without taking his eyes off Alex. “Show me who you are loyal to.”

Lucia smiled. Empty-handed. A student again. “Put the toy away,” she purred, and pressed her body closer to the Maestro’s heat. “Come inside.” She lowered her voice until it became something only he could hear. “I will show you,” she promised, “in front of him, who I choose.”

The Maestro watched her watch the blade and decided, for the moment, that she was to be believed. “Inside, then,” he said.He released Alex’s shoulder as if dismissing a servant. He turned toward the door.

Lucia followed. And as she stepped inside, she understood the truth that changed everything, clean and brutal as a cut. Taking him down had been a plan. Now it was a rescue. Now it was war. And Alex’s life was the price of one wrong note.

Chapter Twenty-Three
The Proof

The room behaved as if nothing holy had ever happened in it. The piano lid shone like a black sea. The metronome waited with a parishioner's patience. The air held that particular stillness old houses keep, the kind that makes even breath feel like an act of permission.

Lucia let the red robe settle at her shoulders and sharpened her smile into the tool it had always been. Silk, skin, collarbone. A suggestion of surrender that cost her nothing she wasn't already spending.

Please, she prayed toward the veranda without moving her eyes. See the mask, not the woman. Trust the rhythm, not the words.

Through the gauze, winter light made a pale veil of the world outside. She could not see Alex clearly, but she felt him the way you feel a person in a dark theater: weight, attention, pulse. He was there. He was listening. He was learning, and that was its own kind of danger.

"Begin," the Maestro said.

The syllable stroked the air. He stood close enough to be a wall. Lucia let it look like shelter.

Her breath went long in her body, the way he had taught it. Four in. Four held. Eight out. She sang nothing yet. She let a vowel hum behind her teeth, a honeyed line the nervous system remembers before the ear does. The room, trained by years of him, leaned forward to receive it.

His palm hovered at her waist. Not touching. Commanding the space where touch might happen. "You remember," he murmured, pleased to find his work still living exactly where he had left it. "Obedience suits you."

"Excellence does," Lucia replied, velvet over blade. She leaned just enough for his blood to mistake strategy for surrender and let a breath brush his mouth like a promise deferred. She kept her eyes soft. Kept her shoulders loose. Kept the part of her that was screaming quiet in the ribs where no one could hear it.

He wanted jealousy like spice. Lucia saw it arrive in his eyes before he named it. "You are not mine unless the world knows it," he said, soft, almost amused, and the sweetness of the sentence made it worse. His gaze slid toward the gauze like a hand checking a pocket for a knife.

"Rosa," he called, bright as a bell. The girl appeared at the door with the eagerness of someone summoned to glory. Practice silk. Braid too tight. The kind of youth that gets called devotion by men who profit from it. She was twenty and more, old enough to be "woman" in rooms like this, young enough still to believe reverence is protection. "Watch," the Maestro said. "Better. Sing the line and let Lucia answer you."

Rosa looked to Lucia. Question. Plea. Worship. Lucia met her with the smallest nod she could afford. I will keep you safe if I can.

Rosa began. A clean, young line climbed the air. Lucia answered not as rival but as sky. Harmony that says there is room. Their voices found each other the way two rivers find confluence: briefly separate, then inevitable.

The Maestro's pupils narrowed. Pleasure. Possession. He stepped behind Lucia, just out of reach, and the absence of touch felt like a threat. "Again," he said.

Rosa's breath shivered, then steadied. Lucia freighted the room with heat that was not spectacle. She kept her tone warm. Kept it controlled. Kept it useful.

He moved to Lucia's front, palm close, fingers near the hinge of her jaw. The baton was on the table where it always was. He no longer needed to lift it. Its presence did the work for him. "Look at me," he said.

Lucia did, and let devotion warm the surface of her eyes while she kept the deeper temperature for herself.*Alex. Hear the vowel, not the lie.*

"Again," the Maestro told Rosa without turning. Rosa obeyed, brave and exact. Her sound was a map of places she had not yet visited. Lucia followed, shading, sheltering, making future.

The Maestro listened like a hawk listens to river current. Not for beauty. For weakness.

"Do you feel it?" he asked Rosa, eyes still on Lucia. "How loyalty sounds when it learns pitch?" Rosa nodded, flushing.

Lucia's gaze slipped. Only a fraction. Only a human thing. It fastened a heartbeat too long on the gauze that hid the veranda. She recovered in the same breath. Returned to his eyes. Smoothed her expression. But the Maestro had built his life on noticing spans no one else accounted for. Something in him unlatched.

His temper changed the room's shape. His hand came up, not touching Lucia's throat, but closing around the air near it as if to remind the oxygen who it belonged to. "Again," he said, and the word had lost its silk.

Lucia's pulse tried to climb. She forced it back down into her count. Four. Four. Eight. "Maestro," Lucia said lightly, coaxing him back toward theater, "let Rosa take the high and I will carry the line beneath. For contrast."

He turned his head at last, considered the girl, and decided he wanted more cruelty than instruction. "Come closer," he told Rosa. "Here." He placed her a breath from Lucia's shoulder. The girl's perfume was soap and sugar and terror she didn't know she owned yet. "Sing to her," the Maestro said. "Make her choose to be yours."

Rosa began. For a moment it was exquisitely dangerous, the way love is when it has not learned to be afraid.

Lucia answered her with a half-smile she had used to save men's lives and wither others' courage. She cradled Rosa in harmony like a hand on a staircase. She felt Alex like a second pulse.

Trust me. Count to four.

The Maestro watched the space between Lucia's eyes and the gauze. Watched the flick of restraint. Watched the lie of warmth. Want came undone in him like a knot cut too fast. He stepped into Lucia and caught her jaw, turning her face toward his like the world owed him the angle. His mouth found hers.

Not a lover's kiss. A claim. A performance. A punishment aimed through fabric.

Lucia did not recoil. She could not. She let it

happen because stopping him would cost breath, and breath was the currency of survival in this house. She counted in her bones. Four. Four. Eight. Kept her body still so her face could sell obedience. But she was human, and the human part of her did one unforgivable thing.

She thought of Alex's hand on a coffee mug. The heat of a kitchen. The softness of a man who did not need her to be obedient to be brilliant. The thought tightened her throat. Her breath changed.

It was tiny. It was nothing. It was everything.

Rosa heard it.

Rosa's note wavered. Not a collapse. A tremor. A vowel arriving late. A breath placed wrong.

The Maestro broke the kiss and turned his head toward Rosa as if she had insulted him. "Again," he said, and the word cracked.

Rosa tried. She tried so hard it was unbearable. The line rose, then thinned. The falter became audible, and the room did what rooms do when they sense blood: it waited.

Lucia opened her mouth to rescue the phrase, to steady the girl, to hold the room together.

The Maestro's arm lashed out. Not calculated. Not ceremonial. The reflex of a man swatting at loss of control. His forearm caught Rosa at the temple as he turned, careless with strength. Rosa's head met the edge of the piano with a sound that reordered the air.

Silence does not always arrive at once. A final vibration. The metronome ticking because it does not know it should stop. Lucia's breath still held in her ribs with nowhere to go.

Rosa blinked once like a question. Her knees

unlocked. She slid to the floor with a softness that pretended mercy.

"No," Lucia said, and the word left her as a sound she had never made on any stage.

The Maestro froze. Not in grief. In error.

"Rosa," he said, as if language could rewind force. He reached, then stopped, his fingers hovering, refusing to touch the mess his precision had made.

Lucia was already down, hands on Rosa's pulse, on her breath, on the place where the world should have continued. Rosa's skin was warm. Too warm. Alive and gone at once. Her eyelids fluttered, then stilled.

Lucia's vision narrowed. Something very old in her stood up. Something very young screamed. For once, they agreed. She rose in one motion and took the nearest weight the room offered: an iron candelabrum from the side credenza, heavy with unlit candles like delayed mercy.

The Maestro turned toward her, mouth opening to say her name as if the invocation itself would stop consequence.

Lucia swung.

Iron meeting bone has its own timbre. Thick. Low. Inevitable. He staggered sideways with more shock than pain, a hand flying to his head like a composer protecting the only instrument he has ever truly loved.

Lucia did not stop. Not because she wanted violence. Because he had left her no other language that interrupted him.

She swung again, not at his skull this time but at his wrist, the hand that had learned to make women into instruments. The candelabrum clipped him hard. His fingers spasmed. The Maestro made a sound that was not a word. He tried to stand into authority.

Lucia hit him again, smaller, more precise, breaking the spell of his balance. He folded to one knee, not elegant, not divine.

Just a man.

Lucia's breath came sharp. She forced it back into the count. Four. Four. Eight. She dropped the candelabrum and moved. Not toward him.

Toward the drawer that had always kept order: scores, scissors, keys, the knife he used for reeds and letters and threats.

She took the knife, he placed back. Her hands did not shake. She looked once at Rosa, on the floor, and something in her chest split open and stayed open. "Forgive me," she whispered to the girl without touching her again, because touching her again would break the part of Lucia that still had to move. She went for the gauze. The veil fought her for a second and then remembered it was only fabric. Alex's eyes were already on her.

He was strapped to the chair. Leather biting. Face bruised. Gag forcing him into silence. He looked at Lucia the way men look at a woman they have chosen to believe even when belief is dangerous.

Lucia cut the first strap at his wrist. "Do not speak," she said, because words cost breath and breath would buy them time. The second wrist. The ankles. Leather fell like bad policy, like a lie being voted out.

Alex surged up into pain because standing into pain is a thing men learn. Lucia ripped the gag free. It took skin with it. He did not flinch. "Rosa?" he managed, hoarse.

"Not now," Lucia said, and the sentence broke both of them and moved them at once.

A shout inside. Not the Maestro's. Lower.

Matteo's.

Footsteps that knew the house.

Lucia grabbed Alex's forearm and pressed the knife into his palm for one beat, then reclaimed it.

"No heroics," she told him. "Follow."

She did not go for the grand stairs. She went for the servants' door half hidden in the stone, down the tight spiral that smelled forever of oil and steam, past a pantry where pickled lemons watched revolutions, into a corridor that refused to be a hallway on any official map. She knew every turn because once she had learned the house for breath. Now she learned it for escape.

Behind them voices braided.

"Maestro?"
"Dov'è?" Where is she?
"Chiudi i cancelli!" Close the gates!

The bell began. Deep and old. The kind that meant fire when cities burned with other problems.

The house was waking. The villa was remembering what it did when it was threatened.

They reached a door that had not been opened since a summer when the house pretended to be generous. It stuck.Lucia put her shoulder into it.

Air hit them with olives and cold earth. The hillside dropped away in terraces. Cypress trees kept their counsel. Somewhere above, someone shouted orders in a voice used to being obeyed.

Lucia glanced back once, toward the room where Rosa lay, toward the corridor that held the injured god.Then she faced forward. "Run," she said.

Alex did.

They moved in a rhythm they had not rehearsed, the kind bodies find when they do not have time to be strangers. Below, a service road promised a car if fortune remembered them. Above, the house gathered itself like a choir preparing to condemn.

Lucia counted under her breath. To four. To eight. To the turn where sightlines broke.

"Left," she breathed, and Alex followed without argument, as if he had finally learned the music.

A shape detached from the trees. A man stepped into the service road as if the road had been built for him. Dark coat. No panic. Stillness made of decisions. His hand was raised, palm out.

Not surrender. Not threat. A signal.

Alex stopped hard. His body snapped in front of Lucia before he could think. Protective. Instinctive. The knife came up in his hand.

"Stop," Alex said, voice raw. "Lucia, behind me."

Lucia didn't move. She held her breath steady and economical while her eyes mapped the man's stance, his distance, the angle of his shoulders.

The man spoke in Italian, low and quick. "Non ho tempo per convincerti." *I don't have time to convince you.*

Lucia's gaze narrowed. And then her body recognized something her mind hadn't named: the cut of his jaw, the set of his mouth, the way his eyes moved without his head. Blood has its own grammar.

The man's attention flicked past Alex and landed on Lucia. "Lucia Conti," he said, and her name sounded like it did in Sergio's mouth. Exact. Respectful. Controlled.

"Who are you?" Lucia demanded. "Say it."

He reached into his coat slowly so Alex could track every inch of motion. He didn't pull a weapon. He pulled out a phone. The screen was already lit.

One missed call. One message thread. A single line in Sergio's Italian, Sergio's punctuation, Sergio's restraint.

Proteggila. Portala via. Protect her. Get her out.

Lucia's throat tightened so fast it hurt.

"Enzo," the man said. "Enzo Ferri."

Alex didn't lower the knife. "Prove it."

Enzo tapped once.

A voice note, short. Sergio's voice filled the air, flat with pain and clipped by distance, but unmistakable.

"Lucia. Vai. Non discutere. Fidati di lui. È mio fratello." *Lucia. Go. Don't argue. Trust him. He's my brother.*

Lucia went very still. "Where is Sergio?" she asked.

"Alive," Enzo said. "Bleeding. Stable for now. I left him with a doctor and two men who still fear him." He flicked his gaze up the hill. "We have minutes. The car is down the switchback. Keys are in. Engine warm."

Alex didn't like any of it. His knife hand didn't shake, but his eyes burned. They fled.

Enzo led without looking back, as if looking back would be a luxury the living couldn't afford.

At the bend, the car sat exactly where it was supposed to, engine running, heat already inside it. They got in.

Enzo took the descent fast and controlled. Gravel spat under the tires. The bell dulled as the switchbacks carried them away.

Alex's voice cut through the motion. "If he's your brother, and you're on our side, why do I look like this?"

Enzo didn't flinch. "Because the story has to hold," he said. "If you walked out clean, the Maestro would know." He kept his eyes on the road. "You were meant to look half dead."

Lucia's gaze slid to Enzo, sharp as a blade. "Sergio agreed to that?"

Enzo's jaw flexed. "Sergio understood," he said. "Believability is survival."

Alex swallowed. Anger and gratitude collided, both too big to fit in one breath.

Enzo killed the engine at the bottom of the road where the village path began. Quiet rushed in, sudden and wrong.

The road down here was only a ribbon of gravel and olive dust. A low stone wall held the field like a breath. Beyond it, a footpath switchbacked toward a village Lucia could find blindfolded by the smell of bread alone.

Lucia turned to Alex and finally let her arms do what her voice had not been allowed to.

Hold.

His face was close enough to see every bruise placed with intention. Every cut of effort. The raw line where the gag had been.

"It looks worse than it is," he said. Then, because honesty had become his only workable skill: "It hurts."

"Good," Lucia said. "If it hurts, you're here." The

reprimand found her next, automatic as breath. “You shouldn’t have come.”

He laughed without humor. “I listened. I didn’t come. I was brought.”

Something in her unclenched at that, some part of her that needed him to have followed one instruction today. The unclenching lasted a single beat.

She looked up the hill at the Cypresses and the red roofline that had stolen years from the sky.

“This ends now,” she said.

Alex caught her wrist. “You can’t go back there. He will kill you.”

“Not if I end him first.” She kissed him then, not as consolation but as a seal. When she pulled away, her eyes were clear. “Listen to me. You do not go to the police alone. Not yet. You go to the village. You go with Enzo. You find a man who answers to the law and not to money. You stay visible.”

“Signora,” Enzo said politely, “I know what to do.”

“You will take him with you,” Lucia told Enzo. “And you will not lose him.”

Alex’s jaw tightened. “No. We go with you.”

Enzo shook his head once, small and sincere. “Operas are tragedies,” he said. “This is not our fight. She must go alone.”

“This isn’t an opera,” Alex snapped. “What is wrong with you?”

Lucia stepped into Alex’s space and took his face in both hands, like she was steadying a cathedral that had started to shake.

“My love,” she said, and the words were both armor and wound, “if you love me, move.”

He stared at her for one dangerous second, the

kind of second where men decide whether to be brave or useful. Then he nodded. Not because he agreed. Because he understood what she was asking him to be. Alive.

"And Alex," she added, because superstition was cheaper than regret, "if my curtain is called, remember this is not your final act. Your opera will have a happy ending."

His throat worked. "You shouldn't do this on your own."

Lucia almost smiled, the ghost of a woman she could have been in another life. "I don't get to leave until the music does," she said.

She put his hand against her cheek for a single beat, leaned into it like a woman who had ever been allowed to, then pressed one final kiss to his mouth. Then she turned. And started back up the hill.

Alex watched her go until the trees took her. Then he did what she told him. He moved along the wall, found the cut in the stone where the field gave way to footpath, and headed for the village with Enzo, the knife hidden in his palm and the shape of his rage held tight inside his chest.

Chapter Twenty-Four
The Last Lesson

The house had reset itself to silence. That was how Lucia knew it was lying. She came in through the servants' door where the smell of oil and steam made it possible to breathe without remembering. She took the stairs two at a time without noise, a lesson she had never asked to learn.

The lesson room waited with its old blasphemies intact. The piano kept its black ocean. The metronome sat like a priest who had stopped arguing with God.

Rosa was on the floor. Matteo knelt beside her, hands pressing cloth to her temple not like prayer, but like a man managing an outcome. When Lucia entered, his eyes lifted. Sharp. Calculating. They dropped first to what she held.

A dagger. Short. Narrow. Built for endings.

"She's alive," Matteo said quickly, before Lucia could become a scream. "She is breathing." His voice didn't soften. "But she needs a doctor. Now."

Lucia crossed to Rosa and dropped beside her, fingers finding pulse, breath, the small stubborn insistence of life. Relief didn't come clean. It came jagged. Delayed. Furious.

She looked up at Matteo like a blade deciding what to cut. "Why?" she asked. Not the accident. Not the blow. The architecture.

Matteo's mouth moved as if he were tasting which answer would cost him least. "Because he cannot stop wanting," he said. "And because I thought I could keep it contained."

Lucia's gaze narrowed. "You brought men."

Matteo didn't flinch. "Not to harm you."

"Then to do what?" Lucia asked, and the dagger lifted a fraction, just enough to remind him questions could become consequences.

"To keep control," Matteo said. The honesty had no remorse in it. "To keep the story intact."

Lucia stood slowly. The room changed with her, as if the air understood that something it had never allowed was now standing.

"And Marina?" Lucia asked.

Matteo's jaw flexed. "Don't," he said. "Don't make her into a prayer."

Lucia stepped close enough that his breath caught. The dagger went under his jaw with a precision that made Matteo go very still. A bead of blood surfaced, bright as a note.

"You did not have to kill her," Lucia said softly. "You could have sent her to me."

Matteo's voice came tight. "I followed orders."

"And now," Lucia whispered, "you will follow mine."

Behind them, the Maestro moved. He was slanted against the bench, one hand cradling his injured wrist, the other braced on the piano's edge like pride. Blood threaded his hair at the temple where iron had taught him weight.

He looked at Lucia as though he couldn't decide whether to be furious or grateful she'd returned to the frame. "You came back," he said. Hope wore his mouth unnaturally. In his hope, he believed they could begin again, teacher and instrument, conductor and sound.

Lucia didn't answer hope. "To end this," she said. "To end you."

Matteo shifted, half rising as if to interfere. Reflex. Ego. The old habit of thinking he could touch the machinery and make it move.

Lucia didn't look away from the Maestro. "Matteo," she said, quiet. He froze. "Take her," Lucia said, meaning Rosa. "Get her to a doctor. Now."

Matteo's lip curled. "You don't give me commands."

The dagger pressed a fraction deeper. Warm blood slid against Lucia's knuckle like a signature.

"I do now," Lucia said.

Matteo's eyes cut toward the Maestro, seeking the only authority he had ever respected. The Maestro's gaze lingered on Lucia, bright with devotion that was really possession. He took a small breath, painful and reverent, and in that breath he decided to bless what he thought he had created.

"Sì, Lucia... amore mio... la Maestra," he whispered, loud enough for Matteo to hear. *Yes, Lucia... my love... the Maestra.*

Matteo went still in a new way. Not fear of Lucia. Fear of what had just been sanctioned. His throat worked against the blade.

"Capito," he said. *Understood.*

Lucia's voice stayed cold. "You are not dismissed from her," she told him. "Only from him."

Matteo lifted Rosa carefully. Not like a vow. Not like redemption. Like a thing he could not afford to let die in his arms. He carried her out through the side corridor, footsteps disappearing into the rugs, swallowed by the house's hunger for silence.

Lucia stayed standing.

The Maestro pushed upright. Every movement was a practiced argument against weakness. Pain had slowed him, not humbled him. His injured wrist hung close to his chest, cradled like a broken instrument, but his eyes still tried to conduct the room.

"You came back to me," he said.

Lucia didn't answer. She watched him the way she had learned to watch storms: without flinching, without mercy, without surprise.

He stopped too close. Then he kissed her.

He had always been better at inevitabilities than requests. His mouth tasted of heat and apology and old orders. He drew her in with the arm that still worked, as if her body could reassure him the world had not moved without his permission.

"You were always my prima donna," he whispered, softened by pain into something that almost resembled truth. "I could never harm you, Lucia." Then, quieter, as if confession could repair the air: "Ti amo." *I love you.*

For a breath, she believed him. Because love is a liar. Because memory is indulgent. Because there had been a time she wanted that sentence more than air.

She let her eyes close, and inside that closing she felt it: the familiar reach, the old claim, the hand inside the kiss searching for the place in her that used to shrink on command. Lucia opened her eyes.

She didn't shove him away. She didn't panic. She did what women do when they are done asking permission to survive. She kissed him once more, soft and deliberate, the last courtesy of clarity. And while his body leaned toward victory, Lucia's hand moved.

Not frantic. Not theatrical.

Precise.

Under the ribs. Angled in and back. Where Sergio had once taught her the difference between rage and ending.

The dagger.

The Maestro made a sound that might have been her name and might have been disbelief. His eyes widened, not at pain first, but at the idea that the world had disobeyed him.

Lucia stepped back and let him meet gravity on his own terms.

"For Marina," she said. No poetry. No performance. A ledger closed. "For Rosa." Then, because the truth deserved the whole sentence: "For me."

He folded toward the bench and slid to the floor, one elegant hand skittering as if reaching for something he could still conduct. The metronome kept ticking, faithful to time instead of him.

Lucia dropped beside him and caught his head before it struck the wood. Not mercy. Control. If he died, he would not die with her screaming. Not because he deserved quiet, but because she did.

He stared up at her, and for the first time his face held something other than certainty. Not softness. Not repentance. Recognition.

"I only wanted..." he rasped. The rest collapsed. Want is always too small a word for what he had built.

"You wanted to own what you could not become," Lucia said.

His breath hitched. His mouth tried to lift into a smile and failed. "I saw the world," he whispered, fighting for air, "and it was ugly. And you were... you were the only beautiful thing that answered me."

Lucia's throat tightened once. She did not let it become forgiveness.

"Stop," she said. Not cruel. Not kind. Final.

He tried anyway, because even dying he could not stop directing. "Lucia... I made you... I—"

His voice cracked into nothing. His pupils fluttered, searching for a stage, searching for a god, searching for the hand that would applaud him back into power.

Lucia held his gaze like a metronome refusing to speed up for panic.

Tick. Tick. Tick.

His breath left him in one long exhale, as if he had been singing his whole life and only now ran out of air.

And then he was gone.

The room did not applaud. The house did not speak. The metronome kept ticking.

Lucia sat there, hands stained with the cost of ending a man who had written himself into too many women's bodies. She did not collapse. She did not celebrate. She stayed long enough to prove she hadn't imagined it, long enough to make the ending real.

Then, with a steadiness that surprised even her, Lucia reached across the piano, touched the metronome, and stopped it.

Silence arrived like a new law.

Chapter Twenty-Five
A Quiet Ovation

Outside, Tuscany held its posture: domes behaving, roofs stacked in patient perspective, light pretending the world had always been orderly.

Lucia stood in it anyway, blood on her hands, breath in her lungs, and felt something that did not resemble triumph.

Return. Not to him. Not to the stage. To herself.

Footsteps behind her. Not the staff first. Not the law.

Men.

Enzo came through the veranda doors with the quiet authority of someone who understood what rooms demanded. Two others followed him, local men in plain coats and work boots, faces set with the kind of seriousness that doesn't ask questions in the wrong order. Not soldiers. Not servants.

Stagehands, in another life. The kind who could strike a set without breaking what mattered.

They looked once, just once, past Lucia, toward the lesson room, toward the body on the floor. Then they looked away.

Enzo's phone was already in his hand. He spoke Italian in a calm cadence that sounded like logistics but moved like choreography, telling the world where to enter, what to say, what to carry, what to never touch barehanded.

"Ambulanza." Ambulance.
"Medico." Doctor.
"Carabinieri." Carabinieri National Military Police

The world beginning to behave like law again. Slowly, reluctantly, but finally. Enzo lowered the phone for a beat and looked at Lucia. Not asking permission. Confirming a cue.

"Rosa is breathing," he said quietly. "She's with the doctor now. She's safe."

Something inside Lucia loosened. Small, unwilling, human.

Enzo's gaze flicked past her, toward the corridor that led deeper into the villa. He signaled with two fingers, subtle as a baton cue. One of the men nodded once and disappeared into the hall without a word.

"Find Matteo," Enzo said, voice low enough to be merciful, flat enough to be final. "Before the law does."

A muffled crash sounded somewhere inside the house. Wood against stone. A shout strangled mid-word. Enzo didn't look back.

"Good," he said quietly, as if a piece had finally clicked into place.

Lucia didn't turn. She didn't need to. She could feel the house behind her, heavy with its history, pretending it had never swallowed women whole.

Another set of footsteps, faster, uneven, familiar.

Alex.

He entered like a man resisting the urge to run. Bruised. Cut. Burning with restraint. Alive. His eyes found Lucia and broke, and he didn't try to hide his fear. He stopped just inside the threshold, gaze slipping past her shoulder despite himself.

He saw the Maestro on the floor. Saw the elegant hand slack. The wrist that used to direct. The face that used to look immortal when it spoke her name like a claim.

"Is he—" Alex began. Then he stopped himself. He looked at Lucia instead, as if he'd learned in one brutal night where the real question lived. "Are you?"

Lucia didn't answer with words. She breathed once, four in, four held, eight out, and held his gaze the way she had learned to hold notes: steady, exact, refusing to break.

Alex crossed the stone without hesitation and stopped just close enough to ask without words. "May I?" Lucia nodded once. Alex gathered her into his arms. Careful at first, as if she might shatter if held too tightly. Then tighter when he felt the tremor she had been holding back since Florence, since the cloister, since the first time the Maestro said her name like a verdict.

And because Alex was not the Maestro, he didn't demand composure. He didn't ask her to be beautiful through it. He didn't ask her to be strong in a way that served him. He simply held her like a man who understood that softness is not weakness when it's chosen.

Tears slipped down Lucia's face, silent, unadorned. Not only grief. Not only relief. Something stranger. Freedom is not always loud. Sometimes it is simply the body realizing the cage is gone and not knowing what to do with the space.

"I need a new memory here," Lucia whispered, voice scraped raw by truth. "On this veranda. Please."

Alex didn't pretend to understand it all. He didn't ask her to translate the sentence into something smaller. He kissed her forehead, slow and deliberate, like a vow without theatrics. Then he pulled back just enough to look at her.

"I'm here," he said. Simple. Unavoidable. "Just you and me."

His thumb brushed her lower lip, not taking, only offering. When she didn't move away, he leaned in and kissed her. Soft at first, then steadier, like he was teaching her nervous system something new.

That it didn't have to brace. That love could be quiet.

When he broke the kiss, he took her stained hands and pressed them against his chest where his heart beat hard and human beneath her palms. "Let this be yours," he murmured. "No one behind you. No one above you."

Lucia looked out to the Cypress valley, heart heavy, emotions flooding, and for a moment the world was only air and light and the fact that Alex wanted nothing from her except her truth. She pulled him in again, holding him tightly against her body, making a final memory on the veranda to replace all others.

Behind them, Enzo's men moved with purpose. One set down a folded cloth on the stone table without looking at the blood. Another opened the doors wider, letting air and daylight into a house that had hoarded silence like a weapon.

Enzo returned to the phone, placing calls the way conductors place beats, making a believable sequence out of chaos. Not lies for the Maestro's sake.

Because monsters didn't only die. They left networks. Paper trails. Men who still believed. And if a story was going to be told, Enzo would make sure it was told in a way that didn't put Lucia back inside a cage, this time built from headlines.

Lucia pulled back enough to look at Alex. His face was torn up and still gentle, as if softness wasn't weakness but choice.

"Thank you," she said. "For loving me. For listening." She searched his eyes like she was trying to learn whether men like this were real. Whether she could build a future without using her femininity as strategy, without turning love into leverage, without paying for affection in blood.

A siren wound up somewhere below the hill, thin and distant, climbing toward the villa. Italy would arrive with its paperwork and its questions and its insistence on cause.

Lucia looked out over Tuscany and felt the strangest thing. Not victory. Not absolution.

Return.

She took Alex's hand. Not for one beat this time. For as long as she could. "Come," she said. And Alex came with her.

They left the chamber behind them: the Maestro, the metronome, the old doctrine baked into stone. They left the memories that had required obedience to survive. Ahead of them, the morning waited, air and light and a world that would try to make meaning out of what she had done. Lucia didn't look back. She walked with Alex into a new opera.

Not one written for her.

Epilogue
A New Score

Alex woke to birds and a kind of quiet he had once believed was a myth. The shutters were cracked just enough to let morning pour in soft and gold, smelling faintly of rosemary and damp soil. A distant bell marked the hour without urgency. No sirens. No camera flashes. No voices demanding a version of events.

Only sound. Not the Maestro's metronome. Something healed. A woman's voice outside, carrying across stone and garden rows like it belonged to the land. Lucia.

She wasn't singing opera.

She was singing her grandmother's song, the one that had lived in her bones long before anyone taught her to count. It rose and fell without performance. No audience. No demand. Just breath and memory and the simple fact that she could.

Alex lay still, listening the way he'd learned to listen this past year, with his whole body, not just his ears. He could hear her moving between notes. The scrape of a basket. The soft clink of glass. Leaves being gathered like the day was something you could collect and keep.

When he finally sat up, he saw her through the open door: barefoot in the garden, hair loose, sunlight catching the curve of her throat as she carried a basket toward the kitchen fresh figs, tomatoes, basil, and a small bouquet of lavender that looked like it had been cut for no reason except joy.

She paused at the threshold and looked at him like she'd been waiting for him to wake. Not as a prima donna waiting to be witnessed. As a woman who'd built a life and invited him into it.

"You're up," she said, soft in the way that mattered. Soft because it wasn't afraid.

He rubbed his eyes, smiling despite himself. "I was trying to hear the end."

Lucia's mouth tilted. "There is no end. It's a loop."

"Makes sense," Alex said. "Your grandmother wrote a hit."

She stepped inside and set the basket down. The kitchen smelled like bread and clean stone. It smelled like a home that hadn't been designed to trap anyone. Lucia came to the side of the bed and leaned down, pressing a kiss to his forehead. Unhurried. Ordinary. Devastating in its simplicity.

Alex reached up, caught her wrist gently, and kissed the inside of it where scars had faded into pale lines of history. He didn't ask what they meant anymore. He didn't need her to bleed to prove she'd survived. "How are you?" he asked, because he still believed in the question.

Lucia exhaled once, slow and measured. Then she smiled, almost annoyed at how honest the answer was. "Good," she said. "I'm... good." It had taken a year for that word to stop sounding like a dare. They lay back down together, Lucia curling into him like she had nowhere else to be, like she wasn't bracing for footsteps in the hall.

"We should talk about San Francisco," Alex said, because reality always arrived, even in paradise.

Lucia's fingers traced his jaw. "You mean your city."

"My former city," he corrected.

Lucia hummed approval disguised as teasing. "You still love it."

"I love what it could be," he said. "That's different." A year ago, he would have said it like a campaign line. Now it sounded like the truth.

San Francisco had fallen and climbed back up again, the way cities do: slow, brutal, stubborn. The scandal had burned Alex's name to the ground. The comeback had been interrupted. Then he made one decision that carried more weight than the election ever could have—the kind that didn't read like heroism on paper, only consequence. He stepped out of the race. Publicly. Unequivocally. He endorsed Maya and pledged what was left of his machinery to hers.

Maya took the endorsement like a blade and turned it into momentum. She didn't save him. She would save the city from the kind of men he used to represent. And somehow, that gave Alex a way to live with himself again.

Lucia watched his face while he thought. She always knew when his mind went back to those months the war room, the headlines, the way power made people speak in lies even when they believed they were being noble. "Do you ever regret it?" Lucia asked softly. "Handing her your *baton*."

Alex stared at the ceiling beams, the kind that held weight without needing praise. He let the truth arrive without trying to polish it. "I miss the city," he said. "I don't miss the version of me that thought he could save it by winning."

Lucia's mouth curved. "You gave her the role," she said. "And she ran."

"She became mayor," Alex said, still sounding faintly disbelieving when he said it out loud.

Lucia's eyes sharpened with pride that wasn't hers, but still mattered. "She is fighting the good fight," she said. "Without performing gratitude for the room."

Alex let out a quiet laugh. "That is the most Maya sentence you've ever said."

Lucia kissed his mouth once, then rested her forehead against his. "The truth is," she murmured, "two men had the same idea." Alex's eyes opened, attentive. "Take the world back from the people who hoard it," Lucia said. "The Maestro believed it. You believed it." Alex's jaw tightened, but he didn't look away. "He wanted change," Lucia continued, "and he chose ownership as the method. He called it art. He called it discipline. He called it love." Her voice stayed calm, and that calm was the proof. "You wanted change without becoming a monster to get it."

Alex swallowed. "And both of us failed."

Lucia's smile was soft, and it was merciless in the way mercy can be when it refuses to lie.

"Two men reached for the same baton," she said. "One used it like a weapon. One tried to use it like a mirror." She shifted closer, the sheet sliding over skin like a quiet curtain. "Maybe the baton was never meant to stay in men's hands."

"And you?" Alex asked.

Lucia's gaze lifted not to an audience, but to the

middle distance where she kept her visions now: practical, fierce, real. "I stopped his tempo," she said. "Now I set my own."

Alex's mouth curved. "La Maestra," he said, half teasing, half reverent.

"Don't start," Lucia said, but her smile betrayed her.

"Too late," he murmured. "You already rewrote the score."

Lucia propped herself on one elbow. "We leave tomorrow," she said.

Alex blinked. "Back to the noise."

"Our world," Lucia corrected, and the smile that followed made it real.

She traced a fingertip over his chest, the place where his heart refused to be civilized. "Sergio and Enzo are meeting us in San Francisco," she added.

Alex let out a warm, disbelieving laugh. "Sergio is getting on a plane?"

Lucia's eyes glittered. "He says it will be his last trip to the States before he officially retires."

"Sergio?" Alex repeated. "Retire?"

Lucia shrugged, innocent in a way she absolutely wasn't. "His word."

Alex's smile turned wicked. "He's never retiring from you."

Something tender moved through Lucia's face affection, exasperation, gratitude. "He'll pretend," she said. "For my sake."

"And Enzo?"

"He'll pretend less," Lucia said, and the way she said it made Alex laugh again, quieter this time.

Alex brushed her hair out of her face. "Tell me

again what you're building," he said. "I like hearing it out loud."

Lucia's gaze steadied. "The estate is no longer his," she said. "Not in spirit. Not in function. It's paper now. It's a building. A resource."

"And the women?" Alex asked, like the question still mattered enough to be asked twice.

"The sopranos are safe," Lucia said. "All of them. The ones who wanted to disappear did. The ones who wanted to stay... stayed. Not as instruments. As architects." She spoke with the calm of someone who had learned that power didn't have to shout. "We're turning it into conservatories. Not one. Several. Italy first, then Paris, then—"

"San Francisco," Alex supplied.

Lucia nodded. "San Francisco."

"And the foundation?"

Lucia held his gaze. "The Metronome Foundation."

Alex's mouth curved. "Because you stopped it."

"Because I stopped it," Lucia said. "And because no one else gets to set the tempo for them again."

He kissed her slow, thorough, like he was sealing the name into the world.

Lucia's eyes gleamed with something lighter. "Emily agreed."

Alex blinked. "Agreed to what?"

"Headmaster," Lucia said. "San Francisco."

Alex stared at her. "You're serious."

"She said it would be fitting," Lucia replied, voice bright with amusement. "If the city is going to heal, it should be through music, not men."

Alex let out a laugh that surprised him with how easy it was. "She's going to run your conservatory."

"Our conservatory," Lucia corrected, then added, almost gleefully, "and she said, verbatim, 'thank you for taking him off my hands.'"

Alex groaned into the pillow. "I wasn't that bad."

Lucia arched a brow. "You were... a type."

"A type," Alex echoed, wounded on principle.

Lucia softened, fingers tracing the edge of his mouth, the place where bruises used to live. "When you see her," Lucia said, "be this version of you."

Alex's laughter faded into something quieter. "I will. I owe her that."

Lucia nodded, satisfied. "Good. I don't want ghosts following us into the new building."

She slid out of bed, bare feet finding the cool stone floor. She pulled on a robe and turned back, looking at Alex with a kind of love that didn't ask.

"Coffee?" she asked, like she meant ordinary.

Alex watched her this woman who had once been forced to earn air and felt the strangest, simplest thing.

Peace.

"Yeah," he said. "Coffee."

Lucia took one step into the kitchen. Then she stopped. The refrigerator clicked, small, harmless, and the sound landed in her bones like tempo. For a second, her breath tried to reorganize itself: four in, four held, eight out. Like someone else was counting again. Lucia closed her eyes and refused. When she opened them, she turned back to Alex. Not afraid. Just reminded.

Alex was already sitting up, watching her with the kind of care that never rushed her into being fine.

"Hey," he said gently. "You don't have to—"

"I know," Lucia interrupted softly. She crossed

back to the bed without hurrying. Without apology. She climbed onto the mattress and straddled him, not as performance, not as penance, not as proof. As choice. Her palms pressed to his chest, over a heart that refused to be civilized. “This,” she whispered, brushing her lips against his once, barely there, “is mine.” Alex’s hands went to her waist and stopped, waiting. Lucia smiled at the restraint. “You can,” she said. Permission given like a gift, not a negotiation.

Alex’s grip tightened, and Lucia exhaled relief turning into heat. She kissed him slowly at first, then deeper, teaching her body the new truth the way she’d taught it to survive.

One breath at a time.

His mouth moved to her throat. He kissed the place where her voice lived, gentle and reverent, and Lucia shivered not from fear, but from the simple shock of being touched without being claimed.

“No more prima donna,” Alex murmured against her skin.

Lucia closed her eyes. A smile, small and stunned. “Just Lucia.” She rocked into him like she was learning herself. Like she was allowed. Like she wasn’t being watched.

Alex’s hands slid under the robe, warm on her hips, then her back, anchoring her. Not directing. He kissed her again and again, each kiss a quiet ovation that asked nothing of her except the truth of her want.

Breathless and awake, Lucia turned her head, her voice uneven and honest.

“In San Francisco,” she whispered, “I’m going to sing for me.”

Alex’s voice went rough. “I know.”

"And if the world looks at me and tries to decide who I belong to," Lucia said, the old steel returning as calm leadership, "I will let them look."

"They can choke on it," Alex said simply. Lucia laughed, a soft sound that turned into a kiss.

Outside, the birds kept singing. The garden kept existing. The day kept arriving. Tomorrow, they would fly back to the noise. Not to resurrect his campaign, but to build something that could not be bought. Italy first. Paris next. Then San Francisco.

The stage had never belonged to him.

And if the world needed proof that the tempo had changed, Lucia would give it to them. Note by note, city by city.

Not as his prima donna.

As the woman holding the baton...

As ***La Maestra.***